THE LIGHT

OVER

BROKEN TIDE

HOLLY DUCARTE

Claire
May this story
find a special
place in your
heart

holly ducarte

Black Ladder Publishing
CANADA

DEDICATION

For Jesse and Verona,
who are lights in my life and
inspire me to write

TABLE OF CONTENTS

TRIGGER WARNING

THIS BOOK INVOLVES SCENES OF MENTAL ILLNESS. INCLUDING DEPRESSION, HINTS AT SCHITZOPHRENIA, ANXIETY, A BRIEF SCENE OF DOMESTIC VIOLENCE, AND A BRIEF SCENE OF ATTEMPTED SUICIDE. THESE TOPICS ARE WRITTEN WITH A GREAT DEAL OF CARE AND ARE NOT GROSSLY EXPLICIT.

ACKNOWLEDGMENTS

Many thanks to Heather Benton and Roth Editorial Services who saw this book in its inception phase (that very rough, ugly phase) and gave their edits and qualified input.

Appreciation toward my cousin, Lacey, who read sections of my earliest draft and gave advice in regard to creative techniques, querying, and writing conferences to attend.

To Paula Munier of Talcott Notch Literary Agency for giving me her time when she didn't have to, and offering me such great advice to enhance this novel and my skills overall.

My respect to Michael Neff who offers Author Salon, an intense and professional commercial writing course that has done more for my writing than I could've imagined.

To my second-brain, Mandy, who uplifted, motivated, and offered brilliant ideas I wouldn't have thought of.

Thank you Samuel H Hurley for writing a beautiful poem that so perfectly embodies the theme of this novel. And all on a whim! You are incredibly talented, sir.

All my Underground Writing Cohorts. Especially Kelly who has willfully gone along for the ride, edited like mad, and brainstormed amazingly. And Suzanne for catching those niggly things that can often go amiss.

I want to appreciate all my super supportive family, coworkers, and clients who had to deal with me talking their ear off about all the ins and outs of my endeavors with book writing.

Gratefulness toward all the amazing people I've met over Instagram, and other social media. You truly make a difference.

Thank you Beta and ARC readers for giving my novel your time and helping promote it to the world. You are very special to me.

And of course, last but least, to every reader who picks up this book, thanks for giving my writerly dream wings. May my words inspire you and offer hope.

Hourglass

Water keeps its memory here;
Each trial of life veiled,
Each vial of heart revealed
And struck wet along the rock.
    So these savage hands turn
    Loved circlet ghouls
    Reversed around the clock.
As the bay brings back the tide
And lost bones born back the love.
As the tilt of time twines blue below
And streams through land above.

—Samuel H Hurley

ONE

We're all like paper dolls. Happiest when linked to another, often unaware of our flimsiness. So easily torn. What happens when we reach out to find there's no one there to hold our hand? I'll tell you what happens; we blow away into uncertain air, then desperately search for anything to pull us out of the chaos. Everyone is afraid of what happens if they don't get pulled out. *I* was afraid.

On a Saturday in early April, Andy interrupted my re-read of Peter Pan. He bobbed his head and crossed his arms over his chest, kicking at the carpet. He'd never entered my room before—as if it were a twilight zone bound to suck him up into oblivion.

Fairy-tale books had become a necessary mode of distraction for me, and the feel of grainy paper, therapeutic. I put my finger down on the page to keep my place. "What are you doing in here?" I asked, leaning against my headboard.

He fiddled with some knick-knacks on my dresser and picked up a foil owl I'd made. "Nice little set up you have. You make all these paper thingies?" He put the owl back in place.

"Uh-huh."

Unfortunately, after reading so much fiction, I longed for it to become reality. I needed it to. So, I'd bought piles of various paper: rice, water-color, tissue, cardstock, etc. While cutting and folding, I tried to make fantastical worlds appear with all manner of creatures. It didn't have the effect I wanted, but I got to know paper. Its thickness, texture, suppleness. I even figured myself to be made up of the flexible variety. Namely, origami. Life bent me. Tore me. Tossed me. It seemed to deviate from following an outline, thus folding me in all the wrong ways.

I went back to reading until he cleared his throat. "Did you *need* something?"

One hand deep in his jacket pocket, jangling what sounded like coins or keys Andy said, "I...uh...got a new job."

I closed my book in a snap. He and I never had conversations about his work. Heck, we hardly conversed at all. We spoke most at the supper table when he'd ask how my school day went. Even then, he tuned out a lot of what I said and continued listening to the news off the 19-inch, bubble-screen television set on top of a breakfast hutch in our kitchen. "A new job," I repeated. "Well, that's good, right?"

"We're moving...at the end of your school year."

"What?" I shot straight off my bed. "After all I've been through? You can't do this to me!"

My doubts about being made of flesh and blood came after Mom passed away. I turned frail then, torn into a thousand paper shreds. Some pieces never to be retrieved again. Relatives worried. They hustled here and there after the funeral, trying to pick up the pieces and put me back together like Humpty Dumpty. The gaps in me had to be filled. And the solution, obvious.

It took five months for them to find Andy, and when they did it happened nothing like I imagined it would in my daydreams; being swept up into awaiting arms and told how much I'd been missed. As a substitute, I got awkward arm scratches, shuffling feet, and a pained smile. No resemblance to the young man with shining eyes and clean-shaven face who used to visit and send me things from time to time. The guy with worn suitcase in hand, who had stood in the doorway of my childhood house, claiming to be my Dad, had cross-hatched lines on his forehead, hair grown past his ears, and greyish-brown stubble on his chin. A total stranger who acted like no time lingered between us. Ignorant to those many years I waited for him to show up, call, write. Still, everyone thought it best we should be together.

Well, they couldn't have been more wrong.

"Look, I know you've got memories here and all, but we had a big project come up on the coast. Gotta go where the work takes me."

"Work, work, work…that's all you've ever cared about. It's probably the *irreconcilable difference* that made you and Mom split. And you think you can just come in here and drop this as casually as a conversation about the weather?" Set adrift without Mom, my paper arm extended out as far as I could muster. Desperate. Since her presence was like several people in one, life felt smaller now that she was gone. As for Andy, the notion of family fizzled out in seconds. He didn't grab my hand. There was just him, and then me.

It was moments like this that made me miss the man I'd hoped he'd be. The man I pretended to have tea parties with using the dainty set he'd sent me on my fourth birthday; the last gift since he disappeared. That gentleman—who pulled out my chair and had me use proper etiquette at the table—would always be my Dad. This imposter I got forced to live with, I called by his first name, Andy. It didn't feel right associating fatherhood with someone who had no clear definition of the word.

My eyes glassed over with tears and my insides flooded with anxiety. I crumbled to the floor, choking on my own saliva. With my head in my hands, the tears flowed. How could Andy be this uninformed? Wasn't it common knowledge that teenagers, above anyone else, required stability and support? Someone willing to hold on as the world pulled them in all kinds of emotional directions.

When he approached, my head shot up and I shouted, "Get away from me. Just leave."

"Rebecca, I—"

"Get *out* of my room."

Andy lifted his hands in surrender and turned on his heel to leave me in ruins on the floor. I peered over at my framed picture of Mom on the nightstand and made no attempts to suppress the gut-wrenching sobs, weak at the notion I'd lost her and now my home full of memories.

That dreaded, uncertain air encircled, and like a tornado, ripped more pieces off me. How could I form into anything with so much gone?

Moving into a side-lying position with knees tucked to my chest, I wiped away a new blur of tears onto my sweater sleeve and a flutter from a dress's hemline appeared briefly before me. The familiar designs on the fabric stopped me mid-cry. Jolting upright off the floor, I looked around. The tiny hairs on my arms prickled and stood on end. "Hello?"

After several minutes went by with no reappearance, I attributed the hallucination to extreme exhaustion and Andy's traumatic news. I yawned, pulled my comforter off the bed, and slept away the rest of the evening on the floor.

I tossed and turned from occasional arm numbness and erratic breathing, waking in a start that next morning, chest tight. The intense sunshine aggravated my eyes until I got up and drew the blinds shut. When Andy called for me to come to breakfast, the scowl deepened on my face. How could I eat, let alone with him? I decided to bypass breakfast and start on the outdoor chores designated for me every weekend.

Andy and I fought the rest of the morning. Subtle remarks, gestures of irritation, until we were all-out screaming at each other. After I finished furiously pulling weeds and last year's dead plants out of the flower beds, I rushed back into my room. I took up Peter

Pan and tried to read where I left off, but hated how Mr. Darling's harshness reminded me so much of Andy.

Staring at my dresser mirror, tears drew out the lighter shades from my spruce-green eyes—the same color as Mom's. I spoke to my reflection as if it were her. "You said we'd always have each other." I slapped my hand on the glass. "So, where are you? How could you leave me with Andy?" I said choking on the words.

When a clear image of Mom flickered briefly behind me and disappeared, I stumbled back and gasped, a hand to my chest. I stared hard at the mirror, turned away, looked back. I thought about the hemline of the dress that fluttered by last night. The designs on it familiar because of the red tanagers. *Mom's* sundress—the one she often wore in summer on account they were her favorite songbird.

"I need a shower," I said, rubbing my eyes, heart thudding.

In the bathroom, letting the water rush over my head, I worried. The gaps in me, pieces unrecovered, I wondered whether they were from my mind. But maybe it had nothing to do with that. Could it be these visions weren't some psychosomatic problem? That even in death, Mom meant to take care of me when I needed her most?

If they were real…I wouldn't have to go along with my makeshift fantasy world of paper anymore. *Rebecca Leah Stafford isn't ordinary. She is now…extraordinary.* That sounded good.

Drying up and getting clothed, I stuffed a chair under my doorknob to keep Andy out. I had to try to figure a way to strengthen this ability. To find a pattern with both instances.

Mulling it over the rest of the day and into the evening, even staying up until 3 am, I always came back to one thing. Stress. But, it didn't work when I forced myself into a tizzy trying to brew up old wounds; fake crying, messing up my hair in a tantrum. Those kinds of things only made me more cognizant of my poor acting skills. It had to be authentic, like after a severe argument with

Andy. And I didn't wish for those to occur more than they already did.

⁂

May arrived quick in a series of wind gusts. I brought the marker's tip down across box number one on the calendar and bit my lower lip. Every day crossed out inched us closer to moving day, which made me dizzy. I fell against the wall and put a hand to my forehead. When I turned my head to the side, Mom stood there holding a cage with a tanager inside. She delicately unhinged the iron door and opened it wide.

I got wrapped up in how to maintain the vision of her. It proved impossible because, as they say, what goes up must come down. As delicate as our bodies are, they are fashioned to regulate—much to my chagrin. Imagine, welcoming stress. What a concept.

Mom began to fade as fast as the tanager flew out of the cage. "Wait...please. Just stay."

A knock at the door and a jostle of the knob startled me. I fisted my hands, already irritable in my failed attempt to keep her here, and asked, "What?"

"Got a pile of your laundry," Andy said. "Why is your door locked?"

"Just leave it on the floor and I'll pick it up later."

He huffed. "Open up."

I shimmied the chair from under the knob and opened the door a crack. "It's not locked. I put a chair there for privacy."

"Privacy for what?"

I yanked the laundry from his hands and through clench teeth answered, "From you."

"You know...I've had just about enough of your attitude these past few days. You've been withdrawn in your room for weeks. You skip meals. Do you need me to say sorry for the move or something?"

"Yah, but you won't mean it."

6

"Because there's nothing to be sorry for."

Without thinking, I blurted, "Mom appeared to me and said she hates the idea of this house being sold. She's very upset with you." Of course, that didn't happen. But it's how I knew she must've felt. Besides, the idea of getting to talk with her again felt good.

"*You're* upset with me. *You.* There's no need to include your mother in this."

"But I really do see her." At least that had truth.

"You can believe whatever you need in order to get you through," he said, plainly. "But it doesn't change the fact that we're leaving at the end of the month."

I threw my laundry aside and pushed him out of the doorway. Positioning the chair back in place, I turned around to see Mom sitting on my bed. Andy's snarky tone resonated. *You can believe whatever you need in order to get you through.*

"My visions of you are real, aren't they?"

TWO

Limbo; a terrifying word when concerning one's mental state and the fact that, technically, you can be in motion and yet be neither here nor there.

I considered this irony as I clutched the handle of my suitcase with white knuckles, rushing past crowds of blurred faces in the Halifax airport on a Saturday at the end of June.

"Rebecca, slow down," Andy shouted.

I maintained long strides to avoid him. If I had any pluck, I might've began to run and kept on going without hesitation. Escape. Perhaps that vision of Mom with the cage signified flying free like the tanager. But I didn't risk it, already having such delicate edges, unable to take another precarious fold.

With a glance at a clock reading quarter after ten in the morning, I exited through the front doors of the airport into a whisper of fog. The humid, salty sea air tingled in my nostrils. Andy drew near.

"I'm not going to run halfway across an airport just because you have PMS," he said and grabbed my arm tightly.

People about to make their way inside stared at us with uneasy eyes. "For your information, when girls are angry, it doesn't always mean that it's PMS." I squirmed his hand off me and strode toward the plump taxicab driver holding up a cardboard sign with our last name on it.

The cabby stood beside his Lincoln sedan, friendly eyes gleaming from under white, bushy eyebrows and wrinkled folds of skin. "Can I take your luggage?"

I pushed mine into one of his big hands, forcing him to drop the sign in a whirling flutter to the ground. Opening the door to the backseat I overheard Andy apologize for my rude behavior. I slammed the door. The pungent combination of pine-tree fresheners and body odor assaulted my nose.

While the driver stowed our luggage in the trunk, Andy got in the front passenger side. When he turned to look at me, the scissor-sharpness of his eyes nearly cut through. "Quit it. You're making a scene."

"I'm making a scene?" I turned to stare out the window.

The cabby opened the driver's side door to silence. His seat let out a whoosh when he sat, its last breath squeezed out. Andy turned to him and in a fake calm tone said, "We're heading to Lunenburg." He reached into his coat pocket. "Here's the address."

After eyeballing the sticky note, the cabby said, "If we're going to Lunenburg—" he turned the key in the ignition and put the car in drive "—then how about going down Lighthouse Route? We'll hit a few tourist attractions. Right along the ocean. Very scenic." He informed us about the sites we'd pass along the way, while I began to nod off in the back. Like the cabby's seat, this day had squeezed the last drop of energy from me.

Disregarding my weariness, Andy poked me awake at the first point of interest. My eyes creaked open and my temples throbbed like an out-of-tune band marched through my head. We were in a rustic community called Peggy's Cove—made of lobster fishers and those leading the quintessential simple life in boxy houses—packed with tourists clambering to see Peggy's Point Lighthouse and the gothic Anglican Church.

"This place looks like it's right out of a calendar," Andy said.

"If you'd like, I can drop you off to do some gallivanting."

"I'd like nothing more than to hop in one of those boats and spend the entire day fishing out here. But, we really should just keep on going. The plan is to tour around once we settle in."

The cabby gave a light nod. "Sure thing, boss. We'll make our way to Chester."

We passed through a few other communities within the Halifax municipality that wore a foggy veil. Then we arrived at the village.

While my eyelids dipped, Andy ogled. "Must be some wealthy folk who live here. Just look at the creativity and detail that went into these spectacular houses. Gives me some ideas," he said glancing at the driver. "I do construction for a living."

"Good line of work. Always needed in these parts," the cabby replied.

"You weren't kidding when you said this road was scenic. Just look at that ocean, Rebecca," Andy carried on. "Makes a person feel so small. Doesn't it?"

It's not the only thing that makes a person feel small, I thought watching the fog evaporate off its surface. I slumped in my seat and closed my eyes just in time to receive another painful poke. I massaged the spot on my shoulder as the cabby explained the significance of the three churches of Mahone Bay. "It's been said that whenever sailors set their sights on them while sailing by, they'd get a strong sense of sanctuary."

I stayed awake through the next point of interest (hoping to avoid another jab) which happened to be our new community. I sat up in my seat and scrutinized. The boisterous buildings with their bright colors laughed when the cab went by them. Windows and shutters stared like curious eyes. Somehow the town knew I was coming, knew of my discomfort. It wanted to make me smile, uplift me, convince me with its rustic charm of bed and breakfasts, fish and tackle shops, antique stores. However, instead of peaceful, I felt panicked about the sense of isolation here.

The driver pointed to one of the fire-truck-red buildings next to the glistening waterfront. "That there is the Fisheries Museum of the Atlantic and the Old Fish Factory restaurant. Finest seafood you'll taste around here. I recommend the crab legs or the scallops. Mighty good."

"We'll have to eat there sometime. What do you think, Rebecca?" Andy's hand reached and whapped the back of his headrest.

"Everything here is too bright...it gives me a headache." I leaned my head against the window, and the coolness of the glass pressed against my cheek. The odd car passed by, obscuring sidewalks with a handful of people walking along them, strangers I tried to read the faces of.

Two old men shared a newspaper on a bench, bantering back and forth, exchanging pages genially, unmindful of the seagull picking at their shoelaces. A mother shepherded her well-mannered children into an antique store, no doubt reminding them (no matter how perfect they seemed) not to touch anything. I imagined this was all there was. Every day the same cars drove downtown, the same two men read their paper, the same woman with her children entered the store. The same everything.

Lunenburg was a cuckoo clock, perfectly timed, never changing. The very idea angered me. Behind the gentle come and go, there needed to be a sudden chaotic event, just like my life. The seagull could jump on one of the men and start tearing the paper to shreds. One of the well-mannered children could start slapping their sibling and throwing a fit in front of onlookers, their mother trying to pull them apart. Anything.

I started to bite my nails. The seat no longer felt comfortable. I shifted here and there. Pulled at the collar of my shirt. The cabby looked in the rearview mirror and said, "Is everything okay back there, Missy?"

When my eyes veered frontward, Mom stood in the middle of the street, the cab coming straight at her. My fingernails dug into Andy's headrest and I shrieked, "Look out!"

"Woah!" the cabby bellowed as if halting a pair of horses, his foot slammed on the breaks. A pallor of shock overtook his rosy-red skin as he surveyed the scene.

I shrunk back in my seat. "Sorry, I thought I saw someone try to cross."

"You could've gotten us into an accident." Andy barely rotated his head, eyeing me peripherally.

"I—" No use arguing this one. I overreacted. But I wasn't prepared for Mom to show up like that.

"This is not the time for your hair-brained imagination games," he said, somehow privy to my outburst being related to my visions.

Minutes later, when our hearts were back in our chests from being catapulted in our throats, we parked alongside the sidewalk in front of a tall, beigey-yellow house with a peaked roof. A basic two-story with three windows on the upper level and two on the bottom. No real lawn out front, except for two squares on each side of the tall, white door, which protruded with an eyebrow window and a peak above it. Ordinary amongst the eccentric colored houses down Montague Street. Would it ever be much more than a building to me? I missed being on the acreage, with all the grass and flowers. Home consisted of memories. Hard to imagine any would be made here.

Andy had bought the house, without even looking at it, from private sellers named the Hockers—an elderly couple who were looking to downsize. They said the best part about the house was it being right near the water.

The Hockers' burgundy car should've been in the small parking space to the left of the house when we arrived. We were to meet them to get the keys and finalize paperwork. "Where is it?" I asked leaning in toward the front to look at Andy.

"Don't know." He scratched his sandy brown hair. "We'll knock at the door. I'm sure they're inside."

I swung the door open and deeply inhaled the fresh ocean air. My well-worn Keds slapped down on concrete.

A balmy wind whipped my long, strawberry-blonde hair in circles and the hem of my pleated skirt, mocking my papery form, threatening to cart me off into nowhere. I held the skirt down with one hand while accepting my suitcase from the cabby with the other. Andy received his suitcase and put it down next to his feet. He reached for his wallet and paid the fare.

"You're sure you want me to head out?" The cabby asked scratching his beard. "I don't mind waiting."

"Yes." Andy picked up his suitcase. "It's no problem. Thanks for everything."

"My pleasure," the cabby said before tipping an imaginary hat and getting back in his car. Just before he pulled away, he unrolled his window. "Welcome to Lunenburg."

Andy gave a quick wave.

I leaned an elbow over the wooden *Sold* sign on our property, stuck in one of the patches of grass, and said what was on my mind, "I hate it here."

Andy started toward the front door. "This can be difficult or you can look at it as a new beginning. Your choice."

"A new beginning," I scoffed and shook my head. *Don't you mean a new end?* If only I said that last part out loud. Instead, I suppressed my emotions and shifted my glance down to my shoes.

"Fine. Choose to be difficult," he said. "I'm not surprised."

"Yah, I'm what's wrong with all of this," I said through a long-winded sigh.

Andy tightened his grip on his suitcase and turned toward the door. "Are you coming in or not?"

I pulled my elbow off the sign and joined him at the door. It opened before we could knock and I—expecting to see a shriveled old man or woman—stood shocked to see a tall boy with blue eyes as dark as the ocean crashing against the shorelines.

The cuckoo clock of Lunenburg struck, opened, and brought forth a pleasant surprise. It suddenly changed its mundanity, ever unyielding in its effort to prove itself more than what I judged it to be.

The boy had one slender hand tucked in the front pocket of his worn jeans, and the other on the doorknob. I swallowed hard and my face went warm. His fingers moved from his pocket to brush away strands of ash-blond hair from cheekbones carved in shadow. His windblown hair gave the impression he'd been sailing all day. And then he spoke. "You're the Stafford family, right?"

THREE

I tried to coax out words to introduce myself, but no matter how hard I willed it, nothing got past my desert lips that I could've sworn were moist minutes ago.

With a curious look on his face, Andy waited for the reply he probably thought I'd make. When nothing came out, he shot his hand in the boy's direction. "Uh, yah—we are the Staffords. My name's Andy and this is my daughter, Rebecca." The two of them shook hands.

"My name's Shawn." He brought his hand out toward me. I smiled, still unable to speak. When I stared down at his outstretched arm, a hopeful burst overtook me. What if he could do it? What if he could pull me out of the uncertain air? Save me. If we touched, I'd stop drifting.

"Rebecca, don't be rude," Andy whispered. "Give the boy a handshake."

I snapped out of my daze and placed my hand in his. At first, I relished in the warmth of his touch and wondered what type of paper he'd be made of. We gave each other a sturdy shake; the kind business partners give one another after taking on a successful venture. "Hi," I managed to say.

Shawn gave a mischievous grin, revealing a perfect set of teeth. "Hi." He motioned for us to follow him inside. "Can I take your luggage for you?"

"That's nice of you to offer," Andy said before picking up our bags. "But we've got it. Thanks."

Shawn led us into a narrow entranceway. A middle-aged man came around the corner. "Thanks for showing them in, Sonny Boy."

"Pop, you know I don't like when you call me that," Shawn gave a half-grin and disappeared where his Dad came from.

"The name's Phillip Barringer," he said mostly to Andy.

"Nice to meet you."

"My pleasure. Now, you're likely wondering why we fellows are here to greet you."

Phillip told Andy the owners left the keys with them because Mrs. Hocker was recovering in the hospital from a minor heart attack, but that she'd be just fine. He stood a couple inches taller than Andy with the same lean physique, though more muscular. Whenever he moved, a light waft of fish and seawater came off his clothes. There were tattoos on his left forearm. A ship with its anchor twisted around his wrist like a shackle. Beside the ship a squid-like beast lurked with upside down tear-shaped eyes and a hint of crimson in them; a toll of disaster with barbed tentacles reaching, about to pull the ship to pieces. I averted my eyes from the squid and up toward Phillip's face. Despite the tough-guy look, kindness pervaded him.

"In the meantime, here are the keys the Hockers told us to give you," Phillip said. He placed two bronze keys in Andy's palm. "They said they can stick sometimes. You may have to jiggle them a bit to open the door. And there's one last thing for you to sign that I'll deliver back to the hospital for them tomorrow."

Andy took the pen and document Phillip offered him, read things over, and used the wall to sign the bottom line before handing everything back.

"Come then—let's all move into the living room."

We took our shoes off and hung our jackets on some silver sailboat-shaped hooks to the right side of the door, then followed Phillip, scanning the rest of the house on our way.

It was partially furnished with a vintage-sailor quality. The paneled walls were whitewashed, which looked to be the general theme throughout. It had that lived-in smell that old people's homes often have; a thousand dinners made and a hint of harsh cleaner.

We found ourselves in the living room where two foldout beach chairs sat facing a barn-wood coffee table sitting atop a braided, jute rug. Shawn leaned against some dusty sailboat-print drapes left over the bay window, looking out. He moved to sit on the coffee table when he saw us enter.

Andy nudged me and told Phillip, "The one pretending to play shy beside me is my girl, Rebecca." I cringed when he ruffled my hair. "I'm Andy."

"You've got yourself a cute daughter there, Andy. Eh, m'boy?" Phillip winked in his son's direction. Shawn wiped a hand over his mouth and turned his attention to his feet.

If only I could disappear at will like Mom, I thought while tidying my hair behind my ears.

"Teasing is all." Phillip smiled toward Andy. "Hope that's alright."

"No problem," he said. "We both could use some humor after the travel we had."

"Good. Good."

"I don't know how to thank you for going out of your way for us," Andy said, his eyes wandered toward one of the foldout chairs.

"Go ahead and take a load off." Phillip said pulling a chair closer to him. "We didn't know if you guys would run a bit late, so we brought chairs over. We're your neighbors—the house on the left of you."

Based on my observations before, I knew the one he referred to. The moss-green Edwardian with window shutters and red-brown edging and trim. I'd considered it a little gaudy, but now, it seemed whimsical, like it belonged in one of my fairy-tale books. "The houses around here are quaint," I announced.

"What?" Andy blinked his eyes and looked at Phillip. "When we arrived, she was prattling on about how she couldn't stand all the bright colors."

"I wasn't prattling on."

He smirked at me and turned his attention back to Phillip before lowering himself gingerly into the chair. "So, we're neighbors? You'll have to let me in on some of the must-sees in town."

Phillip sat in the other fold-out chair. He and Andy got lost in conversation about Andy's new job with a siding and carpentry company, and the things Andy already wanted to change in this house. Phillip mentioned he used to be a fisherman. When the business dwindled due to the cod moratorium of 1992, he kept it only for hobby, and now made money building boats at The Dory Shop.

I sat down on a piece of carpet next to Andy's chair. Out of the corner of my eye, I saw Shawn get up from the coffee table and walk toward me. I looked up and stopped breathing for a second when our gazes met. He casually pointed down. "You mind if I sit next to you?"

The ends of my mouth stretched into a twitchy smile. "Sure. Go ahead."

I kept my eyes on him this time. He was rugged, amusingly unkempt, and looked as though in pursuit of something great. Like an explorer out to discover new worlds.

A loud screech of brakes came from outside and stole me out of my daydream. Andy rose from his chair and sauntered to the window. He pulled back the drapes to reveal a moving van. "Great timing. Looks like the rest of our belongings have arrived," he said.

Phillip walked over to where Andy stood as Shawn and I shifted in our places looking for something to say to one another.

"The Hockers, the couple who used to live here, told us you guys were coming from Ontario," Shawn said loosely crossing his arms over his chest.

"Yah, Oakville. Have you ever been?"

He shook his head. "No—I've never been anywhere but here."

"It's pretty there. I lived in a simple place on an acreage surrounded by trees, nothing fancy. But it was home, you know?"

"Sounds like you miss it." He leaned back on his hands.

"Miss it?" I shrugged. "I suppose maybe a little." My heart pumped faster and faster and my ears started to burn. I couldn't find a compliment about this town without saying something silly like, *this place is much better to me now that you're in it.*

"Lunenburg doesn't look like much to some." Shawn's eyes wandered around the room and I wondered if I'd offended him with my lack of comment. He whispered, "Beyond the beaches and tourism stuff, like the old-world heritage part of town, there are things that people here try to keep hidden…forgotten."

Before I could ask him what he meant by that, Phillip sauntered over, bent a knee, and threw his arm over Shawn's broad shoulders. "Ready to help the Staffords haul some stuff in?"

"Yep."

When we all got up and went outside, the movers opened the doors to the back of the van. Back and forth Shawn and I went carrying boxes out, while Phillip, Andy, and the movers took the heftier furniture pieces.

The moving van took off after everything had been unloaded neatly in the living room. Andy gave a sigh of relief, moved a few things out of the way, and fell onto our maroon sofa. I joined him seconds later.

Phillip tucked his hands in his jeans. "Did you need help with anything more, Andy?"

Shawn kept staring at me from behind his Dad with an amused grin. What was on his mind?

"You've both done more than enough," Andy said.

"Alrighty. The boy and I are going to head home and shower. You know where to find us if you need."

Andy gave a quick nod. "You bet."

After they'd gone, I lugged my suitcase to the steep stairs and brought it up into the room with the stunning view out to sea. Easing it to the floor, I pushed away the sheer curtain, and opened the window. My shoulder rested against the sill. I continued to mull over Shawn's mystifying comment about stuff being hidden around here—told like a secret meant to be kept between him and me. Lunenburg grew more interesting by the minute.

A glowing shine from the sun created a shimmery ripple on the dark waters of the ocean. The silhouette of trawlers and schooners drifting past calmed me. Especially the schooners. I related now to the way their sails whipped about in the wind but stayed firmly attached to the boat, thanks to Shawn. At the door when we'd met, I pondered whether some of the missing pieces of me had found their way back.

I left my room, paying no attention to where I went. Andy and I collided into one another. "Geez, where are you off to so fast? Here," he said placing a box carefully into my arms. "It's all clothes."

I grabbed it and turned back upstairs, Andy followed.

He ran his hand along the wall as we walked into my room. "Could use some new paint." He peered out of the window and cocked his head. "But look at that view. I'd say it's the best in the house."

We kept moving my things up until our doorbell chimed around 3 o'clock in the afternoon. "Who's that?" I asked stowing a dress away on a hanger in my closet. But I knew, or rather, my heart knew. All kinds of celebration went on inside.

"I'll go and have a look," Andy said.

He left to answer the door and I rushed out of my room to watch from the top of the staircase, being careful not to be seen.

"Oh, hello there. Come on in."

Mrs. Barringer introduced herself as Margaret and carried a pot of steaming soup and what I guessed to be a loaf of freshly baked bread wrapped in kitchen towels. "It's clam chowder for a late lunch," she said. "We also brought along a few other non-perishable odds and ends knowing you wouldn't have had time to shop just yet." Phillip followed her into the house carrying Foodland grocery bags.

"How about I put this on the counter?" Margaret said and walked past Andy to get to the kitchen. After Phillip went with her, Andy spotted me and signaled to come down. Where was Shawn? The party inside me shut down.

I shuffled downstairs, taking my sweet time to get to the kitchen. Once there, I peeked in to see Andy sitting next to Phillip at our oval table close to a tray of food. He slapped his thigh in excitement while reaching for a spoon. "I haven't had homemade in a while, and I'm as hungry as a horse. Thank you for bringing all this over."

His reaction was laid on way thick. Just like his ruffling my hair while introducing me to Phillip, and then the comment about my room being the best view. Blah. Blah. Blah. It was all a manipulation. He wanted me to forget he failed to grasp my hand when I'd wanted him to, forget he extracted me from my comfort-zone.

"Our pleasure. We're just so happy to have new members of our community," Margaret replied. She was a slender pixie-like woman with pointy, ethereal features. "Shawn hasn't been his usual self since his brother, Aaron, left for university back in September. Those two were peas in a pod. But you know, schoolwork and bookings for his band…it's tough for him to make it out here for visits. Besides Aaron, Shawn doesn't spend much time with others. Fairly independent—you know the type. It'll be nice to have someone around his age he can help get acquainted with town."

Phillip nodded. "That's what I say. It will keep the boy from sulking around the house or getting into mischief."

Margaret pursed her thin lips at her husband's assertion and then said, "I'll have to make more soup for you and your daughter. You can freeze it for a rainy day—and there is no shortage of those around here." She poured soup into two bowls. "By the by, where is your daughter? I would love to meet her."

I figured now was the time to enter and took a seat next to Andy. He introduced me to Margaret and afterward said in my ear, "Nice of you to *finally* join us." After we shook hands and greeted one another, Shawn's Mom went back to removing our dishes from a dusty box and putting them in the sink for washing.

Andy placed a bowl full of clam chowder in front of me and pushed a spoon over.

"Didn't Shawn come along for something to eat?" I tried to sound nonchalant about it.

Phillip's body language revealed he knew why I asked. Smiling eyes, a grin struggling not to show itself. "He already ate, and is in the back cutting the unruly grass for your pop."

"Yes, that's very nice of him. It was meant to be your job," Andy said to me with a no-nonsense look. "After you're done eating you go out there and see if he needs a hand."

The party commenced in my heart with even more fervor than before. I played with my soup, absent of an appetite. Still, I forced myself to eat it so I wouldn't appear rude to Margaret.

She approached, looking at me with the same dark-blue eyes her son clearly inherited. I handed her my bowl. "Great soup," I said still tasting the buttery richness of the cream and the delicate sweetness of clam.

"I'm glad you liked it." She placed the bowl by the sink and began to dry the cups she just washed. Her silky pale-blonde hair caught a glowing white shine coming from the window above the sink. I barely knew her, but it comforted me to have a woman around, cleaning and worrying over me...like Mom used to. If I blurred my vision a little bit, I'd swear it was her.

I got up, walked out the patio door, and sat on the deck. The sun, like a golden eye above my head, stared upon the dark purple of my shirt. I turned to my right where I heard the drone of a lawn mower. Shawn's t-shirt sleeves were rolled up like a muscle shirt, and he gave the mower a strong push in a straight line. Severed dandelion heads scattered seeds through the air as he went along cutting. The sweat on his brow forced his hair to fall damply over his forehead.

After getting around some lilac bushes, a hydrangea shrub, and tree in our new yard, Shawn took a break. He didn't look up to notice me sitting on the steps, and I wasn't about to get up and bother him now to say I was here to help. For the time being, he was a work of art to study. Unmoving, as statuesque as The David.

He eventually walked over to the fence separating our properties and reached for a bottle of water sitting atop the uppermost board. He poured it over his head for refreshment from the hot sun. When he shook the water off, I exhaled, awestruck.

He straightened up as soon as he turned and saw me.

"Hi." He strolled back toward the lawn mower. "How long have you been there?"

I took a long time to speak, and didn't even answer his question. "Andy sent me out here to help you."

"I have things pretty much handled," he said. A drop of water fell from his hair and trickled down his jaw. "Thanks though."

We lived in the clique-class of the mid 90s, where the trend was to be forced into some stereotype. Shawn would be *The Daring*; an embodiment of unbridled charisma, needing no one. I was *The Book-Worm*; hiding in between the pages. Naturally, his type intimidated the types like me who weren't as confidant, but needed people. I needed him.

After finishing up, Shawn pushed the mower toward a tarnished shed at the right corner of our lot. The wheels creaked, leaving clumps of cut grass on the ground behind it. He glanced over his shoulder and saw that I left my spot on the deck and sat closer on the grass, watching him. "Rebecca, did you want to do something with me later?"

"Sure," I said, regretting the speed of my reply.

He nodded and carried on storing the mower away before breezing past me and up the patio steps from where I'd come.

Andy and Phillip stepped outside from the kitchen and met up with Shawn, who laughed at something Phillip said, bearing all his teeth. When he started back in my direction, he reached into his jeans pocket to pull out a toothpick and placed it in his mouth. He chewed on it, carefree. Like nothing changed for him like it had for me when we'd met. I envied that. "We don't get this kind of heat all the time. Do you want to swim?" he asked, rolling the toothpick between his lips.

I made sure not to answer too quickly this time. "Okay."

"Cool. I'll get my trunks while you go grab a bathing suit. Meet me out the gates of your backyard." Shawn began walking away. "There's a dock we can get to down the bank," he said as he glanced over his shoulder.

"Sounds fantast—uh, sounds good." I hurried inside the house, up the creaky staircase, and rummaged through moving boxes in my room until I found the dreaded full-piece (which may as well have been from the Medieval ages). Was there nothing else? *For the love of God let there be a suit I didn't even know I had.* Without any luck, I tossed the dull suit aside and decided the black sports-bra and panties I wore would do better. Together they practically looked like a bikini. I surprised myself in my attempt to be bold. Would Shawn tell the difference? Did girls around here wear bikinis? Atlantic water was known to be cold.

Downstairs, Andy, Margaret, and Phillip rearranged the big furniture in the living room when I approached. "Shawn wanted to take me swimming. Can I go?"

Andy barely lifted his head to look at me. "Yah, go. Shawn already asked permission when we met up on the deck."

I didn't linger; I ran out the patio door and down the steps toward Shawn, who leaned against our back gate with a towel slung over his shoulder.

"Shoot, I forgot to grab one of those," I said. Before I turned back, Shawn offered me a towel from his house.

"You can follow me in, if you want."

He opened the gate and led me over into his backyard. We strode by a garage and then I stopped to look up at a square balcony with spindle railing extending out from the very top floor of his house. "What's that?" I said, pointing.

Shawn stopped. "It's called a widow's walk. Lots of homes around town have them. They were used by the wives of sailor's back in the day."

"What did they use them for?"

"They'd look out toward the ocean and hope to see their man's boat coming back home."

"That's so sad."

Shawn nodded. "There's lots of old stuff like that around here...if you like that sort of thing."

We went up onto a deck like the one at my house. As he turned the doorknob and I walked inside, it felt natural, like we'd been friends for years and it was common for me to come over.

We entered the clean, white kitchen that had marble countertops and farmhouse sink. Daisies in a vase decorated the dining table painted the same moss-green as their siding. Beyond it, a staircase led upstairs and next to the stairs was the living room. Black and white art prints of Old Town Lunenburg, seashell décor, and perfectly placed antique fishing equipment hung from the walls. The sun peered through the lacy-white drapes over the windows, leaving complex designs on the distressed wood floor. If Lunenburg had a sailor's museum, it probably looked like this.

Shawn put a hand on the railing of the staircase. "I'll be right back."

After five minutes, my attention diverted to a display of prized fish mounted to my right.

"I see you've met the fish." Shawn said, coming back down with a towel for me. "My pop caught all of them."

"They're all real?" I asked.

He nodded.

"Can I touch one?"

"Sure," he said.

I found a big Atlantic salmon on an oak plaque and was about to touch it when a giant, red lobster began singing, detecting my motion. In a nasally voice, it belted out the lyrics to a nursery rhyme I recognized: "Sailing, sailing over the bounding main..."

Shawn smiled.

I blushed, with a hand to my beating chest. "You knew it would go off."

"I forget that thing is there sometimes and I jump just like that," he said handing me the beach towel.

I put the towel over my shoulder, like Shawn, and followed him out.

"It's a little steep walking down to get to the water—just so you know," he said.

We continued to the other end of his yard and through the gate, which brought us to a flight of weathered, rickety stairs.

I hobbled clumsily onto the first step, trying to avoid getting a foot stuck between the large gaps in the wood. When I lost my balance, Shawn took my hand to steady me. We were both silent for a moment, still holding hands. I knew more than ever. *I'm safe with you.*

"Thanks," I said after he released me.

"Don't mention it."

We made it down to a path of jagged gray rocks. Shawn stopped me. "These rocks can be slippery. I can carry you over if you need…"

Flustered by the enticing offer, I said, "That's okay. I'll be fine."

Minutes later, I looked a complete fool as my ankle rolled on something sharp and I had to limp over the rest of the rocks. I sat on a boulder to inspect it.

"How's the foot?" Shawn asked, wincing. "Pretty bad?"

"It's fine," I lied slowly lifting myself. Why didn't I just take him up on his offer to carry me?

Shawn pulled off his T-shirt and threw it over some tall grass. I pulled mine off next and his dark blue eyes widened. He turned away toward the ocean like a gentleman. Apparently, he knew a sports-bra from a bikini. Once I had my skirt off, I threw my clothes and shoes in a pile next to his. "It's a new style," I said pulling on my bra strap. "Looks like underwear but it's not." He didn't reply. I wished I hadn't said anything about it at all.

We took up our towels and stepped down the narrow strip of beach armored by small to medium cobbles. We approached the edge of the water in silence. Gentle waves swept over the modest portion of sand, depositing light and dark brown pebbles over our bare feet. Shawn turned to face me again, his look intense, examining all of me. My stomach went buoyant and began to tickle me from the inside. I had the urge to wrap up in the towel and hide.

"Should we...uh, go in then?" He still stared, as he pointed out, with a deep, uncompromised focus. Heat radiated along my curves, right to the tips of my toes until all self-consciousness faded. I felt beautiful.

"Yah." I nodded.

Shawn led me down a long salt-stained dock. My ankle ached, but I forced myself to walk as normal as possible. Halfway, he took to a run, passing a few boats tied to posts, and did a cannonball off the edge into the ocean. Water erupted everywhere.

"Is it pretty cold?" I asked when he came up, spitting water from his mouth.

"You just have to dive right in. The faster the better, to get used to it." Water dripped off his face. He swam back to the dock and rested his arms on it.

Bell buoys chimed as fishing boats puttered by. A few seagulls dove down and propped themselves on the cobbles, using their beaks to scavenge the rocks for scraps. Once nearer the dock's edge, I put my towel down neatly and used my hand to shield my eyes from the sun. "I'm too chicken."

"Come on—it'll be fine."

I stared down at the dark water with hesitation. "If you say so." I got to my feet and before I could dip my toe in, Shawn sprung up, grabbed my hand, and pulled me in.

My body slapped into the water. I kicked and thrashed toward the surface, the sensation as severe as stepping outside into frigid winter temperatures stark naked. Every muscle in my body contracted as if to tear off my bones. I chided myself for the foolish choice of swim attire. "I can't believe you did that," I gasped upon reaching the surface.

He laughed and rubbed a hand over his eyes. "If you do the toe test, you'll never go in. Trust me."

I swam toward the dock, trying to make an escape. "You are nuts to want to swim in this icebox."

Shawn propelled toward me and grabbed my ankle, gently forcing me back under with him. As soon as he had me fully submerged, he let go and our noses grazed. I found my way through the darkness back to the sun-warmed surface. "Stop doing that," I said playfully, parting my long hair away from my face.

"Do you really want me to stop?" Shawn asked seriously.

I grinned and splashed water in his face as a response.

"So, that's how it is?"

"Yah, that's how it is," I said.

He and I played this splash and run-away game for several minutes and by then, my skin was numb. I laughed. "You're right. I can't feel the cold anymore." I flicked my wrists. "That's so weird."

"See? I told you." Shawn swam around me. "Race me back to shore?" he challenged, arching one eyebrow.

"You're on," I said.

We lined up next to one another, treading the water heavily. I watched him out of the corner of my eye. This time my heart raced from pure competitive energy. "Are you ready?" Shawn said. "We swim 'til shore. On your mark, get set…go."

Water came up through my nose and washed over my face as I did the front-crawl as hard and as fast as I could. There were times I could see Shawn beside me. His breathing sounded erratic and his determined eyes were fixed on the beach.

Long ago, Mom put me in swimming lessons and I completed it top of my class. I forced my way past him, just in time to see the staggered expression on his face. He was practically at my heels when I reached shallow water and came crashing down onto the unforgiving shore.

I let out a big gasp of air. "I win."

"Just…barely," Shawn said searching for his breath, too. He climbed, rigidly, onto the pebbles and flopped on his back. While I got out of the water and stretched, he looked up toward me with chattering teeth and nearly blue lips. "Must be part mermaid."

"And don't you forget it, Sailor." I smirked down at him, noticing my legs were turning the color of his lips.

We walked down the dock again and grabbed our towels to wrap up in. The feeling finally came back to my skin, and I began to shiver again.

"Three of these boats here belong to my pop," Shawn said while scrubbing his head with his towel. "Come, I have something to show you."

He tapped a finger on a bright blue tarp in between a lobster boat and an inshore fishing vessel.

Sauntering my way to where he was, I asked, "What's under there?"

"It's my humble opinion, that under every tarp, there should be an adventure," he said.

My eyes lit up.

Shawn pulled away the tarp and tossed it to the side, onto sand. "There she is."

The white paint on the outside and navy-blue paint on the inside of the boat had flaked off in a lot of places, communicating many long fishing voyages. The splintering planks of wood and worn seats invaded by barnacles made me question getting inside. "She's got character, I'll give her that," I said.

"It's a wooden dory Pop made a while back. He used to take me on many fishing trips in it. I call her *Old Broken Down* now."

"*Old Broken Down?*" I let out a giggle. "I can see why you call it that."

"Hey, she still has some life left." He grabbed the side of the boat and rocked it back and forth in the water. "Maybe you'd like to test her out with me."

"Go out in that old thing? Really?"

"It'll be fun," Shawn said playfully.

"I don't know. Maybe we should ask your dad if it's alright first."

"He won't mind. Honest."

I crossed my arms over my chest, and eventually let them fall to my sides. It was easy to give in when I wanted so much to impress this jaunty boy. "If we get in trouble it's your hide, not mine."

"Deal." Shawn held *Old Broken Down* steady. "Well, go ahead and get in."

Placing my towel down, I covered the seat and sat. Shawn got in facing me and untied the boat. He picked up the oars attached to the sides and rowed us away through the water. With each stroke, the boat glided further and further from shore.

"Where are we going?" I asked slightly disconcerted.

When our eyes met, a brief, perhaps foolish calm came over me. It was on account Shawn treated me like someone he'd been connected to all his life. Like, to him this wasn't the first day we met. Could that be why when I'd walked into his house it felt so natural?

The oars repeatedly hit the water like a hypnotist's pocket watch going back and forth. He stopped paddling to point out a flashing red light and rock-strewn peninsula, blurred in the distance. "You see that?" I nodded, following his gaze. "We're heading there," he said, mystery in his voice.

FOUR

Clearly, Shawn asked me to go swimming as a ruse. All along his real plan was to take me out on the water in *Old Broken Down* to get to a place with large, concave stone eyes—reminiscent of *Skull Island* in Peter Pan. And that's exactly who he reminded me of; a modern-day Peter. Sprite-like and full of youth, taking me to his Never, Never Land.

He stopped rowing and asked me a question that confirmed the likeness. "How about we play a game?"

I twirled a strand of hair, picked at the barnacles on my seat, and relished how I'd somehow stepped into a make-believe world. "A game?"

"Yah. To ease you up. You look a bit tense."

"I'm not tense," I lied.

"You're fidgety," he said. "You haven't said much in the last few minutes or so."

"I'm just a bit curious about you," I replied, to divert the conversation away from my unease. I intended to find out what made Shawn tick.

"How?" He asked with that boyish sparkle in his eyes.

While under a heavy curtain of intrigue, I could've kissed him right there. "You're so...animated. It's like you see everything painted a color no one else can see."

"You're not far off about being able to see things differently, and if you're curious about me, you'll like the game I've got in mind," Shawn said. "Truth or dare. I'm sure you've heard of it."

"I have."

"Then I'll start. Truth or—"

"Hold it." I held a hand up, smirking. "I'll start. Truth or Dare?"

"Dare,' Shawn answered. "I always choose it. My rule of thumb is to never back down."

"I dare you to tell me why we're going toward that red light."

"Ah, you're a sly one. But that's reserved for a truth." Shawn arched an eyebrow and the corner of his mouth crept up into a smile. "Besides, the fun is not telling you until we get there. Dare me anything but that."

"So much for your never backing down rule."

He laughed. "I break rules all the time."

When he turned from looking at me, it freed me from his magnetism for a time and I stared around at the inky water that surrounded the old boat; the dory's wooden parts creaked like dry bones. A different dare to ask evaded me. I might've been a strong swimmer, but the ocean had an ominousness attached to its beauty. A power, that if wielded, couldn't be controlled.

The boat teetered at the sudden onset of wind that churned the surface of the water and my hands shot out to clutch the sides of the boat.

"Rebecca, you alright?"

I didn't answer.

"Becky, you okay? You look kinda pale."

I relaxed my hands off the boat and said, "Becky?"

"It's a nickname for Rebecca," Shawn said looking behind as he steered. "No one's ever called you that before?"

I blew hair away from my eyes. "No."

"Well, I like it," he said. "It suits you."

"I like it…coming from you."

"That's good." He bobbled his head in a self-assured way and cleared his throat. "Now that we have that figured out, I asked if you're alright."

"I am."

"You haven't been in boats much, have you?"

Nothing ramshackle like this. "Never on the ocean."

"Shawn! Hey! You get that dory back here right now." A voice echoed in the air. Phillip Barringer stood on the edge of the dock.

Shawn took another leisurely stroke, unmoved by his dad's apparent discontent.

It felt like we'd gone miles, but upon looking back we weren't as far off as I thought.

"Let's see you rowing like hell, boy."

"Pop, stop hollering. I'm turning around." Shawn forced the oars back in the water and dug as hard as he could.

Andy rushed down the dock and stood next to Phillip. "What's going on, Rebecca?"

"We're coming back," I hollered. "Don't worry."

"Good. And when you step foot back on this dock you're grounded for a week."

I stood up in the boat. "But—"

"Sit down, you're going to tip," Andy shrieked.

Shawn beamed at my rebellious action. Because it appeared to please him, I rocked the boat a bit, arms outstretched. "Woah, woah. I think I'm going to fall in."

"Rebecca!" Andy shouted. "Stop that."

Shawn chuckled as I sat back down. He continued to row us back, breathing hard and seemingly holding in another laugh.

When we reached the dock, Phillip didn't give Shawn time to tie up *Old Broken Down*. "No lifejackets," he said pulling him out by the arm. "What were you thinking? I ought to make you work the whole summer away. Taking Rebecca out there without asking Andy's permission…" He clicked his tongue and shook his head disapprovingly. "You could have gotten yourselves in danger and we'd have known nothing about it." Phillip eyed us both. He was no one to fool around with when he was upset, tattooed-skin taut and veins appearing around his face. "Did you think of that?"

"It's not that big a deal, Pop," Shawn grumbled trying to wriggle his arm free from his Dad's grip. "Plus, you let me take your boats out plenty of times."

"Yes, but you know this old dory isn't safe. I have work yet to do on it." Phillip crouched over on the dock after Shawn squirmed away, grabbed the rope inside *Old Broken Down*, and began tying it to a post.

"Mr. Stafford," Shawn said. "I want you to know I told Becky to come with me. I persuaded her to get into the boat when she never wanted to." He indeed kept his word about his skin being on the line and not mine.

Andy glared in my direction. "Becky?"

I shrugged. "It's just a nickname."

"I don't care if what Shawn said is true or not. Do you have rocks in your head? Don't you have a mind of your own?"

Once the dory was tied, Phillip laid a heavy hand on Shawn's shoulder and pushed him ahead, walking down the dock. As Andy and I followed behind, I overheard Phillip say, "This better not be about that lighthouse."

"What if it is?" Shawn replied.

Phillip let go of his son. "Shawn, you've been fixated on that damn ruin since you were a little kid. Now you're trying to get Rebecca into it, too? I don't think so. Best you stay away from there."

Shawn looked down at the wooden boards beneath his feet. "It's not a damn ruin."

"Fine. But Son, we're not going through this again. I don't need the Coast Guard on my back. Forget about it. Stay away from there."

"Sure, Pop," he acquiesced. "Whatever you say."

I had a feeling Shawn said what he had to, but did what he wanted. The small feud between him and his dad interested me, greatly. Why was this lighthouse so forbidden? Was this what Shawn referred to when he said stuff was being kept hidden and forgotten in Lunenburg? Suddenly, some of his wild nature came out and bit me, infecting my inhibitions.

While we both picked up our clothes purposefully slow, Shawn whispered, "I'm real sorry about getting you into trouble."

"Don't be sorry. It was actually…fun," I replied, and then waved him closer. "Meet me at the dock at midnight. I have an idea."

"Seriously?"

I nodded.

"What kind of idea?"

"Shhh, just be there."

His grin said it all. I was speaking his language. "You got it."

Andy made me put on my top before continuing. When we reached our backyards, Shawn gave me a wink before we parted ways.

I followed Andy into our kitchen, feeling too good to worry about the lecture sure to come.

"Don't get me wrong, I like our neighbors, but I don't like how easily manipulated you are by this boy," he said. "If you didn't want to get in the boat, why did you? And what's with this nickname business?" He slid his shoes off and walked them over to the front door.

"You're making too much of nothing." I removed my shoes and did the same.

"Yah? Well, explain why the hell you're wearing underwear instead of a bathing suit." He waved his index finger swiftly in front of me.

"My old suit was way too worn out."

"Then wear a t-shirt and shorts for Heaven's sake!"

"Why do you care? I can wear whatever I want."

A heavy frown created shadows over Andy's grey eyes. "You're just sixteen, and still under my rules whether you like it or not."

I gave a snide laugh. "We just got here and suddenly you want to do the *father* thing? Well, it's a little late."

"You don't speak to me like that in my house. Understand?"

"*Your* house. Yah, because you forced me out of mine. You took everything from me."

"Bah!" He waved me off. "It's not wrong that I don't want you parading around barely dressed in front of teenage boys. I know what's on their minds."

"I bet you do. But Shawn's not like that."

"Oh, and I guess you'd know from spending time with him for just a few hours."

"You're bitter toward Shawn, but really, you should be thanking him. I haven't seen Mom since he and I met," I said adjusting my backpack on my shoulder. "Isn't that what you wanted? For these visions to go away?"

"I'm done discussing this. Right now, you're going to be put to work. Got that? We still have moving in to do."

"Sure, Pop," I repeated Shawn's line. "Whatever you say."

The comment whizzed over Andy's head.

"Phillip is introducing me to some guys at work tomorrow afternoon and taking me to look at used vehicles. I'll have a *You're Grounded* list on the table. I expect everything on there to be done when I come home."

"Uh-huh."

An awkward pause lingered between us. We stared at one another.

"If you're done being snarky, how about something to eat?" Andy offered. "You must've worked up some kind of appetite. I can warm up the rest of the chowder."

"Not hungry."

He pointed a finger in the direction of our stairs. "Go organize your room, then. You're lucky I did some of it for you."

"I didn't ask you to."

I made my way up and closed the door. The bed was made with linens and the smell of old was overtaken by fresh air and laundry. I changed from my soggy clothes into a new pair of underwear and an oversized sweater and leggings.

I peeled the tape off a box marked *Rebecca's paper*, found my book of origami patterns and a sheet of navy blue paper with a white backing. I crossed my legs on my bed, turned to page 21 and began folding. Once complete, I held a very simple boat in hand. "Why hello, *Old Broken Down*." I reached over to my nightstand, placed the paper dory down, and set an alarm. No matter how nervous I felt sneaking out, I would keep my promise to Shawn.

I fell on my pillow, my hair cold and damp against my neck, and anticipated midnight. Remembering how Shawn looked at my body, how close we were in the water, noses skimming against each other, made me grab the pillow next to me to smother my giddy scream.

I tossed the pillow back in its place, turned on my side and ogled the clock changing from one minute to the next.

***

Tiny seashells crunched underneath our feet as we raced past patches of yellow grass peeking out of pebbly sand. Shawn held a flashlight in one hand and in the other he clutched my wrist, urging me to run faster and faster. My hair beat against my back. The ruckus of wind echoed overhead. We were in front of the ocean, *Old Broken Down* waited at the dock, curling back and forth on a wave, like a finger summoning us to come join in. The discordant collision of waves crashed against the shore.

Shawn pulled me, coaxing me on. When he left my side to untie the dory, red, origami tanagers swarmed in front of me. The wild flutter of wings became the wind whipped fabric of my mother's dress until her whole body materialized. The warning on her face spoke volumes. She didn't want me to get inside the boat with Shawn.

I reached out to touch her, but the vision dispersed and the tanagers flew off into the grey of the sky. In a blink, Shawn and I were halfway out to sea. His arms rowing faster than humanly possible, his expression morphing into lunacy. Before we hit one of the large boulders of the island, my alarm clock went off and woke me. My hand slammed down on the nightstand meaning to stop the buzzing and instead, crushed the paper dory.

FIVE

There was a dull glow around the quarter moon, casting thin wavy lines of white over the ocean's surface. Everything eerily quiet, apart from lapping water against the sides of boats and underneath the dock. I sat with my back against one of the posts, hoping I'd see Shawn making his way down the rickety stairway and past the treacherous rocks I sprained my ankle on hours ago. I directed the flashlight I'd taken from Andy's tool box in that direction, intermittently. The grating of rocks against one another and driftwood cracking like knuckles brought me to stand. A bobbing shine came from a lantern.

"Shawn?" I turned my flashlight to see a shadowy figure approach over the last layer of rocks.

"Yah, it's me." He used his free hand as leverage and hopped over the large boulder I'd rested on prior. The wick in the lantern snapped and wavered.

"Part of me thought you weren't going to come," I said as he reached the dock and walked across to where I stood.

"You kidding? Part of me thought you weren't serious." His black hooded zip-up sweater camouflaged him well. "No offense, but you don't strike me as the overly—"

"Gutsy type?"

"Yah."

"I can be, sometimes."

"Suppose so. Like when you stood up in the boat and rocked it. That was something else." Shawn chuckled. "Your pop almost blew a gasket."

"Andy's always blowing gaskets," I said. "In fact, I think all he's made up of is machinery."

"So, what's your idea?"

"At this point, do you have to ask?" I said, an eyebrow arched. "Take me out to the lighthouse."

"Don't have to tell me twice." Shawn put the lantern down on the dock to uncover *Old Broken Down*. "By the way, I get a kick out of you calling your pop by his first name. What's the story there?"

"No story. Just drama. Wouldn't want to bore you with the details."

"Ah," Shawn said nodding. "Seems like our pops aren't too different."

"How do you mean?"

Shawn struggled to untie the knot in the rope anchoring the boat to the dock. "My old man isn't comfortable with my idea of fun. He'd rather me do what regular boys do like filling their heads with sporty cars and a hard day's work."

With Peter Pan still fresh on the brain, I said, "I think grown-ups like them forget the joys of being young." I added, "But I don't think your dad is like Andy at all. I can see he cares for you, deeply. He knows you. Andy doesn't have a clue who I am."

"And who are you, then?" Shawn asked.

"That's a pretty broad question."

"Well, if you could describe something about yourself in one sentence, how would you do it?"

"Hmmm." My eyebrows rose for a beat. The first thing that sprung to mind was, *I'm a nerd.* I wanted to say extraordinary, but instead went with, "I've been told I'm pretty smart. I like to read…especially fairy-tales and fantasy books.

"Dig deeper," Shawn said.

"I don't know." I shrugged. It's like he knew I wanted to share something important, but held back. "I've always wanted magic to exist."

"A girl after my own heart," Shawn said. "But what if it does?"

"I get the feeling this is something to do with that lighthouse."

Shawn tapped the end of his nose to confirm my question, and I wanted to laugh because no one did stuff like that anymore. He was right out of a story.

With the knot finally untied, he got inside the dory and removed a thick bar with a hook from under a seat and slid it into a holder. "Can I get the lantern, please?"

"Sure." I flicked off my flashlight and set it down. It didn't need to be brought along.

After I handed the lantern over, Shawn hung it on the hook, helped me inside, and gave me a reflective-yellow lifejacket. "Safety first, this time," he said, putting his own on.

"Yah. I thought your dad was going to string you up by your toes when he saw we had no lifejackets earlier." I zipped mine.

Shawn nodded. "No doubt. He was pretty disappointed in me."

"What was all that, don't get Rebecca into the lighthouse stuff, that he said?"

"Drama." He flashed a grin. "I wouldn't want to bore you with the details."

"Touché."

We both eased onto our seats, and even though this was my idea, *Old Broken Down* made me uncomfortable as ever. I didn't want to pay the nightmare any credence, but it had a lot to do with why.

Shawn propelled us away into the foggy night, and my fears were left on the dock to wane into nothingness.

"I overheard your mom tell Andy you have a brother. What's he like?" I asked.

"Aaron? He's like all big brothers, I guess," Shawn said. "They rough you up a little bit and bug you most of the time...but they're cool." I noted a hint of sadness in his voice. "But it's different now that he's in university over in Halifax. He doesn't come around as much anymore." He looked behind to gauge our direction.

"I see." I dipped my fingers in the water and a few minutes later asked, "What do you do when Aaron comes home? Did you ever go to the lighthouse with him?"

"No—he showed no interest in going," Shawn said hurriedly. "But he tolerated my fascination, and knew it was always on the corner of my mind, itching. He'd let me talk about it to scratch the itch inside. We'd usually bike trails and end up sinking our feet into some random beach out of town, build a fire. Aaron taught me how to play the acoustic guitar, so we'd jam together outside. That sort of thing."

"Maybe someday you can play me a song he taught you," I said, liking the way the white-blond hair on Shawn's arms glowed in the lantern light, as if covered in a layer of pixie dust.

"I guess I could. I'd need to brush up, though. I haven't played since he left. My mind's been occupied elsewhere," Shawn's voice drifted off.

A white pyramidal tower at the tip of the breakwater began to take shape, emitting a reddish light. The same one I saw at a distance, yesterday. A fog-horn wail sounded out.

I figured this to be the lighthouse, but when we moved around the other side of it and kept on, I wasn't sure. Black waves crashed against the precipice of the tree-laden peninsula in a continuous cycle, getting raucous as we drew nearer.

"I always wondered what it would be like to have a sibling, but my parents divorced and neither remarried," I said to fill the silence that settled between us.

"Can I ask you what happened to your mom?" Shawn pushed a strand of his hair behind his ear without losing the rhythm of his rowing.

"We were very close. But, there was a car accident…she never made it."

"Wow, that's awful. I'm so sorry." Shawn lowered his head. "Now I feel like a jerk asking about it, and complaining that I don't see my brother as much."

I shook my head quickly. "Please don't feel bad. It's okay to miss your brother. That's normal for anyone. Besides, I still feel my mom with me." I wanted to tell Shawn about my visions of her. With his last comment about magic, he might've been the type to understand.

When the dory hit the rocky shore without warning, my body jerked forward. Shawn's swift hands kept me from falling face-first to the bottom of the boat.

"Are you okay?" He hoisted me up and his hands lingered on my waist. "Those rocks just came out of nowhere. I rarely take this route, but with the fog and whatnot..."

"That's the second time now you've protected me from a fall." I looked up at him, his eyes black in the darkness. "Thanks."

"Welcome."

We both removed our lifejackets. Shawn checked the lantern over to make sure it hadn't suffered any damage by the impact. Afterward, he said, "Feel free to use my shoulder while getting out."

I took the offer and watched as he hopped onto shore, no trouble at all with those sea-legs of his. Tying the dory's rope around a hefty, lichen-encrusted rock, he directed the lantern at the bow. "I knew I heard something. Looks like we added another scratch to *Old Broken Down*."

I shuddered. "How big is a scratch?"

"Nothing too serious." The ambiguity of Shawn's statement offered no comfort.

He began toward a far-off wall of gray rocks. "We have to climb up that cliff ahead to get to the lighthouse. It's not the easiest, but there's a rope ladder halfway up that I made. Come on."

White mist crawled off the ocean's surface and slunk on shore, covering our shoes while we walked. I looked up when we reached the cliff.

It looks worse than it is," Shawn said. "I'll go first. There's a point where there's a natural ledge. Once I reach it, I'll kneel and hover the light from above enough that you should be able to see where you're going." He held the lantern handle between his teeth and began the climb with astonishing agility, being careful to grab the strongly wedged rocks and step into clefts in the rock face. I started climbing only when the orangey beam shone down on me.

"I'm right here if you need help," he said.

I chipped a few nails trying desperately to grasp and hold on as I moved up. It was a struggle getting to the ledge—not as easy as Shawn made it seem. But once there, I saw the braided ladder in his hand. "Do you want to go up first this time?" he asked.

"You go ahead. I need a breather." Several minutes went by before I had the energy to climb again. When my hand finally seized the very top of the cliff, Shawn pulled me gently over onto sodden grass.

Flashing the lantern toward the forest, he started toward it.

I stood up and swept myself off. "Where are you going?"

"The lighthouse is about a hundred yards away, veiled by these tall trees."

"Wasn't the tower I saw back there the lighthouse?"

"Not even close."

"Why don't I see shafts of light coming through the woods then?"

"The real lighthouse hasn't been working for years," he said.

"Can we wait a bit before carrying on?"

"There'll be plenty of time to rest when we get there, I promise."

Thick gnarled branches bent here and there and the smell of damp leaves made me think of this as an enchanted forest. Ocean gusts slunk between the trees, whispering to one another about *The Great White Father* being home; how everything was back to how it should be. I took long strides to keep up with Shawn, not really watching where I stepped. My feet knocked the heads off large mushrooms and mashed them as I traipsed on in the shadows.

In a clearing, Shawn held the light up toward a barn-wood shanty. But my eye turned to the forbidden lighthouse next to it: cylindrical, rust-stained, and grand. I stood agog in its presence, having never seen one in person before.

"There's some coal and dry wood in that old place. I'll grab a few logs and I'll make a bonfire," he said.

We reached the shanty and Shawn tried the door, the top of which had a broken window. "Stuck," he said. He handed me the lantern and began using his shoulder to ram the door. It swung open with a loud, agonizing creak.

Shawn stepped inside, while I looked on from my spot on the rotting porch and lifted the light. He walked across overturned boards covered in exposed nails, partly used beeswax candles, and broken dishware. A Celtic wool tapestry with an eagle hung on a far wall off kilter.

He picked up six dry pieces of wood from a heap next to a brick fireplace and piled them in his right arm. "This should be good enough for now."

Shawn led me behind the lighthouse and down a slight hill to get to a pit of ash surrounded by stones in front of a Northern bayberry bush. While he piled the wood tepee-style in the pit, and broke off the bark to use as kindling, I sat cross-legged and kept the lantern on him so he could see what he was doing. Reaching into a pocket of his jeans, Shawn pulled out a matchbook, opened it, and ripped off a match. It took some tries before the wood caught, but once it began, the fire spit and crackled into a roaring flame, eating up the dryness.

"So, why aren't we going inside the lighthouse?" I implored, this question gnawing at me.

"You aren't quite ready."

"I'm not?"

"Give it time," Shawn replied. He reached back to grab a fistful of leaves from the bayberry and sprinkled them over the fire like a wizard throwing ingredients into a potion. I wanted to ask why he did that until a waft of the fragrance found me.

He drew puffs of smoke toward his nose with his fingers and breathed in. "It's like Christmas morning."

"That's exactly what it smells like." I paused to enjoy the aromatherapy and turned the knob of the lantern until the flame went out. "So…do a lot of other people come out here? Your dad made it sound like it's a place to avoid."

"The officials in town, along with the Coast-Guard, prohibits entry." Shawn poked at the coals with a damp twig he picked up from the ground. "Most people follow the rules. I'm not like *most* people."

"I noticed," I said rubbing my hands together in front of the fire.

"You did, did you?" he grinned.

"Yah, but in a good way."

"Well, you surprised me," Shawn said. "And I like that, because not many can. You're turning out nothing like my first impression of you." He grinned. "In a good way."

"Your first impression of me was bad?"

"No, it's that…well, I didn't know if I could trust you."

"That's an odd thing to say. And you trust me now?"

He eyed a whorl of sparks that drifted off and disappeared in the dark. "I do."

"Still, we don't really know one another."

Shawn shrugged. "Trust is a gift you give someone at your will. It doesn't have to take years. I'm a bit of an intuitive guy, and my instincts say I can trust you."

"Thanks," I said, eyes on the fire. "I don't know what all that means, but thanks."

"It means, even though we haven't talked about everything under the sun, I'm comfortable with you," Shawn said. "I heard that similar minds gravitate toward one another, like some magnetic thing."

My palms got hot and, as badly as I wanted to, I tried not to smile ear-to-ear. "I can see that being true. I mean, I sensed your openness to me and that made me feel I could trust you, too."

"It's part of the *real* magic in this world."

I nodded. "I think so."

"I want to share a big part of who I am with you, that nobody else understands. But if my intuition is solid, something you might totally get." Shawn's eyes impelled me to look right at him as if to say without words, *I know you want to share a secret, too. It's safe to tell.* "It's about this place."

"Yes, I've been dying to know," I said. "There are so many questions swimming in my head."

"And I hope I answer them for you," Shawn said. "I'll begin by mentioning the technical name of this area is Battery Point. Still, I know it *only* as O'Sullivan Island. It's not exactly an island, per say. But its remoteness makes it feel like one. Anyway..."

He cleared his throat and in an ethereal, story-telling voice continued, "A long time ago, around 1870, an Irishman named Jack O'Sullivan traveled to Nova Scotia by boat from Kilbrittain, Ireland. He settled here, and became the next lighthouse keeper.

"On the voyage, Jack brought with him a vial of rain-water from the limestone hills known as the Mendips, south of Bristol and Bath, which the Celts believed to hold special properties. Whoever or whatever it touched, would be gifted health and longevity." Shawn stoked the fire. "Legend has it, Jack anointed the lighthouse's Fresnel lens with this water so the light may never falter for seafarers coming and going from the harbor. He also anointed himself. When Jack died, folks say he got to live 110 years, maybe even more, and hadn't aged a day from when he'd taken the waters."

The shadows in between the fire's blaze played with the features on Shawn's face, drawing his eyebrows and ears to point a little more. "Eventually, word spread about the unusual lighthouse keeper who didn't grow old. Resources speculate a curious seaman happened upon the island, spotted the lighthouse, and found Jack penning a journal entry. He overheard him utter something under his breath about the day being his 99th year. Meanwhile, not looking more than forty. The lighthouse became quite the tourist attraction after that. Jack was forced to hide the vial itself, afraid it might fall into the wrong hands.

"People from all corners of Nova Scotia came begging to take the waters. Mostly the sick. They rushed to the island in droves to camp the night, and then eventually were told that the vial was no more. Another option to receive the water's properties was given. The custom started with everyone drinking ale, singing Jack's favorite Irish songs and some he'd made up, and then listening to his stories around a fire—like what we're doing now. It ended with Jack leading the campers up to the lantern room. Because the Fresnel had been anointed and it appeared no harm befell anyone out at sea around Lunenburg since then, Jack believed it might be enough to have them touch it."

"Did it work?"

"There aren't any reports that say it did or didn't. But I think it would've if the water held that much power."

I leaned on my side and rested an elbow in the wet grass. Did this legendary world of Jack O'Sullivan feel more real to Shawn than his own life back at home? "Tell me more about the stories Jack told the visitors."

"Some of them were life stories, others more mystical. He changed it up with every new crowd, I assume. Since there were many, I won't go into every one. I'll just tell you my favorite," he said. "The Grim Reaper visited Jack one night, either in a dreamful state or while fully conscious, depending what book you read it from."

"Which do you like to go with?"

"You already know the answer to that," Shawn said with a wink. "So, the Reaper demanded the vial and the lighthouse's lens. It angered him that those two things kept people out of his clutches by upsetting the natural order, keeping people alive longer." He paused and blew the flame out on the end of the twig he poked the fire with and set it aside. "I know it all sounds far-fetched..."

"I've read stranger tales from the Irish. I think them interesting," I said smiling as Shawn reached and threw two more pieces of wood on the fire. "Go on, please."

"Jack cast the Reaper away, shouting, "O let any man who touches the waters be safe from head to toe; may his path be lit to journeys ahead, where darkness may never go!" The fire snapped embers near us and Shawn snuffed them out with his shoe. "Too bad in later years, the town labelled Jack a charlatan, and the special properties of the water a fabrication from an unsettled mind. Instead of keeping the history pertaining to him, after he died, they called it strictly legend and said the lighthouse was no longer here. That all that's left is the one on the breakwater."

"Yet here we are looking at its magnificence," I said.

"Everyone calls me a kook for believing imaginary drivel and here they're lying the whole time."

Andy wasn't *everyone*, but I related to the feeling.

"At fourteen, when pop allowed me to boat out without supervision, I needed answers after all I'd been told and read. I went out there and discovered the farce at so-called Battery Point."

"You'd think more would've done as you have. Surely, there are some who still believe."

"There are few in this world, Becky, who believe in anything anymore. Never mind the old stories."

"What is this legend to you? Like, what makes you think it real?"

He moved closer to me, avoiding a cloud of smoke smothering him. "My Grandpa Barringer—who isn't with us anymore—used to tell me tales of Jack when I was little. I soaked all that up like a sponge. My pop asserts, along with everyone else in town, that Jack is folklore. Myth. Not to be believed. That grandpa wouldn't want me turning into one of those Oak Island nuts, who wasted their time excavating for Captain Kidd's treasure only to come up with diddly-squat. I think my grandpa believed Jack's stories. And if he were here, would support what I'm doing. Anyway, it's not treasure I'm after. Not really. What would I do with gold? No, it's much more profound than that."

I sat up. "How so?"

"Legends aren't implausible. Not to me. Every story comes from a truth."

"Even the supernatural kind?"

"Especially those," Shawn said.

"Hmm." I absorbed his answer and my audacity to consider my visions supernatural. Didn't I already know what to call them, but feared doing so? In the meanwhile, I asked, "Unearthing the truth hidden in the legend, that's the treasure you seek?"

"I already know the truth. The vial is real, and I'm going to find it. Get the chance to become part of something more. Take a page out of O' Sullivan's book and share in his legacy. People try to convince me to drop it by saying I'll be wasting precious life. I don't believe I'll have wasted anything. If I find that water, the time I spent won't matter, because I'll be given more years," he said slyly.

I thought of our paper hands linked and then ripped away by death. My death. "All the people you love…you'd outlive them."

"Not if I share it with them." Would I be one of the lucky ones? I hoped. "Don't you worry that after all these years the water in the vial might've dried up?"

He sprinkled more bayberry leaves over the flame. "This kind of water doesn't dry up."

I pointed up at the lighthouse. "Why not go up there right now and touch that Fresnel lens if it's been given powers, too? That makes more sense."

"It's gone. Has been for years."

"Gone?" I bit my lower lip. "Wow. The Coast Guard, or whomever is in charge, obviously wants this legend as dead as Jack."

"That is the *logical* explanation, or..."

My eyes widened. "The Grim Reaper has it."

"The Reaper could only return after Jack died due to the protective proclamation he'd spoken. Darkness could never come at any man who'd encountered the water, either from the vial or the lens. The vial, hidden very carefully, remained unfound. But not the lens. Jack made a mistake. He should've included in the proclamation that not only any man but any*thing* that touched the waters was off limits, too."

"I better help you find this special vial, then," I said with conviction, allowing myself to get wrapped up in the story. "We can't have the Reaper finding it before us."

"I knew I could trust you." Shawn flared out his chest, apparently proud of his intuition not leading him astray. "Still, I'm curious. What makes you want to go along with all this crazy stuff? I have a sense it's not just my charming good looks luring you in."

Perhaps, now was the time to be clever, like Shawn, and let my impulses guide me. Spill everything about my visions. I smiled. "It might be."

He gave a flattered chuckle.

I turned to stare through the orange fingers of the fire glowing in front of us. *Rebecca Leah Stafford is not ordinary. Remember?* The decision was made. "Frankly, I'm no stranger to the extraordinary myself…"

SIX

We kicked ash over the weak fire. A final, skinny curl of smoke dissipated before us into the dawn.

"You can't just leave me hanging," Shawn said. "Tell me what that means."

We'd been so wrapped up in our discussion that we lost track of time. "Even if I'm not overly anxious getting back into your leaky little boat," I teased, "I'll tell you another time. I should get back home. If Andy wakes up to find me gone, it'll be the end of the world as we know it."

"Tell me on the way."

"I'm not the most comfortable out on the water in *Old Broken Down*. It wouldn't come across how I want."

"Ok, fine. But you owe me an explanation sooner than later because now I'm going to be up all night thinking about you."

I knew Shawn meant he'd be up thinking about what was extraordinary involving me, but I liked how he'd said it. I wanted very badly to be the Wendy to his Pan, and have this island be ours alone. A place I could be with someone who made me feel like I belonged in this new town. Someone equally unusual, but who didn't hide or question it. Rather, relished being that way.

During the trip back, Shawn brought up books to divert my attention away from the wooden groans of the dory as the water squeezed it like a vice. Apparently, our tastes toward the classics were similar. We talked about the recent stories we'd read and why we liked ones over others. When the conversation turned to poetry, we recited our favorite lines from *Romeo & Juliet*, *Hamlet*, and *Macbeth*.

It felt like mere seconds getting back to shore after the fun talk we had. Shawn's hand grazed mine once we were home, in front of his backyard. "See you around?" he said.

Our eyes met, and the shiver up my arm lingered. "Yah."

I slipped into the house just before four o'clock in the morning with my skin and hair smelling of smoke and the sea. A few stairs creaked lightly on the way up to my room, but Andy's door was shut and I heard snoring. Relief washed over me as I crept into bed. I hoped to dream about being in Shawn's arms like when he'd caught me from falling in *Old Broken Down*.

***

I walked downstairs and found the patio door open, rapping against the wall in a slow, spooky fashion. A deafening draft whistled and nipped my feet as I closed it. The odd sensation of being watched trickled down my spine. Peering out at our back yard, I saw that everything outside looked like an assemblage of different colored paper pieces. A collage of cut shapes. The deck and the lawn had vanished, replaced by a long stretch of fragmented beach and ocean with waves rising in zeal and then fainting upon the shore.

Part of me wondered if I'd become papery shards when I made my way outside, but my bare feet crept along on the flat pebbles, still flesh. I had on an all-white gown, blank against the multi-colored blue and black sky.

The ocean continued its melodic tempest, but I heard someone call my name in between the howls of the wind. Looking left, I saw Mom in the distance dressed in white, too.

"Stay there," I called out. "I'll come where you are."

But my ears perked and heart skipped the moment I heard, "Becky." Only one person used that nickname. I turned to the right.

"Shawn!"

He stood at a distance on a misshapen dock, also in white clothing. When I started in his direction, I questioned my choice and froze mid-step. My head turned from side to side, Mom to Shawn. Both ran toward me and grabbed hold of my arms. They yanked, pulled, urged me to go with them. "Stop it. Stop!" I begged.

Everything went silent at my command; the noise of the sea, the wind. Without warning, we turned into two-dimensional beings; weightless, picked up by a soundless gust. We whipped around manically, yet Mom and Shawn kept tugging me right then left, wrestling. An epic battle in the air, we fluttered and bent into strange contortions.

When my body began to tear in a horrific *chhht*, I jolted out of the dream. The humming shred continued, though I rubbed the crust from my eyes, and realized Andy turned on his electric razor in the bathroom across from my room.

"That thing sounds like a rusty paper-shredder," I hollered. "Ever think about getting a new one?"

"Not if it gets lazy teenagers out of bed," he replied. "I might just loan it out to every other father in town. Could make a pretty penny."

"Har, har." I threw my pillow over my head.

"Now that you're awake, I could use a hand setting up the patio furniture in the backyard and feeding the birds after I'm done in here." By turning his razor back on, he didn't give me a chance to request a few more essential hours of rest. Then again, with him occupied in the bathroom, it gave me time to try and reach Mom somehow.

The shower turned on and vibrated the water pipes in the walls. I got dressed, rushed downstairs, grabbed a granola bar from the groceries the Barringers bought for us and went outside to find a hidden place.

Behind a lilac bush outback, I sat down and ate my snack. I knew seeing Mom willy-nilly wouldn't happen. She came only when I needed her. When my nerves shook with unease. Like when she'd appeared in the middle of the street on our arrival in town. All the same, I had to try. I just couldn't shake the guilt I woke up with after that dream.

I had to get myself worked up somehow. I began to rifle through memories of Mom and I. Giggly moments before bed, heart to hearts about boys, laughing and crying during our favorite movies. A compressing ache sat on my chest and I stopped breathing for a time. Until…Shawn.

I realized I'd never again have visions of Mom so long as my thoughts directed to him; who may as well have been Ativan—those anxiety pills Andy took when he got wound too tight. Shawn was my calm. Euphoria. All pain and emptiness deteriorated at the mere whisper of his name in my head.

If I hadn't woken when I had, would Shawn have held more of a piece of me than Mom after the tearing finished? I knew the answer. I'd walked toward him first, hadn't I?

All the rest of that day, while I worked around the yard with Andy, I reprimanded myself about it. *You're a bad daughter.*

***

I spent three days in my room mindlessly doing origami, trying to muster even a glimpse of Mom (whenever I had a spare moment away from Andy's never-ending list of "You're Grounded" chores). I pressed and folded, folded and pressed, trying to keep my thoughts only on her.

On the fourth day, I placed my last red tanager on the dresser brimming with others, and left back to the lilac bush outside.

Instead of merely trying to think about her, I spoke aloud as if she stood in front of me, hoping this might prove more successful.

"That time you found me putting on your pink lipstick, wearing your straw sun hat at five years old…you laughed and laughed. Thinking it was so cute because I tried to act like you in the mirror. *Rebecca, it's time to put your toys away and go to bed or no more story time.*" I let out a suffocated laugh, and a stitch of pain weaseled into my heart. Just like before, right on time, Shawn inundated my thoughts. "Focus," I reprimanded myself. "You can do this."

I slapped at my cheeks as if that might help, and continued. "When Eric King gave all the other sixth grade girls Valentines and not me, you said it was because he liked me the most and was too shy to let me know it. Or, how you loved dancing. You'd take my hands if there was music playing in a store, wherever we were, you'd swing me around. I wish you'd appear now. I wish we could dance." My words choked out, lungs constricting. Hot tears pooled. This was it. Any moment now, she was going to show up.

Instead, an epiphany casually presented itself, like a bowing gentleman, and removed all my guilt from the premises. *Maybe your mother sent Shawn to you.*

She of all people would never want me to be set flailing about, no direction in life. Lost.

Rather than the Hockers greeting us at the door, Shawn appeared like a wish granted. Someone with the power to ease the burden of Mom's passing. Who made me feel like living. Someone willing to take my frail, paper hand.

It all made sense now.

Or, was it that the missing pieces of me came from my mind and Shawn put them back where they belonged. The issue remained what to tell him.

I have visions. They are real, but you're the reason I don't have them anymore. Actually, I'm a fraud. Nothing about me is extraordinary, but I want to be so badly that I make things up. I want to impress you. I need you to love me.

Through the blur of stubborn tears unwilling to drop, feet materialized in my line of site. "Mom?" I said, hopeful butterflies in my stomach.

"Mom?" Shawn said.

I jumped up from sitting and wiped my eyes on my shirt sleeve. "Shawn."

"I heard you saying something. You sounded upset, so I came right over."

"Oh, really?" I shot up from the ground. "That's nice of you."

"Did I interrupt some kind of ritual you have regarding your Mom?" he asked. "Cause I can go."

"Uh…no. No ritual." We walked out from behind the lilac and sat on the steps of the deck. "How much did you hear and see?"

"Not much other than you reciting something out loud while crying. A prayer or something?"

"I wasn't praying." *Maybe I should've been.* I took both of his hands. "Remember, I wanted to tell you something extraordinary?"

"Remember?" He chuckled, looking down at our hands and then up at me. "How could I forget?"

"I wasn't sure I could tell you at first. I wondered if you would truly understand. I mean, I know you aren't the judgmental type, or at least you don't seem to be. But after you told me about Jack…"

Shawn cut me off. "Becky, slow down. Just tell me." His eyes were wide.

"I see my Mom." There, I said it.

The grind of gravel onto the lot and the sound of a bubbly muffler meant Andy was home. He'd bought a used pickup truck the day Phillip took him to look at vehicles. I knew the sound of it already.

Shawn continued to pepper me with questions I couldn't answer now with Andy around, who I heard exiting his truck. "What do you mean? I thought your Mom was dead?"

"Well, she is but—" The front door slammed shut and Andy called my name from inside. When I turned to look over my shoulder, he was glaring from the patio door window and then opened it.

Shawn spit out a couple more staccato questions. "So, if you see her...do you mean you see her ghost? Can you see other spirits?"

Andy towered over us and tilted his head toward the door. "Get inside."

I let go of Shawn's hands.

"Now," he said before turning on his heel, and back in the house.

"Are we in trouble?" Shawn asked.

"Not *we*. Me." I sighed and got up. "We'll catch up later."

"That's almost exactly what you said last time. You got me on pins and needles."

"I know, and I'm sorry." I waved and joined Andy inside. "What now?"

"Don't give me lip," he said, at the sink, tinkering with the dirty dishes. "I wanted supper started and these clean by the time I got back from work. Instead, you're busy holding hands with the neighbor's son."

"I was excited to tell him something. Chill out."

"That you see spirits?" He grumped. "Just get over here and help me. You still have a few more days of being grounded."

I grabbed a dish-cloth. "And you keep reminding me."

After dishes and a quick supper of spaghetti, I went out on the deck and sat on the rattan lounger, one leg dangling, taking in the harbor sounds and the smell of lavender soap coming off the laundry drying on the clothesline. I wondered what Shawn's plans were tomorrow for Canada Day.

A babble of conversation and clatter coming from the front of the house interrupted the serenity. I slid out of the hammock and went to see what was going on. The Barringers had their truck parked in front, the tailgate down, and were pulling sheets of wood off it.

My eyes scanned Shawn up and down, hungrily. He changed his clothes from last I saw him. Blue jeans with a tear at the knee and a well-worn white shirt that clung wonderfully to his skin.

"Hey Becky," Shawn said noticing me approach.

I thought it neighborly to ask, "Did you guys want a hand?"

"No need, but thanks," Phillip said while he and Margaret carried five long pieces of lumber in the direction of their backyard.

"Your dad building something?" I asked Shawn.

"Uh…" He slid some pieces off the truck onto the ground. "I'm helping him with something for work."

"I see." I shifted my position, smiling. "Maybe after you're done that, you and I can sneak off somewhere. Say, the island? I can finish telling you what I wanted to before Andy rudely interrupted. If not today, tomorrow. For Canada Day and all."

"Shoot," he said. "Is it Canada day tomorrow already?"

"It is."

"Gee, I'd love nothing more than to take in some of the festivities," Shawn said. "But, this project with Pop is going to keep me busy pretty much all Friday and this weekend." He knelt to pick up the wood.

It wasn't like Shawn to stay tied to a project forced by his dad. My smile faded. "Oh."

"But there's always the fireworks. Can't very well miss those," he said. "The Yacht Club shoots them off every year around 11pm. Did you want to go with me?"

My spirits rose again. "Sure."

"Then it's a date. I'll knock on your door a half-hour before then." Shawn balanced three two-by-fours in his arms, moving in the direction his parents went.

A date. I floated to the backyard, fell on the grass, and gazed heavenward, wrapped in the damp embrace of the evening.

"Mom," I said softly. "Thank you for sending Shawn to me." I'd already told him I was extraordinary, in so little words. *The die is cast.* "It had to be you. You're known to do thoughtful stuff like that. I only wish I hadn't stopped seeing you after meeting him." A loud sigh escaped me.

At the rustle of jean fabric, I turned my head to see Andy coming down the steps of the deck, brows furrowed. Had he come outside to use the patio furniture while I spoke with the Barringers? I didn't know he was in earshot.

"You always tell me this *seeing-your-mom* nonsense is over. But then you tell Shawn about it, and now you're talking to her out loud for the neighborhood to hear."

"If you listened to the last thing I said, you would've heard I stopped getting visions. I'm only talking out my thoughts to Mom. I'm allowed to do that, aren't I?"

"Why don't you talk to me instead?" he asked. "I'm right here."

I chuckled and then realized he meant what he said.

"You want to start having heart-to-hearts?" I sat cross-legged. "Fine. Why did you and Mom divorce? Why did you stop coming over to see me when I was little? Why do you treat me like crap all the time? Why do you hate me?"

"Alright, alright," he said and threw his hands in the air. "Play your games. Be sarcastic. But you have a lot to learn about real life. This isn't one of your fictional books. Life isn't always about happy endings."

I rolled my eyes. "Believe me, I know."

"Do you?" He lowered his tone for the next part. "You seem to think that neighbor kid is your knight in shining armor."

The blood in my body grew hot. "Why are you bringing Shawn into this? What do you have against him?"

"Keep your voice down," he said. "It's not him, really. It's you. How you act around him. Cling to him."

"Cling? You know what…at least Shawn makes me feel special. He doesn't belittle me or make me question who I am."

"And I do all that?"

"What do you think you're doing now?"

"I heard you say that you think your mom sent him to you, like it's some destiny thing. I don't want you getting your hopes up, falling in love with this boy."

"I can fall in love with whoever I want." I stood, arms akimbo. "Since when do you care what happens to me? You break my heart all the time."

Andy's lips dropped, and a whiteness came over him.

"Besides, what do you know about love?" I carried on without keeping my voice down. "You gave up on Mom, you gave up on me. You're the last person I want to take relationship advice from. This conversation is over." I breezed past him and slammed the patio door. Offended and heart wildly pumping, I closed my eyes and tried to breathe. When I opened them, on the verge of passing out, Mom stood behind with arms open to catch me.

SEVEN

I woke in bed the next day, afternoon sun glaring through the window. How did I get to my room after fainting?

At some point, when I came to, Andy...no, Mom carried me. Yes, it was Mom. She'd worn a gauzy, angelic dress, and had caught me before I hit the cold hardwood of the kitchen. She drifted me here, as soft as a cloud.

My sleep must've been hard due to being spent from anger. I didn't like how Andy revived my anxiety so bad it forced Mom to return. Shawn came into my life on her behalf, and I would not allow Andy's bitterness to sully any part of that. Mom deserved to rest in peace now.

I kept to the backyard, steering clear of Andy while he re-painted the living room on his day off. With a quilt laid out, I pretended to read Peter Pan, staring down at the same page for minutes on end. I made it a point to wear my best summer dress that laced up at the back—the dark teal one with pale-pink and beige flowers. The screeching of power tools and saws cutting resounded from the Barringers' garage. A haze of sawdust seemed to hover over everything, like pollen during the spring. While Shawn helped his dad, I ate my heart out waiting for that half hour before 11 o'clock when he said he'd take me to the fireworks.

During small breaks, Shawn waltzed up onto his deck and into the house, unaware I watched him. The one time he did notice me, while on the top step, I looked down and turned the page. When I looked up again, he smiled while giving me a salute-like gesture, walked down the steps, and disappeared back into the garage. I pressed the book to my chest and fell back on the quilt, pining.

When Andy came outside to wash some paintbrushes with the hose, I packed up my quilt and book in one motion.

"I could use a hand in there."

Silence.

"Still ignoring me, are you?" he asked.

I stormed off into the house, grabbed a package of Pop Tarts, and spent the remainder of the afternoon in my room leaned against the wall under the window. I didn't care that the tarts had a tang of paint from the fumes saturating everything in the house, I ate them cold. Crumbs fell on the page I'd been stuck on while swooning over Shawn. I read out loud:

"She clung to him; she refused to go without him; but with a 'Goodbye, Wendy', he pushed her from the rock; and in a few minutes she was borne out of his sight. Peter was alone on the lagoon. The rock was very small now; soon it would be submerged."

I turned my eyes to the ceiling. *She clung to him* echoed in my head. Andy's cruel words followed. *It's not him, really. It's you. How you act around him. Cling to him.* The book fell from my hands.

As the sun dipped further in the sky, Andy opened the door with a plate of supper in his hands. "You don't have to like me right now. We don't have to talk. But don't starve because of it."

I had a look at the clock on my nightstand. Almost 7:30. "Set it on the dresser."

He followed my instruction and left.

With the tart a distant memory in the depths of my stomach, the rumbles of protest had begun hours ago. I hustled over to the dresser, picked up the plate, and sat on my bed to eat. Once the remnants of sauce and dressing were licked, no proof whether any food had been there, I cast the plate into the hall and closed the door again.

It wouldn't be long now before Shawn came to take me on our date. I brushed my hair, put gloss on my lips, and spritzed peach body spray over my dress. To pass the remaining time, I went back to reading until the clock turned 10:20.

Just after I threw on a cardigan and misted myself once more with body spray, Shawn knocked at the front door. I rushed down from my room to answer it.

"Who's here at this hour?" Andy grumbled from the living room.

"Hi Shawn," I said, swinging wide the door. *Remember not to cling.*

"Wow, you look nice."

Andy came around the corner. "Hey there, Shawn. What brings you here?"

Shawn looked at him confused. "Didn't Becky mention I was stopping by to take her to the Canada Day fireworks?"

He turned to me. "No, she didn't. But I suppose since you're already here, why don't you come in while she gets her shoes on."

"Sure, thanks."

"Where is this being held?" Andy scratched under his chin.

It took me all of five seconds to slip on my Keds. "K, we can go."

"The Yacht Club. It's not too far from here," Shawn said and tucked his hands into his jean-jacket pockets. "They do it there every year. You wanna tag along, Mr. Stafford?"

My eyes bugged, and I stiffly shook my head at him.

"Thanks, but I'm settled in for the night. Got one call to make about a job and then I'll be hitting the hay."

How boring, I thought. *How can he stand himself?*

Shawn clicked his tongue. "Alright."

"You driving?"

"Yup."

"How long will the fireworks go for?"

"An hour tops," Shawn replied.

"What's with all the questions?" I asked. "Sheesh."

Shawn swiped a hand in the air. "I don't mind."

Andy slid by me and whispered. "When they're done, I want you straight home."

I barely had my cardigan buttoned before ushering Shawn out. "Let's get going," I said. "I can't stand being in that house a moment longer."

"Fine by me." His body buzzed under my hand, a shook-up bottle of pop, sizzling. I wondered what had him so wired.

We took off to the Yacht Club in his dad's truck. I unrolled the window and leaned an elbow out.

"What smells like peach cobbler?"

"My perfume. Do you like it?"

"Yah. It's tasty."

I smiled half-heartedly and after a heavy sigh, Shawn glanced over at me. "So, are you going to tell me what has you avoiding home? Does it have anything to do with the shouting I heard last night?"

"You heard us? Ugh. How embarrassing."

Shawn stopped and eyed me from the side. When I looked at him, he said, "Just want to know you're okay."

"I'm okay. But let's not talk about Andy. I'm just happy to be with you." *Don't be clingy.*

He asked nothing else, nor said anything more, just kept driving and being watchful of the road, tapping on the steering wheel. A nervous *bad-a-bum-bum-bum*. Vehicles lined the streets and whizzed by. People were everywhere celebrating. I smelled barbequed cod and french-fry grease in the air. Folk music echoed. Canadian flags whisked proudly in the wind from poles and on small sticks held by children gleeful they got to stay up later than usual.

The Yacht Club overflowed with families and groups sitting on chairs and blankets waiting on the big square of lawn in front of the building. We exited the truck, the street lamps and light from inside the club cut through the dull dark. A spotlight upon us.

Shawn slid his hand in mine and led me into the crowd. People turned their heads as we approached, whispering. All knit-together brows and judging grimaces. Maybe even pity, because to them, I was basically *Naïve Nancy*. Shawn's blind follower. Their faces morphed into Andy's, chanting, "Cling, cling, cling." My hands dampened.

"So much staring," I whimpered and let go of Shawn.

With an impervious demeanor, un-fazed by any of the scrutiny, Shawn said, "Forget all them."

He took up my hand again and weaved me through the cluster to get to a spot under a small tree, and I tried to avoid eye-contact with anymore onlookers.

When five tall, broad-shouldered guys in football jackets confronted us, I cowered closer to Shawn's shoulder.

"Hey there, good-looking," the one with the buzz-cut and prominent crook to his nose said, looking down at me. The stench of stale ash and nicotine from the cigarette he held burned the inside of my nose and back of my throat. "What's a girl like you doing hanging out with *Bonkers Barringer?*"

Short guffaws erupted out of the other four, and from a few bystanders.

"He put you under some spell?" He tossed his cigarette to the ground, snuffed it, and threw a heavy arm over my shoulder to pull me away from Shawn's grasp. This guy exuded cockiness. No doubt used to ditzy bottle-blonde cheerleaders (maybe girls in general) fawning over him enough to do whatever he wanted them to do. "Come and spend some time with the big boys."

I lowered my shoulder and squirmed away behind Shawn, who—though leaner and a touch shorter in stature—bumped his chest against the jock's and glared at him with fearlessness. "Don't get too close there, Jeff. Wouldn't want some of my crazy to rub off on you."

"Oh yeah?"

A loud click made Jeff raise his bushy eyebrows and his face showed insecurity. "What's that?" He turned to Shawn's right jacket pocket. "You threatening me?"

Shawn's hand in that pocket had me wondering what exactly made that noise in there. A weapon? Would he go that far to protect me?

"What does it look like, beef-head?" Shawn said. "Get out of our way."

Jeff's friends surrounded Shawn until one of the club's male staff—a skin-flint of a man with round eyes and a receding hairline—approached. "Hey, hey, come on guys. Break it up."

"This loopy-loon threatened me, Carl," Jeff said.

Carl adjusted his glasses and put both bony hands up, "Alright. Alright. We don't want any squabbles."

"Fine." Jeff nodded. "You got it."

"Atta boy." Carl smiled and elbowed him a few times in the ribs. It was like a cheesy 70s film. "Your father coming to the bowling tourney next weekend?"

Jeff shoved Carl playfully in the shoulder. "You bet. He wouldn't miss it."

Shawn smirked and thumbed toward the two.

Carl turned his attention immediately to Shawn and his smile turned to a scowl. "People are trying to enjoy themselves here, Barringer." He wiped a finger above his lip. "Keep your nose clean."

After Carl got lost in the crowd again, I scoffed. "What the heck was all that? Jeff started it."

"It doesn't bother me."

"But Shawn it isn't fair. That Carl guy excluded you completely."

"They always do."

"Why? Just because you enjoy the thrill of a good legend it makes you bonkers and subject to their ridicule?" I shook my head and sat alongside him on the grass. "If you ask me, it's this town that's the problem. Not you."

"Meh." He shrugged off the comments as easily as his jacket. "Here, sit on this."

"Thanks." I tucked my dress and lifted my hip so he could slide it under me. "Why do you entertain it? How the townspeople think of you, I mean?"

"There's no changing their minds. I might as well have fun with it."

"What was in your pocket that had Jeff scared?"

"Oh, it was only a little Swiss Army knife. I wasn't going to use it on him. Again, just pulling his leg a bit. Getting him going."

"Shawn, you really shouldn't."

"I don't need their approval. As long as I've got yours, I consider myself a pretty lucky guy. But enough about those chumps. My mind's been spinning since you told me you see ghosts."

"I've seen *visions* of my mom, Shawn," I said twirling a piece of hair. "Under duress, when I really need her. I don't see ghosts."

Shawn stared with a wiliness in his eyes. "But do you know that for certain? Have you tried seeing anyone else? We need to explore this."

"Look, before you get ahead of yourself...let me explain." I gave him no time to butt in. I could tell he wanted to. "When Mom passed away, I was a wreck. Andy hadn't fathered me in years. He comes out of nowhere and decides to be my dad again, and throws my life in a whirlwind by saying he's moving me from my home. That's when she showed up to me, clearly. In all her fullness. Not as a translucent apparition. Besides, ghosts have such a negative connotation to them. Haunting and scaring people. Visions are more, people you love watching over you. Like, angels."

"You two talk to one another though, right?" Shawn said, his mind going on its own tangent. Had he even heard what I said? "That's what you were doing by that lilac bush."

The idea of talking to mom always appealed to me. "Yes," I replied. The lie dug its claws in me, deeper and deeper. I feared I might never pull it away.

I had to somehow get Shawn off this idea. "When I confided in Andy about having visions, he said it was all in my head." A sickening wave in my gut overtook me when I recalled the vision of Mom carrying me after I'd fainted. They were interrupted by flickers of Andy's clean-shaved face wearing an unusual expression. One I'd never witnessed on him before. Real worry. A hint of love. Had it been him all along? "As much as I hate to admit it, I fear he's right."

"Don't believe that for a second. Andy's completely wrong. What you have is a gift. A supernatural gift."

I nodded, shoving aside the uncertainty of who *really* carried me to my room. I mean, this was Andy we were talking about. The unemotional tyrant. That guy would've left me out-cold on the floor. Right?

"You and I meeting, it's kismet." Shawn splayed out his arms, eyes to the night sky dotted by stars. "There's no time for firework watching, we've got to get to the lighthouse." He rose and reached out for my hands to hoist me up.

"We do?"

Shawn scooped up his jacket, flicked off the blades of grass stuck on, and tugged me with his free hand toward a small curve of beach with sailboats lined up and tied together. "I see something in you, Becky. Written all over you. Seeing your mom is just the beginning of your gift. Scratching the surface of what you're capable of. Given the chance, with a bit of practice…you'll see other ghosts in no time," he said.

Shawn ran his fingers along the ropes that bound the sailboats to shore. The ocean was calm. My insides were not.

"You want me to try to get a vision of O'Sullivan." I crossed my arms over my chest. "I've been trying to tell you. It's not something I can make happen out of the blue."

"You've never had reason to try. Until now."

"Shawn, I'd hate to disappoint you…"

"You won't," he said. "Someway, somehow this is destined, Becky. You were meant to come to Lunenburg and move next to me. You. Not just any ordinary girl. The *gifted-ghost-seeing* girl."

I hoped I could be all he thought I was. "These boats…you aren't considering what I think you are, are you?"

"Yup." He removed the knife from his pocket and cut the rope from one of the boats. "Hurry and get in."

I felt a rush and glanced around before frantically shimmying inside while he pushed it out on the ocean. No one was around to see us, preoccupied with waiting for the fireworks. Shawn trudged through the water, getting his pants soaked and then hopped in as well.

The first hiss and snap of the fireworks began as Shawn directed the sails with not a worry in the world.

EIGHT

With the sailboat tied on the island slick with seafoam, we bustled our way to the ledge and up the ladder. Shawn hadn't slowed down since we arrived. He talked on and on about my visions, all the what-ifs. I began hating myself for telling him. If I failed—and I had no doubt I would—I didn't know where that would leave us.

For the moment, he seemed to treat me less like a Wendy-type and more like Tiger-lily. Exotic and special. He hadn't stopped finding a reason to touch me, grazing my hand, throwing an arm around my shoulder that eventually graduated to my hip. When we stood on the cliff-edge, the thicket behind us, the fireworks were on their finale, booming like ethnic drums. Colors splattered against the dark sky and lit up the angles of Shawn's face like tribal paint. I imagined the lost boys dancing around him, hooting, hollering, and crowing like Pan.

We sat to watch them, until I scooted myself closer and closer to where he sat, grass pulp deep under my nails. He began to ignore the light show and move in my direction, too, with love-drunk eyes. My body ached for his lips. When he drew me in by the waist, I propped myself onto his lap and wrapped my legs around him. My hands left the grass and stroked his face. Our chins bumped and then our tongues touched before our lips did.

I'd never kissed like that before. Hallelujah trumpets resound. This was salty and sweet at the same time. My body wasn't my own, feeling things it never felt before. Shawn's warm hands crept up my dress and slid along my outer thighs, and I can't say how long we stayed kissing. All I know is the firework finale was over by the time our lips parted.

Shawn slowly pulled his hands away saying, "Sorry, I...I don't know what came over me."

I swept my hair back. "I'm not sorry."

He gave a chuckle at my comment. "I just never met someone like you. Of all people, you moved next to me. It's amazing, it's unbelievable, it's—"

I put a finger over his lips. "I said it was okay."

He swallowed hard. "Okay."

"I really like you." I slipped off his lap and tidied the hem of my dress.

"I really like you back," he said watching me fuss with it. "I have so much I want to show you. Come on. You're ready to see inside the lighthouse"

Shawn and I blazed through the woods, leaves thrusting along with the rambling ocean. Fireflies emerged from out of shrubs and flickered around our heads.

Once at the shack, he picked up a worn tablecloth off the floor and tore a strip off to wrap around a broken broom handle. I kept touching my lips as he busied himself. *We kissed*, I mused in that teen-girlish way. *Shawn Barringer kissed me.* I couldn't get it out of my head.

With torch in hand, he hurried me into the lighthouse. A rustic, red spiral staircase went all the way up to the top, like some stairway to heaven. Nautical dials and unfamiliar equipment sat atop a circular table in the middle of the floor.

"This place is amazing," I said wide-eyed.

"Ladies first." Shawn gestured toward the stairs.

"We're going up?"

"Of course," Shawn said. "Don't you worry. I'm right behind you."

I put my hand on the railing and took each steep step with caution. Shawn lifted the torch high. My shoulder brushed the cold stone walls as I looked out each window at the spiny trees and tiny lights coming through from town.

Before I knew it, we were in a circular, brick chamber that looked as if it once belonged to Captain Ahab. A draught of damp wood and dust coated my throat, making it scratchy and bringing on an urge to cough. Starting from the left were book shelves, a small desk, a wash basin, a Victorian chaise longue piled with sea-themed pillows, a fiddle stand, a wooden pillar holding a bust of St. Patrick; all these were placed like Tetris blocks in perfect spots creating an illusion of more space. A cast-iron, pot belly stove cloaked itself more to the right, inside the shadows. Paintings of whales and ships, along with an old clock hung on the walls. Antiquated artifacts were spread out on the Cherrywood floor.

Using the torch, Shawn lit a lantern with a thick beeswax candle that covered everything in an orange glow. He opened the one window, snuffed the torch in the old wash basin under it, and stood next to me in the center of the room.

"This is where you keep O'Sullivan's stuff," I said kneeling to pick up a tattered journal.

"What I've found so far. Most of it was in here and the shack. Some scattered around the island," he said while I leafed through the journal. "I tried keeping these things at home so I could spend more time organizing and going through stuff, but Pop wouldn't have any of it."

"*I ignite the way, each and every day. Gladly I do it, you see. For I know what it be that keeps ye all safe. Tis the light beaming down upon ye,*" I read aloud, and then looked up at Shawn. "It sounds like a song."

He nodded. "It's a verse from a song O' Sullivan wrote. One of the many he sung around the fire as tradition when campers came."

"I can see him playing that fiddle over there. It's clear he had a passion for music and history, among other things."

"Oh, yes."

I flapped a few pages ahead. "Hey, there's some sections torn out, did you know?"

"Yep. That poor thing is pretty beaten up." Shawn snatched up the lantern and kneeled next to me. He pointed at a pile of similarly sized papers. "At first, I figured these were the missing pages, but I found them all rolled up inside a pneumatic tube. Besides, they feel different."

I closed the journal, set it down, and picked up the papers. Unlike the worn journal's pages—like Shawn said—these felt like fingernails painted over several times with that peel-off polish. Stretchy and smooth. "I work with paper a lot, and have even read up on the histories behind different types. These might be coated in a resin of some kind. Maybe to keep them from aging?"

"I knew that," Shawn said and swiped them from me. "They're drawings. Blueprints of the lighthouse and some of the artifacts I haven't found yet."

"Wow, is this the vial the special water is in?" I said fingering the top sketch of a glass cylinder with a carved, Celtic knot top and bottom. "It's so decorated, like something you'd find in a museum. I didn't expect that."

"It is. Man, I need to get my hands on it." Shawn cleared his throat. "That's where you come in."

The passion in his kiss planted something in me. This ember urging to be stoked into a roaring flame. *I am as special as he says. I do have a gift. I can do this.* "I want to try."

"That's all I ask." Shawn picked up a velvet satchel. "Hold out your hand."

When I did, he turned the satchel upside down and a brushed metal medallion with a *Tree of Life* engraved on it slid into my palm. "O'Sullivan wore this all the time. It's actually a pocket-watch if you press that clasp there."

I pressed where Shawn showed me and it creaked open. None of the hands moved.

"I've toyed with it a time or two. Couldn't get it to work."

"I suppose it wouldn't after all these years," I said.

"I visualize it ticking its last tock the moment Jack's heart did. Symbolic, right?"

I closed it up.

"Anyway, if your mom comes when you need her…maybe if you get familiar with all this, you'll need the water as bad as me and O'Sullivan will appear," Shawn said and lowered the lantern to the floor. He spread the artifacts and papers around and then snapped his fingers. "Here." He plucked a tiny scroll off the ground and handed it to me. "The words Jack spoke when casting the Reaper away in his dream. Maybe if you read it out loud…"

He waited with scrupulous eyes. I unrolled it, cheeks flush, and then recited, "*O let any man who touches the waters be safe from head to toe; may his path be lit to journeys ahead, where darkness may never go.*"

"It's gotta be said with feeling," Shawn said raising a fist in gusto. "Your heart wasn't in it."

"I'll tell you what…why don't you leave this watch and scroll with me to start, and I'll study them in quiet at home. I want to do this right for you."

"Great idea! And take as long as you need," Shawn said, "Well, maybe not too long."

"I'll be very careful with them. I promise."

"I told you before…I trust you."

I slid the watch and scroll carefully in one of the pockets of my cardigan and buttoned it closed, proud because Shawn glowed with enthusiasm at my willingness. "Tell me about some of these other relics."

"Where to begin." Shawn's fingers wiggled and hovered over everything. "Let's take this for example…" He lifted a heavy, jade ankh. "Jack seemed to think this as a sort of amulet for strength. I suppose it's not enough to have long life, you want to feel healthy, too."

"Did you find that in here or out there?" I tilted my head in the direction of the open window.

"Out there."

"Maybe the vial is somewhere close to the spot you dug this up. Since both share a unified meaning?"

"I already thought of that," Shawn said.

"Of course you would have. Silly me."

"I totally scavenged and dug until my hands blistered and my eyes veined up." He put the ankh back in its place. "I've always figured it wasn't going to be easy."

"Until now," I thought out loud.

"Yah…until now."

"You'd think all this stuff would be proof to Lunenburg the tales of O'Sullivan are real."

"They view it all as useless junk, of no value or importance, because they belonged to Jack."

"*Pfft*. Such narrow-mindedness. It's sad, really."

"But if I find that water, town officials might sing a different tune. Even beg me for a drop." Shawn snickered.

"Keeping it between you and people you trust might be best. They won't believe it's the real thing. Or worse, might try confiscating it."

"True."

"Tell me what's in here," I said holding up a small jar with flakes of what looked like crushed leaves or herbs."

Shawn picked up an interesting pipe off the ground with a long stem and cylindrical bowl. "This is an old Peterson pipe called a Churchwarden. The tiny carving on the side says it was made in Dublin. In the journal entries, Jack often mentioned his enjoyment of a good ol' puff now and then. What you're holding in your hand is a jar of his aged tobacco."

"Really?" I inspected it further, gave it a shake.

"Yep," Shawn said. "I've been tempted to give it a little try."

"You want to smoke this stuff? Who knows how old it is."

"The seal hasn't been tampered with. Tobacco can be stored, even aged like wine. When Grandpa Barringer was alive, he used to can and store his *baccy*—as he liked to call it—all the time."

I set the jar next to Shawn. "I never knew you smoked."

"I don't. This'll be the first time. But what a first it'll be." He glanced around. "Becky, do you mind grabbing a few pillows off the chaise? We can sit on them for comfort."

"Sure." I got up, grabbed them, and plopped them down next to Shawn.

"Thanks." He scooted the square one with tassels underneath himself and I sat on the round one with an embroidered ship over curling waves.

"I won't be trying it, just so you know," I said.

"Oh, that's okay. You don't have to." He put the pipe's stem in between his teeth and then with a grunt opened the jar of tobacco. The smell of vanilla was evident right away, and then the subtle hint of clove.

Shawn removed several pinches of it and stuffed it inside the bowl. "Mmmff," he mumbled. "What will I use for a light?"

"A scrap of paper, maybe? Or…" I looked around the floor where I sat. I pulled up a splinter of wood, opened the lantern and drifted it over the candle. "A makeshift match."

"Clever girl." Shawn winked at me and took the fiery splinter, hovering it over the tobacco leaves. He then whipped the splinter around until the flame went out. With every quick draw, he puffed out smoke. Suddenly, he spat out the stem, coughed a few times, and rolled over laughing.

I began to laugh with him.

"What? What happened?" I managed to say with a hand clutching my aching stomach.

He could hardly answer me between laughs. "It bit me."

"Bit you?"

He wiped tears from his eyes with his wrist and calmed down. "Grandpa Barringer said if you smoke it too fast your tongue gets a good lashing. And you better believe it stings something fierce."

I picked the pipe off the ground and handed it back to him.

"Ah, but it was worth it though," he said with eyes still glistening.

When I covered a yawn, Shawn slapped his thigh. "You can rest your head on my lap if you're tired."

I snuggled up while he told me stories about the other treasures he'd found and puffed—properly this time—on the pipe. The room grew hazy, and smoke coiled and drifted away through the window. My eyelids closed, and all I remember was feeling his coarse hands comb through my tangled hair.

I forgot where we were. I forgot the time.

NINE

Jolting out of sleep, I threw Shawn's arm off me, frightening him awake. "Andy is going to kill me!"

Shawn's face went shades lighter. "And then my pop's going to kill me."

I hurried out of the room to find a window, and looked out toward the sky. Dawn approached fast.

"Shawn, come on. We have to go." I practically slid down the railing of the staircase.

Due to our rush out of the lighthouse, we questioned if either of us closed the door. I could tell Shawn wanted to turn back to check, but we were already at the ladder.

The brisk breeze over the ocean stung my bare skin like a winter wind. The hollow caves around the island sung a melancholy, Gregorian chant as we departed on the sail boat. We didn't say two words to each other, but I kept close to Shawn for body heat and wondered if he could feel my heart beating through my clothes. What was going to happen to us? I didn't want to think on it. All I wanted to do was listen to the water licking the bottom of the boat and pretend Shawn and I were sailing off somewhere we could be together with our dreams.

My fantasy evaporated the moment the Yacht Club came into view. Red and blue lights whirled off cop cars parked in the lot. I thought I heard Shawn mumble a curse word under his breath.

"They called the cops," I repeated several times.

Shawn stared, unblinking. "It's going to be okay."

"How can you say that?" I asked, heart about to jump through my chest and overboard. "Look there's even a crowd waiting. Is that your dad?" Afterward, upon seeing this troubled expression wash over him, I realized Shawn probably just said what he did as a hope, a prayer to calm his nerves.

"Crap, that is your dad. And there's mine coming from behind him. We're dead meat."

The sound of splashing water under the boat was no longer a reverie of any sort, but a knell of doom. Every swish brought us closer and closer to Phillip and Andy, whose faces looked a brighter red than the exterior of the Fisheries Museum of the Atlantic.

Carl waved over an officer and pointed out at us. From where we were, I heard him say loudly over the buzz from the crowd, "There, see. It's that Barringer kid, like I suspected. He left his jacket behind." He turned to Shawn's dad. "That's why I called you, Phillip. I may not have witnessed it, but I had a hunch. He was up to no good last night, picking fights and what not."

I wanted to holler, *shut up, Carl. Just shut up.* I wished Phillip would've. But he just kept looking out on the water. Watching Shawn with those dark eyes like a shark stalking a seal.

The police started to usher the bystanders back to their vehicles as we got closer. Carl stayed behind, next to Phillip with arms crossed over his chest. Andy paced, kicking the sand. Was it the coolness of his exhales in the air I saw hovering around him? Or was it angry steam whistling out of his ears?

The wind helped shove the sailboat onto the shore with a loud *shush*. Shawn hopped out and lent me a hand down.

Carl stormed over to Shawn and shook a finger at him. "You're in big trouble, Mister. Stealing a boat at all hours of the night. I called the police, and your dad isn't too happy either."

Phillip shoved Carl aside. "I don't need you to speak for me, Carl. Why don't you help those cops manage that crowd over there, huh?"

Carl huffed and puffed, and then left.

Shawn swallowed hard. He and his dad were eye to eye. "Well, boy…you going to tell me just what the hell is going on here, and why you smell like the inside of a casino?"

I huddled behind Shawn until Andy took my wrist and made me stand next to him. I heard him take a sniff around my hair. "You were smoking with him, weren't you?"

My mouth was too dry to say anything.

Phillip winced. "This better not be about that lighthouse."

The one officer whom Carl spoke with earlier—a brick-house, tanned-skin guy who might as well have worn a wrestler's costume—joined us and said, "I think it's best we discuss matters at your residence, Mr. Barringer. Too many people noodle-necking the situation. You understand?"

"Certainly do, Constable Moon." Phillip said and then leaned in closer and whispered something in his ear.

Constable Moon eyeballed Phillip for a while with uncertainty and then nodded. "Alright, Son," he said to Shawn. "You're going to ride along with me."

Shawn shot a glare at his dad. "What? Seriously, Pop?"

"Do what the officer says, boy. You want to act like a criminal, you'll be treated like one."

"This is nuts. We were only having a bit of fun," Shawn fumed. "I didn't steal. I borrowed with every intention to bring it back."

"Enough. We aren't discussing this here. You've humiliated me enough." Phillip turned away and heavy-footed it to his truck. He didn't even watch Shawn get shoved in the back of the cop car.

But I did, as Andy yanked on my wrist in the direction of where his truck was parked. "We're going to speak with the officer at the Barringers, too. Come on." I didn't know I resisted him, until he stopped pulling me on. "Look as much as you want now," he said with a chin-thrust toward Shawn, "because you won't be spending much time with that boy after today."

All I could do was cry.

***

Constable Moon let Shawn out of the police car in front of the Barringers' house. Andy and I were next to Phillip, who stood at the front door and ushered all of us in, trying to keep Margaret from Shawn.

"Phillip, he's just a boy," she said.

"Stay back, Margie." Phillip gently pulled her reaching hand off Shawn's shoulder as he passed. "He broke the law. There has to be some form of punishment."

Margaret's lips were a tight line.

Phillip brought everyone into the living room. Just as I began to sit down next to Shawn on the sofa, Andy shook his head disapprovingly and moved to take that spot. I sighed, crossed my arms over my chest and sat on the armchair next to the fireplace. Margaret sat on the arm of the couch with her hand on Shawn's shoulder much to Phillip's apparent distaste.

"This is why he does these things. You humor him," Phillip leaned in to Margaret and whispered loud enough for everyone to hear.

"Don't act like you didn't do anything foolish as a boy," she argued.

"Foolish yes, but I was too busy helping my old man *fix* things to break any laws," Phillip maintained.

Constable Moon cleared his throat and interrupted. "The Yacht Club has decided not to press any charges regarding the taking of the boat. However, if there are any damages to it, they will seek compensation for said damage."

"That's very gracious of them," Margaret said.

Phillip sniffed. "You mean lucky."

"Should there be any damages, my daughter will pay her share, even if it means she gets a job." Andy piped in. "It's only fair since she was involved."

He looked at me to see if I would make a stink about that, but I said nothing.

Constable Moon nodded. "Carl and a few others who witnessed events last night have written statements for the file. We will get Rebecca and Shawn's accounts as well." He reached into a pocket of his jacket and handed Phillip a paper and then gave one to Andy. "Try to get those to us as soon as possible," he said.

"I want to mention something from one of the statements and, frankly, it doesn't make me very happy." Constable Moon glanced at Shawn. "Son, do you want to tell me about the concealed weapon you used to threaten somebody with at the club?"

Margaret put a hand to her mouth. "Oh, Shawn…"

Phillip's scowl deepened.

I wanted to stay quiet. I wanted to be smart, but I let my emotions take hold. "Did this statement also mention Shawn was the one who started the fight? Because if so, whoever wrote that is full of it. These brutes came up and tried to force me to go with them. Shawn put a stop to it and then they razzed him for sticking up for me."

"Save it for the paperwork and let Shawn speak for himself," Andy said.

Shawn cleared his throat. "It was my Swiss Army knife, officer. I always carry it on me. But I'd never harm anyone."

"You bet your ass you wouldn't. I didn't buy that for you to use it as a weapon," Phillip said.

"Okay, Shawn…but take into account that someone felt like they were in danger. In a split second, a thought could turn to action. That's not a road you want to travel down." Constable Moon scratched his large, bulbous nose. "I also want to give a word of caution to the both of you," he said eyeing Shawn and me with those wise, coal-black eyes. "The ocean is a dangerous thing to toy with. Going out at night the way you two did is roulette. As calm as it was during the fireworks that can change without a moment's notice. You ought to be more careful."

"That's exactly right," Phillip said. "If you think it'll serve as proper punishment, you have my permission to keep Shawn at the station overnight. Give him some thought about what he's done."

Margaret slapped Phillip on the arm.

Constable Moon chuckled. "No, that won't be necessary. But keep in mind, Son..." he turned to Shawn, "behind bars will be exactly where you end up if you continue doing these careless things."

Shawn nodded. "Yes, Sir."

"All the same, I'm going to make it feel an awful lot like prison for him." Phillip smirked. "He's going to be put to hard work at The Dory Shop and at home here."

"Alright, then," the Constable said. "I'll leave it at that. Best be heading back to the station."

"Let me see you to the door," Margaret offered getting up.

When Andy said we'd discuss things at the Barringers, I expected him to be far more involved with the conversation. Instead, he appeared at a loss for words, sitting there, staring off.

After Constable Moon left, Phillip and Margaret argued about Shawn's behavior as if nobody else sat there.

"He will not continue strutting around without responsibility and no regard for the family," Phillip said. "I've got a business to run, but does he care? He abuses his freedom, and therefore has to earn it back." He approached where Andy sat. "I apologize about him. I really hope you don't take it personally if these two," he thumbed at me and Shawn, "don't spend as much time together."

"Don't worry, Phillip," Andy spoke. "I don't take it personally at all. In fact, I told Rebecca the same thing before coming here."

Shawn and I gazed at one another with reckless abandon. We said with our eyes, *they can try all they want. But we will fight to be together*. We were made stronger by unison. Unwilling to be torn asunder by wind or by parents.

"Let's go home, Rebecca." Andy headed for the door.

I got up, smiled at Shawn, and patted my cardigan where the pocket-watch rested. When it made a clink against the button, Shawn put his head down to mask a grin.

Andy and I strode across to our lot and into the house. "I don't know what to do about you. This neighbor kid is getting to be a damned obsession. I can't wrap my head around it."

"Whatever, Andy, do what you normally do when you can't handle me and go to work."

"You keep being smart like that, I may actually find you a job. That'll keep you so busy you won't have time to be swept up by that boy's influence," he said, the veins on his forehead protruding.

"So I can become a workaholic like you?"

"You bet," he said purposefully trying to annoy me. "A workaholic."

"You accused me of smoking, but I didn't. If I'm so influenced by Shawn, wouldn't I have done it with him, too?"

"I don't know," Andy said. "Maybe you did, maybe you didn't? How can I trust what you say? You sneak around, disobey—why wouldn't you lie about that?"

"I should have smoked." I tossed my hands in the air. "Might as well be the person you think I am."

"You play the victim card with me all too often. Well let me tell you, it wasn't me who got into a stolen boat with somebody I barely know in the middle of the night. Who, by the way, carries a knife he threatens others with."

When Andy put it that way, I could almost allow myself a small slice of understanding. Then again, he was disparaging Shawn. "He didn't do anything like that. I was there."

"You know what, Phillip can deal with Shawn. I'll deal with you." Andy threw his coat down, instead of on one of the hooks. "Maybe I ought to find you a summer job."

"I'm not going to work at some grubby job."

"Newsflash, girl. That's reality. That other stuff you're getting wrapped up into, that's make-believe. It's high-time you take life seriously."

"What about you, huh? When will you stop taking life so seriously?"

Andy stormed past me into the kitchen, grabbed the apple juice out of the fridge and poured himself a glass. "I don't have time for that." He reached next to the sink and popped the cap off his anxiety meds.

"It's pitiful," I said watching him take a drink and swallow the pill down. "You want me to be exactly like you, seeing everything in such a miserable way. But I won't and it bothers you."

"What bothers me," he muttered, "is a daughter that won't listen worth a damn."

"You know what bothers me? I said. "A so-called father who tries to control every aspect of my life but doesn't even know who I am...and never will."

"Oh, I got you pegged. Don't kid yourself."

"Ha! Why am I even talking to you right now over something so stupid?"

"You got that right. It's stupid." He put his cup in the sink. "Go grab me the newspaper from the living room. You and I are going through the classifieds."

TEN

I never thought my first job would be at a grocery store. I'm not sure what I had in mind, but it wasn't that. Andy chose Foodland because it was minutes from our house. I hated how I smelled coming home; over-processed deli meat and fish. I hated how the boys I worked with harassed me so much, I took to eating lunch behind the garbage dumpster. Most of all, I hated how rarely I saw Shawn these past three weeks. Not once did I even spot him shopping with his parents.

Mere glimpses through windows at home eventually turned into no glimpses at all. It wasn't for lack of attempting to bump into him every day. Even when I spent time outside in the backyard, he wasn't out in his.

The weather took to my dismay, and the sky began to bubble grey and pour rain. Those lonesome days after work, I slid the pocket-watch out and spun the dial, studied the designs, used the restless energy within me to meditate on the legend of O'Sullivan. I said the words on the scroll out loud, repeatedly, while pacing my room; recited it with feeling—as Shawn suggested—every night.

Instead of him, I often dreamt of Jack in the lighthouse. I'd come along as one of the campers he told stories to before given the chance to view the lens. When the time came, up the stairway we'd go, but there would never be a top. Endless flights of red stairs. Maddening.

When I saw Shawn again, the last thing I wanted was to have nothing to report. He entrusted me with these few things and I remained determined.

Coming home today, soggy from being in a light drizzle, I told Andy I ate supper at work, even though I didn't. No time for food. I slunk off to my room and locked the door.

All those days gone by, something should've happened by now. *The visions are all in your head,* a voice taunted as I stared at my pale, tired face in the mirror. *He's going to wonder if you're a fake. Little by little his interest in you will dwindle.* "No!" I shouted.

A knock at my door made me curl into myself. "What?"

"Just came by to see if you wanted something. I heard you shout."

"Nothing. Go away." I put an ear to the door, hearing Andy mosey right back down the steps from whence he came. I began spouting off Jack's words verbatim, without even so much as a peek at the scroll. My eyes whizzed to all corners of the room, hopeful.

I moved on from the scroll to the watch and analyzed the designs again, bringing it under lamplight in my room. The wind spat rain at the window, and low rumbles of thunder broke through the thick, simmering clouds.

Etched under the tangling roots of the *Tree of Life* was the most miniscule writing, so small it could be easily missed if one wasn't careful. I placed the watch on my dresser and went down to find Andy in the living room watching world news; something to do with the newly appointed president of South Africa, Nelson Mandela.

Resigning myself to the fact I had to ask Andy for help made me swallow the thick, reluctant lump in my throat. "I need a magnifying glass. Do you have one?"

"Are you going to bite my head off again if I don't?"

"No."

"What do you need it for?"

My brain already hurt. I didn't need Andy's line of questions right now. "Do you or not?"

He turned his attention from the TV screen. "Kitchen. Third drawer down from under the toaster."

I darted to the kitchen, threw open the third drawer, and scavenged. "They're reading glasses," Andy shouted from his chair. "You see them?"

The hope of using a Sherlock Holmes magnifying glass collapsed. I picked up the coke-bottle glasses with brown frames. "I got them."

Hurrying back up to my room, I scooped up the watch and put the glasses on. My enlarged saucer-eyes twitched hard before adjusting. The etching was messy, not engraved nicely, but done by hand. Quite miraculously, too. How could anyone write so small?

To reveal what's underneath,
use what you're trying to find

As I wondered what this riddle meant, my thumb inadvertently pushed the clasp. The top clicked open with a jerk and caused me to juggle the watch until it dropped on the hardwood. I winced and tensed my jaw, but then widened my eyes and slackened my mouth when music came forth.

I knelt and touched around, fumbling, trying to get my eyes to work along with my body. When my finger grazed metal, I swept the watch up, hands trembling. It repeated the same metallic chords over and over like the sound music boxes with a cylinder of pins being plucked makes. In awe, not wanting to move a muscle, I listened as the music contended with the thunder.

How long would it play? I couldn't wait to tell Shawn. He'd be beside himself. If I never so much as got even a sighting of anyone, I had something to report. The watch was alive!

I got up from kneeling, being sure not to close it, and a flicker of someone appeared in front of me and then disappeared just as the music from the watch stopped. Suddenly, my eyes dizzied uncontrollably and I stumbled around the room. My focus going in and out, in and out until I hobbled over to my trash bin beside my bookshelf and vomited stomach acid. My throat went raw, prickling as I coughed and choked. After a quick wipe of the mouth on my shirt sleeve, I remembered I still wore Andy's reading glasses. I yanked them off my nose and threw them onto the bed. Had my wonky eyesight made me think I saw something? Or…maybe the music brought forth a vision of O'Sullivan.

I slapped the watch, spun the dial on the side. No music. "Play, damn you."

I hummed the beginning of the song, but what was the rest? I raked a hand through my hair. Paced. Sat on my bed. Repeated the sequence.

"What the heck is the rest? It's not that long, shouldn't be this difficult."

I stayed up all night lying in bed, humming the beginning, trying to work out the remaining melody. My eyes glazed over while staring at the ceiling. Watch at my side, annoyingly dead all over again.

In the morning, I feigned having the flu. Told Andy I got sick last night and asked him to call work for me and let them know I wouldn't be coming in. With the house all to myself, I strode through every room, humming the only part I knew. I pecked at cold, leftover chicken in the fridge. Hours were spent trying to figure the whole song. My brain more scrambled than an egg on a skillet.

At one point, I just stared at the watch in my hand and wished Shawn wasn't so absent. He knew everything about this stuff. Did he already know about the etching? What the riddle meant?

Everything felt wrong. Disjointed. Out of sorts.

That night, I collapsed back on the bed with exhaustion and a dry mouth, letting my mind wander wherever it felt like going. *Shawn kissing me.* It always seemed to want to go there now. My body sunk into the mattress, my head heavy on the pillow. I rolled onto my side and in a relaxed state for the first time in days, hummed the watch's tune in all its glorious fullness, lips chapped. The faint movement of someone at my bedside made me shoot up in a sitting position. The hair on my arms and back of my neck bristled, a stupefied smirk plastered on my face.

As the image faded in and out, bright then dull, I distinguished the vision as that of a man. When it stabilized, I memorized him, trying not to blink and miss any features. He had slicked russet brown hair, a bushy red beard, and wore a coat with many buttons down to his knees and tall boots over beige slacks.

Jack O'Sullivan. I guessed him to be around mid-forties, even with ruddy cheeks and wind-burnt skin. In principle, he should've appeared as an old salt, not be younger than Andy. Yet, even in the dreams I'd have, I pictured Jack this way. Perhaps it was due to Shawn mentioning the guy didn't age normally after taking the waters.

I drew my shoulders down but they crept back up close to my ears. My mouth dryer than ever. On one hand, I never wanted to stop humming, afraid the vision would disappear. On the other, the urge to speak with him took hold. Unlike with the visions involving Mom, I had an unusual confidence he'd respond. A confidence because of Shawn.

"Who are you?" I asked, voice cracked. Even though I felt 99.9% sure, I needed that last speck of certainty.

"Name's Jack." His reply came in a wavy tone of loud and soft.

"Why are you here?"

He pointed to the pocket-watch in my hand. "Sure there's no other I'd rather have find me sacred water than me buyo, Shawn."

"What does this etching mean?"

"Water." The figure of Jack dulled to black and white, blurry, and then he was gone.

"Water?" I realized my immense thirst just then, shoved the watch in my jean's pocket, and rushed downstairs to the kitchen. I clambered through the cupboard for one of Andy's large jar-shaped mugs, filled it up with tap-water and guzzled two full glasses. I dropped the mug in the sink and slid down to the floor, panting.

Why would Jack have said *water*, other than reminding me how parched I was? Instead of wracking my dismantled brain, I needed to see Shawn in the morning. I prayed he'd be home.

***

I grabbed an umbrella. Rain beat down on the top of the black, nylon canopy. The town as silent as a cemetery. With long strides, I hurried to the Barringers' door. I knocked once and Margaret answered with an apron on, cloth in hand.

"Good morning, Rebecca. It's so nice to see your pretty face."

"Thanks, Mrs. Barringer. It's nice to see yours, too."

"Oh, call me Margaret," she said smiling. "Are you okay? You sound out of breath?"

"I'm fine." The truth; I wasn't fine. Half-alive, I felt shot down like a Wendy-bird. Until I saw Shawn I wouldn't feel better.

"You here looking for Shawn, by chance?"

Regarding the tone of her voice, I said, "Actually, yes. But I assume he's with Phillip at The Dory Shop."

"Well, he had been for a few weeks, but his big brother, Aaron, called five days ago and convinced Phillip to let Shawn go to Halifax as a roadie for his folk-band. He promised it wouldn't be about fun and games, that it was hard work lugging around all their equipment for them. Since the two boys don't see one another too much anymore, Phillip agreed to it on the condition that Aaron kept to his word about Shawn being put to some hard, honest work." She giggled. "But if I know my Aaron, he's being easy on his little brother, make no mistake."

"In Halifax…being a roadie?" I said with a sour taste on my tongue. "When will he be back?"

"Oh, not for another week or so."

"I see." Without thinking, I asked, "Did you need a hand with anything? I'm done my chores at home and don't mind offering you some help."

"That's so sweet. I'm just drying some dishes."

"I can finish those up for you."

"You don't need to do that," Margaret said. "But come on in out of the rain. I'll make us some tea to warm up."

I shook off the umbrella before going in and propped it by the door. It was nice to be in Shawn's house. His presence lingered here, and I knew I probably stared too long at the pictures of him on the walls as I went by them. I wondered if Margaret knew how enamored I was with her son. Sometimes the way she smiled, it made me think so.

"Go ahead and grab a chair at the table, Rebecca. I'll put some water to boil."

"Sure." I slid one out and sat down.

"Do you like Earl Grey or did you want a fruit tea."

I never really drank tea before, but I answered, "Fruit sounds nice."

"Fruit it is."

I drummed my fingers on the table watching Margaret put the copper kettle on the stove. My eyes darted to the staircase. "Can I use your bathroom?"

"Of course, dear. Up the stairs, second door to the right."

Pleased their bathroom was upstairs like ours, I went up to the top and glanced behind to make sure Margaret wasn't at the foot of the stairs to see me slink off in search of Shawn's room.

I discovered his was the one with the door half-ajar and minimalist furnishings, a queen bed and a nightstand full of books. The walls, though, were plastered with maps and old fishing gear not unlike the living room's decor. Exactly how I pictured they'd be. A guitar leaned against the bed with a pick stuck under the taut strings of the uppermost fret. I knew I couldn't loiter long, but I fell onto the bed where one of his t-shirts had been thrown and took a long inhale. Something like *Irish Spring*. No doubt the way he smelled coming out of the shower. Images of clothes on the floor, his bare body only hidden underneath a towel occupied my thoughts.

I had to leave. Part of me wanted to take his shirt home with me. But how to pull it off without being found out? I didn't bring a purse or bag. Sliding off the bed quietly, I plucked the pick from under the guitar strings, stuck it in the back-pocket of my jeans, and scooted out of the room. Once I found the bathroom, I flushed the toilet for appearances sake, ran some water from the tap, and then made my way downstairs.

I talked with Margaret about trivial things—going to a new school, how I came to like Lunenburg, no, I haven't made any other friends but Shawn—until my tea became a tepid pool of crushed leaves. Then, I scampered back home to my room, flicked Shawn's guitar pick in between my fingers and delighted in having been on his bed.

***

The Barringers were hosting a twenty-fourth birthday party for Shawn's brother, Aaron, in the evening and wanted Andy and I there. I didn't know Aaron, but I wanted to run up and give him a huge hug the moment I met him. His arrival in town brought Shawn and I back together at last.

We entered their backyard making squish noises as we went; the ground still moist from all the rain, the smell of minerals diffusing from it.

My gaze met Aaron's immediately. He and Shawn shared many features: same blue eyes, tone of voice, tall stature, and angular faces. Unlike Shawn, Aaron had dark hair, cut short like his dad. I wanted him to like me right away.

"They're here," Shawn said, while ushering his brother over to us.

I refrained on the hug and shared a friendly handshake with Aaron instead. "Becky, right?" he asked.

"Yes."

"I've heard so much about you."

I blushed. "You have?"

"This one over here won't stop talking about the girl next door." He elbowed Shawn.

Shawn shrugged. "I don't deny a thing."

Andy pursed his lips at the exchange between the brothers. When Aaron introduced himself, the grimace faded into a genial smile. "Nice to meet you. When did you get in from the city, again?"

"Late this morning," Aaron answered.

The two of them took a seat on giant logs that Phillip set up around the campfire. Some of Aaron's old high school buddies were gathered there.

Shawn bumped his shoulder into mine. "Hullo, stranger."

"Hello back," I replied.

He swept the hair away from his face, remnants of wood clung to a few strands. His smile lines were more visible from the light layer of dirt on his face, telling me he'd helped Phillip chop logs.

"It's nice being here and meeting your brother," I said.

"I've missed you. Aaron and I had some good times, though. Man, it was nice to watch his band play, and afterward go and party at one of his friend's houses. If Pop knew how little I was put to work, he'd tan my hide."

My laugh sounded deflated even to me.

"You okay?"

I cleared my throat. "Uh, yah. I'm fine. It's just...I have so much to tell you."

"Like what?"

I flipped through the events in my mind, unsure what to say first. When my pause grew longer than I'd hoped, and Shawn's curious stare turned to an *I'm-waiting* look, I said, "The watch played music for me."

Shawn staggered back a few steps and then threw his arm over my shoulder, closing us into a huddle. "No way..."

"I'm not joking. And that's not all..."

"Don't tell me." His breath grew rapid. "You saw him?"

"I saw Jack. He spoke to me. I don't think it would've been able to happen if you hadn't believed I could do it."

Shawn gasped in a long puff of breath, looked behind at everyone and back at me. "We've got to get out of here. You and I have to sneak away somehow."

"But what about Aaron's birthday?"

"Rebecca, why don't you come here where everyone else is, huh?" Andy said.

I sighed and even after Andy gave me serious eyes, I sat next to Shawn, who quivered as if caffeine-induced.

Phillip barbequed burgers and shrimp. Margaret handed around drinks. Everyone listened to Aaron fill us in on university life and his time spent with Shawn.

I pictured Aaron sitting on a tall bar stool as he played guitar in a dimly lit pub, being admired by female patrons. It was no secret these boys had great genes. When he told a story about a twenty-five-year-old woman vying for Shawn's number at one of the gigs, not aware he was seventeen, I ground my teeth together and completely phased out the rest. The group started up in laughter and I realized I had to snap out of it and snickered along anyway, gazing at Shawn. I loved how he showed his whole teeth when laughing.

Back at O'Sullivan Island, inside the lighthouse, I had him all to myself. I wished for that. There was no greater longing within me than to have another kiss or have his fingers comb through my hair again while I described what happened with the watch in further detail.

I let out a deep sigh, purposefully louder to get his attention.

Shawn's pleasant laughter faded and he turned in my direction while Aaron continued talking. "What's up?"

"I feel a little like Wendy Darling," I said. "Peering out my window, hoping to be swept off by magic."

Shawn's eyebrow rose. "Swept off by magic, or swept off by Peter Pan?"

"Aren't they one and the same?"

I noticed Andy held this peculiar leer and tilted his head in our direction, as if trying hard to listen in on what we talked about in between the discussions from everyone else. Maybe he reminded me of Mr. Darling a lot of the time, but right at this moment with that expression on his face, he turned pirate.

With bright eyes Shawn replied, "I suppose they are."

"Yah well, Captain Hook plans to steal Wendy so that she might read him stories." I gave Andy the evil-eye. "But the thing is, he hates stories. He doesn't believe in them. I don't know why he wants her."

Shawn caught on quickly. "Neverland is in unrest, and it will remain that way until Peter makes things right. He has this hiding place; one Wendy hasn't heard of quite yet. It's a fort. Call it...*Hangman's Tree*. He once spent all his time studying maps to find lost treasure. He is going to save her and he is going to take her there."

Andy snuck behind me to grab a drink out of the cooler Margaret had placed by their patio table. Before he made his way back to his seat, he cracked the can open and said over my shoulder, "I may not have heard everything you two said, but I know you think I'm this Captain Hook character. You're not as sneaky as you think." When he was seated back on his stump, he glared at me. Always watching.

Shawn gave me a sidelong glance and slid his hand slowly into mine. All my worries disintegrated.

"Psst!" Andy shook his head and gestured for us to release hands. Shawn nodded courteously and did as he was asked, but I seethed with irritation.

To abate my embarrassment, Shawn whispered in my ear. "Just keep thinking about *Hangman's Tree*, Wendy. It will be our special place."

"But when are we going?" I whispered back, ignoring Andy's constant stares.

"When school is back in."

After everyone ate like royalty, Andy announced we were leaving. "Hate to eat and run," he said, "But got some things to do at home. Nice of you to invite us out. Happy birthday, Aaron."

He gave a wave, "Hey thanks."

On the short walk back I asked, "What is so pressing at home? And why couldn't I stay longer? Margaret and Phillip are there to supervise."

"I see the way you look at Shawn, Rebecca. Frankly, how you two are when you get together worries me. We visited for a bit, that's good enough." He opened the front door and waited for me to go inside.

Nobody wished for the beginning of school as much as I did.

ELEVEN

Shawn offered to drive me to school to save Andy the travel, but was refused. Before heading out to work, Andy drove around a dulling field of grass to get to the parking lot full of pickup trucks and old cars. He dropped me off in front of a set of glass doors hidden under a stony pergola.

"Have a good first day."

I exited the vehicle and watched him leave before making my way toward the oblong, red-brick building that reminded me of a fire-station. Its large windows resembled the automatic doors firetrucks exit out of. The surrounding trees' leaves had ends singed gold from the first sweep of autumn's flame. Damp air clung to the skin. Amidst the lingering smell of ocean, the subtle hint of baked apple broke through.

For what seemed like forever, I'd waited for this. My dreams of Jack were favorably replaced by Shawn, and some of them were not easily forgotten. Ones I felt slightly ashamed to rerun in my head.

All the same, school felt foreign to me. Not just because it was a new place full of new faces, but because Shawn and his adventures made summer feel like the only season that existed.

Every eye was on me as I approached the front doors. Loud whispers circulated about Canada Day and *the follower* of Shawn. A few girls purposely rammed into my shoulder and made me drop my backpack. I hadn't spotted Shawn and wondered if this was a glimpse of how he got treated. Maybe he hid somewhere.

The bell wailed outside and everyone hustled through the front doors, except me. I picked up my backpack, and after my ears cleared the blaring sound, gentle music from a guitar caught my attention. Parked five vehicles away, I noticed Shawn sitting inside the box of his parent's truck. Well, the top of his head at least.

When I propped up on the bumper to peer inside, his guitar sat on his lap and he fingered the strings with eyes closed while whistling. Even at a place as ordinary as school, he made it whimsical, and those *dreams* came flooding back, reddening every nook and cranny of my face. The thoughts of his bedroom made me consider the pick I took. Did he wonder where it went?

"Hi, Shawn."

He opened his eyes but kept playing guitar. "There you are. I've been waiting."

"It was a zoo out front and I couldn't see you. Besides, I was busy trying to ward off all the daggers everyone shot at me."

"Guilty by association." Shawn grinned and stopped strumming. "People think you're trouble, like me."

"If *trouble* means I'm not as boring and predictable like them, then I'm trouble."

"That's the spirit," Shawn said.

"You said you were out of practice, but you strum that guitar so well. Would you play a song for me?"

"I could, I guess…" he shrugged.

Crestfallen, I said, "You don't have to."

"No, it's just…I kind of wanted you to talk more about the watch's music and seeing Jack."

Throwing a leg over to join him in the box, I said, "Uh, right. Of course."

"I suppose one song won't hurt anything." His fingers good-sportingly went back to the strings.

I spun my backpack to my front, held it close, and sat, leaning against the tailgate. "We'll be pretty late for class. And I still have to register at the principal's office."

His attention remained on the strings. "I'm in no hurry to be amongst the living-dead. You?"

"Not at all."

As most girls probably would, I imagined he'd play me a romantic ballad to sweep me off my feet. Instead, I got something that sounded like his own personal theme song. A lively, sailor ditty.

When the music stopped, I gave a bashful grin and swept a strand of hair behind my ear. "Is there anything you aren't good at? Shawn, it's like everything you touch gets bewitched."

Shawn slid the guitar off to the side with eyes locked on mine. Inching closer, his thumb traced my bottom lip. "And I bewitched you?"

"Isn't it obvious?"

Just as we were about to kiss, a plump woman with glasses too small for her face stood with her hands on her hips a few feet from the truck. "Why aren't you two inside?" she asked. "Mr. Barringer, I don't want this to be like last year where I have to get after you every day and usher you to class."

Shawn's hand flew off me so fast, I felt the wind. "No, Mam," he said. We both stood.

"And Miss Stafford, is it? Your father called the school and was very adamant about us making sure your attention remains on your studies and not on this young man here. That includes lunch times, I'm afraid. There are activities we offer…like student council or sports, to name a few."

"He called the school?" My mouth hung open. "As if."

The woman, who was obviously the principal, straightened her glasses on her nose. "Indeed, he did. Now off you two go. Say your goodbyes and get inside to class."

Shawn snuck a kiss on my cheek. "Hangman's Tree."

"No more riddles," I said with pleading eyes. "Tell me what that means."

"Miss Stafford, go to class *please*." The principal said tapping her high-heel on the pavement.

"Meet me here at lunch hour," he said packing up his guitar.

I slid my backpack straps over each shoulder and hopped out, trailing behind the principal. Shawn waved at me when I looked back, and without overthinking it, I mouthed, "I love you."

He almost dropped his guitar case, stunned. I turned my back on him and jogged to the glass doors before he could reciprocate. If he would at all. Maybe that's why I couldn't look at him anymore, or maybe my adrenaline about to bring me to my knees was a factor. Either way, I meant what I said. I loved him.

***

My nerves were getting the best of me. I doubted whether I should meet with Shawn after saying those all-too-important three words. While waiting for him outside, I found myself edging closer toward a thick tree to make a getaway. But with a grab of my hand, I swung left and right between clusters of kids smoking cigarettes (seemingly in slow-motion) until I stood with Shawn in front of his truck.

"We're going to my place and we're going to pack a few things for our journey," he said.

"A few things? Are we going to the island? Is that where Hangman's Tree is?" Part of me already knew.

"Aren't you sick and tired of people interrupting, telling us what to think, who to be, whether we can see one another?"

"You have no idea," I replied.

"I mean, taking your lunchtimes away? Come on."

"I know. That's getting ridiculous."

"Alright then." He pressed me against the cool metal of the truck with his body and whispered the next part. "Let's take off and stay on the island. Send a rebel's message to all of them. They can't keep us apart."

My mind was a blur. "What are we waiting for?"

Shawn ran a hand through my hair and caressed the back of my neck. Desire crept under my skin and down my spine. "First, we finish that kiss," he said.

Mesmerized by his oceanic eyes, I met his lips with fervor. We heard the ridicule and quiet laughter from students passing by. It only made us kiss harder until all the noise dampened around us.

We got into the truck happily numb for a few minutes. Once the fog lifted, Shawn zoomed the streets to his house, and I wondered when he'd say he loved me, too.

Once at his place, he ushered me inside. "Mom is gone to a sewing club thing, but shouldn't be long. We don't have much time."

"How long are we planning to stay on the island for?"

"Heck, as long as it takes until we get caught. *If* we do at all. I know that island better than anybody. Even the Coast Guard."

Shawn dashed upstairs and came down with a duffel bag and a lunch cooler. We went to the kitchen and opened the pantry and threw whatever we could into the duffel. Shawn tore the plastic off a flat of water and tossed half of the bottles in. He then yanked open the freezer part of the fridge and had me empty a bag of ice into the cooler before filling it with non-perishables. "Stick one of those blankets off our couch in the bag while I grab a few rain ponchos and a change of clothes from the laundry room," Shawn said.

"Sure." I rushed into the living room and pulled off the blue and white striped afghan. My mind was trying to catch up with Shawn's plan, but couldn't. The idea was romantic and what I'd wanted during Aaron's birthday party. Surely, he loved me. Still, I needed to hear him say it.

After I zipped up the duffel with the afghan inside, Shawn sprung up behind me and said, "Let's head to your place now and grab a few things." He slung it over his shoulder, while I carried the cooler.

Shawn waited on the step while I went through my drawers for appropriate clothing. Dresses and skirts were out of the question. I pulled out some underwear, a few slimming long-sleeve shirts, jeans, and leggings. Gathered up toiletries. We barely had room left in the duffel, but I wanted a book. I grabbed Peter Pan. Other luxuries had to stay behind.

It baffled me just how much I'd do for Shawn. How much I'd give up. Capable of everything, just as long as he was there.

***

While stepping over the rickety stairs and past the unfriendly path, Shawn eased my mind about food and other needs that may come up, depending on how long we stayed on the island. He planned to travel back out to shore in the event we needed more supplies. After expressing concern he'd be caught and reported to his dad by store clerks, he assured me no one would recognize him in a hooded sweater and sunglasses. "Stop worrying," he said.

We arrived at the dock, set down what we carried, and Shawn removed the tarp of the dory. I put my hands over my mouth.

"*Old Broken Down*...she's brand new," I said. "When did you do this?"

Shawn began folding up the tarp and set it aside. "You remember that time I hauled planks of wood and said I was helping my pop with something? We were fixing the old dory and I wanted it to be a surprise. It would've been done sooner, but Pop stopped helping me with it after the Canada Day incident."

I ran a hand along its unbroken white surface while he undid the rope that bound the dory. "She looks beautiful."

"I knew you weren't comfortable with the shape she was in prior, and..." He stood and rubbed the back of his neck. *Say you love me*, I implored within. *Now's the perfect time.*

When Shawn didn't finish his sentence, I kissed his cheek and he touched the spot afterward. After we were inside, he shot his arm straight out in a sweep. "Off we go, Wendy. Second star to the right, and straight on 'till morning."

As he sculled ahead, I told him more about my encounter with Jack and then hummed the full melody of the pocket-watch. Cold water sprayed on us and left the sting of salt dried as white crust on our skin. *Old Broken Down* (deserving of a new name) bobbed up and down through the gloom of the overcast afternoon. It became a large ship in my mind, with the wake crashing up on the boards of the stern. If I stayed perfectly still, I was the intricately carved figurehead upon it, hair perpetually windblown, carrying Shawn in the direction of his precious vial. As I continued to hum, the sound became haunting while over the Atlantic and distorted my imagery. At any moment, the *Jolly Roger* was going to sail alongside the dory and cast its horrible shadow upon us. Leaving us to realize our ship remained nothing more than the diminutive little boat it really was, on the giant expanse of ocean. The rowdy bellow of buccaneers ringing in my ears overshadowed the sweetness of the watch's tune on my lips.

> *"Avast, belay, when I appear,*
> *By fear they're overtook;*
> *Naught's left upon your bones when you*
> *Have shaken claws with Hook."*

Doubt leaked in and I thought about how I might actually be a figurehead to Shawn. Having one meaningful function, and to remain kept at a distance. I mean, I love you wasn't all that hard to say.

Being no stranger to feeling small from Andy, I loathed the feeling coming from Shawn.

"Man, I had that watch for so long and got nothing. Not a peep."

"Imagine that," I said.

"Still so many unanswered questions. Like, are the visions of Jack linked to the music? Would he say something more if you reached him again?"

"Beats me." I shrugged. I grew jealous of O'Sullivan, the lighthouse, the watch, all of it. They always got Shawn's full attention. As for me, I could only think of him. I said I loved him. He hadn't said it in return.

"I can't believe I missed the riddle on the watch…"

"Uh huh."

"Looks like you've got other things on your mind." The sincere innocence to his stare made me feel terrible for being jealous, but I couldn't help it. Why couldn't he just say he loved me? Why didn't he even bring up the fact that I'd said it, and it meant something to him?

"It's nothing."

"Look," Shawn said. "My Pop mentioned once that if a woman says 'It's nothing', something's up."

I exhaled a heavy-hearted sigh.

"Oh?" Shawn tensed his lips downward. "Something isn't just up. Something's wrong."

I couldn't look at him. It hurt too much. I reached and swished my hand in the water and said, "No, nothing's wrong."

"Alright." He left it at that.

We came around a different side of the peninsula where the caves were. Two large black, hollowed-out eyes scowled down at us wannabe explorers claiming this land as their own. The third opening, the smallest of the caves and bottommost, was a thirsty mouth, sucking up everything in its path.

"Hold on, it's going to get a bit rough," Shawn warned.

At first, when the mouth inhaled us toward its slick black, unforgiving face I dropped my head in between my knees and covered it with my hands. But as the mouth exhaled, I relaxed enough to see Shawn steer us powerfully inside it. Water slapped around us, and the echo of the dory clattering against a line of stone teeth (a footpath that looked to lead out of the cave) made us both cover our ears.

Shawn's reddened face came back to normal color, though his breathing remained hoarse and deep. My heart didn't slow its pace.

He pointed toward the footpath. "We'll walk along there, but it's wet…so we've got to be…careful," he said loudly, his voice resonant with the din.

"Just catch your breath first, sheesh," I said. "You're going to pass out."

He nodded and leaned back for a rest. It was a good thing he'd fixed the boat. There was no way, in the shape it was in previous, it would've withstood the cave's constant lashings.

"You ought to go ahead of me and just wait it out at the top, I'll deal with the cooler and bag. There isn't a rope ladder or nothing, but if you take your time, the climb isn't too steep. You okay doing that?"

"Don't have much of a choice, really, do I?" I replied. Why was I biting at him as if he were Andy?

"Why don't I help you get to the top, and then come back?"

"I'm not that fragile," I said. "I can go myself."

"I meant no offense, Becky. Only offering help."

I hated the tension inside me—this jack-in-the-box emotion, waiting to bounce up with its disquieting grin. "I'm good."

"Well, I'm going to hop out onto the path and find a place to tie *Old Broken Down* and then you can get out."

His fingers meticulously slid their way along the dory's rope. "I think I'll leave the cooler here in the cave. The food will keep longer. Whenever we need anything from it I can make a run back down here," he said. As he tied the rope in a knot around a large rock, my stomach related to the squeezing, tightening. A horrible thought beleaguered me. *You're being used. He plays you even better than his guitar.* My body didn't even have the strength to get out of the boat just then. *No. It isn't true.* But something told me it might very well be.

Water slipped up along the footpath and spit at us.

"Becky, you can hop out," Shawn said offering his hand.

I stared at that hand, the scar in between the thumb and index (from what, I don't know), the sanded down fingerprints from guitar playing, the swollen-looking knuckles. Water droplets coming together in the middle of his palm. When I stood, my knees buckled and I had to lean against the dory's side.

"You don't have your sea-legs yet?" Shawn teased.

I moved his hand aside and crawled out. After wiping myself off, I rushed down the footpath, not taking heed to his instructions to be careful on the slippery surface.

"Woah, Becky...wait up."

I paused momentarily but carried on until Shawn grabbed my shoulders and spun me around. "Hey, come on. What's this all about? I made a joke."

I tilted my head up. "I'll be waiting at the top."

"You're usually all for a little light ribbing."

"I don't care about the joking, Shawn."

"What's going on, then?"

"I said it's nothing."

Shawn shrugged. "If that's the truth, then I'm going to stop asking."

No. Don't stop asking, I thought. *You just don't get it. Why don't you get it?*

He pursed his lips and kicked a pebble—the sound making a tinging ricochet—before rotating around and back to the dory.

I gathered myself enough to climb the incline, taking each step warily. Part of me felt bad that Shawn would have to scale up with a heavy duffel. My ears popped as I got higher, and I realized after being out in the open just how loud the inside of the cave had been. I wriggled a finger inside each ear and sat on a boulder for a break before carrying on, the cold of it coming through my leggings. I spotted some wild daisies popping up between the rocks and knew I wasn't far now. I got up, plucked a few, and returned to my spot. I set them beside me and picked one out of the bunch. The nicest of them.

"He loves me. He loves me not," I said ripping at the petals, envisioning tearing bits off my own papery heart in the same way. "He loves me. He loves me not. He loves me. He loves me n—" I hissed at the last petal and crushed the flower under my shoe.

"What are you doing?" Shawn grunted, setting the duffel down.

My head shot up and I swept the persecuted daisy aside. "Resting."

"Oh." Shawn eyed the rumpled flower, then heaved the duffel over his shoulder again and waved me on. "We're almost there."

I ambled behind him. At the corner of my eye, while lunging over loftier stones, I saw Shawn reach down and pull something from the rock.

The craggy ground transitioned to crawling vines and then grass up to our knees, sweeping against us and leaving damp fingerprints over our pants. Shawn positioned the duffel's strap more comfortably over his shoulder. We drew closer toward a copse and he looked back at me briefly, saying, "Hey, maybe on the way I can try to see if O' Sullivan's pocket-watch will play again. Give it a rap against some tree-trunks or something. Whatta you say?"

"Here."

Shawn stopped and turned around as I dug in my jeans pocket and tossed him the watch, an apparent lack of enthusiasm. With one hand, he caught it and with the other presented me with a drooping, bluish-purple flower. "It's called a Hare Bell. The flower of memory."

I took the dainty stem and pressed my lips together, overwhelmed with conflicting thoughts of anger and yearning. "It's so pretty…"

"They're rare to spot. Maybe you want to stick it inside the book you brought along?" He strode ahead, shook the watch, opened it up, tinkered, got lost back into his world of legends and left me hanging just like the forlorn looking flower bouncing up and down as I walked on.

Once we were deep in the heart of the damp woods, he stopped at a large oak and knocked the watch twice against the ridged bark. *Dack, dack.* Bounding toward the next large oak as if he wasn't carrying a heavy duffel, he tried again.

"Hmmm." Shawn examined it over again.

If the darned thing broke in two I wouldn't have complained. With devious intentions, I said, "I think you might try hitting it harder. Maybe that's what it needs. A good blow like when I dropped it the first time." My eyes peered at him over the head of the Hare Bell as I took in the faintest sweet aroma.

With a curl on the side of his lips, I wondered if he was on to me. "The force from a drop would probably work best. We'll try at the lighthouse."

"Lighthouse? Shawn, weren't you taking me to see Hangman's Tree? You said that it was our special place." I worried whether it was just something hypothetical he'd come up with to distract me at Aaron's party when Andy got on our nerves.

"Oh right," he said, nonchalant. "Well, let's start going left, then."

He hummed the watch's song and skipped ahead, an ignorant boy with true Peter characteristics. It was uncanny. Peter Pan was ignorant to Wendy's feelings, oblivious to the fact Tinkerbell adored him. This was no different.

All the anticipation I'd felt toward Hangman's Tree, about it being special was soured with his forgetting. Embittered, I thought, *If I wait any longer to hear you say you love me, that tree's name is going to become a heck of a lot more significant.*

TWELVE

Songbirds skittered above us going from branch to branch. Twigs snapped as we tread over them and forced them into the damp, mossy earth. We passed under trees bowing down as if before monarchs, ferns fanned against our shins. How easy to get lost in reverie here, easy to overlook my discontent for a time. It was a piece of Eden.

Shawn stopped humming and said, "We're almost at the trail I made from all the times I went out here."

When we were on the skinny track, there were no obstacles in our way save for a few stones bursting out of the ground. It took us mere minutes until we stood before the most veiled and thickest tree I'd seen so far in the woods. Silvermound decorated the forest floor around it. Wooden stepping boards nailed up one side of it were covered in vine. The grandeur, how this tree pulsed with nature, sent shivers up my arms. It resembled the *Tree of Life* on the pocket-watch. "Wow."

"Just wait until you're up into it," Shawn said and began the ascent. "The leaves are hiding the fort."

The steps were sturdy and not difficult to climb, very unlike the rope ladder on the cliff. Curling branches full of deep green leaves dipped and weaved. Moss and shelves of mushrooms crawled up the tree trunk and covered the underneath of the fort, camouflaging it other than the square hole to climb through, which emitted the faintest light. An almost tropical, grassy aroma surrounded Shawn and I as we stood inside. Circular windows let in shafts of sun, reflecting the color of green within. Blankets, pillows, and stacks of books crowded one corner with old maps tacked up on the wall, behind a small, wooden staircase that led to a loft above. Washed out throw rugs scattered the floor. "This is magnificent. Totally exceeded my expectations. It's right out of a fairytale." I approached Shawn and unzipped the front pouch on the duffel and pressed the Hare Bell onto the first page of Peter Pan, as he'd suggested.

"While searching the island, I found it. O'Sullivan wrote about a place he fashioned just to meditate and escape."

"I'm just relieved to know you didn't lie about it."

"Lie? Becky," Shawn gave an exasperated sigh and faced me once I zipped the pouch back up. "I've been trying to pick your brain about what's the matter and you keep giving me the cold shoulder. You can say all you want that you're fine, but I don't buy it."

I crossed my arms over my chest. "What's even more bothersome is how you don't know what's bothering me. How can you *not* know?"

"Know what?" He threw his hands in the air and then let them fall heavily at his sides.

"Are you using me to reach O'Sullivan? To find that sacred water? Is that all I am to you now that you know about my visions?"

"Woah." Shawn bit his lower lip, eyes blazing a brilliant blue. "So, that's what you've been stewing about."

"Stewing? Shawn, you talk about Jack all the time. All you've done is ask me about that watch. You're obsessed with finding that water." I didn't like how the words obsessed slithered out of my mouth. Now I sounded like Andy.

"I thought you were on board with finding the vial. If I remember correctly, you told me about the visions of yours willingly. Why are you throwing all this in my face now?"

"I'm not. It just hurts…you know?"

He removed the duffel and stood in front of me. "What do you think all this is, huh? Escaping to this island was for you. It was supposed to mean something."

"I know all that. And it does, it's just…"

"Spit it out. Just say it."

"I love you, okay." I started crying. "There's my second time saying it and you never said it back."

"Becky." Shawn cupped his hands on my cheeks and his thumbs wiped the tears away. "I didn't think I had to. I thought you knew."

"You didn't catch on to why I was upset all this time, because I kept it in. How then am I supposed to know you love me if you don't ever say it?"

Shawn's hands swept past my cheeks, through my hair, and down my back. "I had it bad for you already when we shook hands at the door upon your arrival in town. When I mowed the lawn at your place, I tried to impress you, pretend I didn't know you were watching me. And when we swam together, when I first touched your bare skin, I knew I wanted to touch you more. I loved you the moment you asked me to sneak off to the island at midnight. I love you, Rebecca Stafford. You're my inspiration to find that water, even more so than ever."

My heart had never felt more full. "I am?"

"After we find it, we'll lather ourselves with it. You and I. And we'll live long lives together. Heck, if there's enough left, we might never die. We'll be the first to say our love will last forever and literally mean it."

Shawn tilted my chin up and left a feather kiss on my lips.

"I shouldn't have doubted you, or treated you the way I did. I'm sorry."

"Don't be. We figured things out. I want us to enjoy being here now. Bask in our much-deserved liberty." He left one more kiss on my lips and turned his eyes up to the sky when a loud rumble of thunder shook the fort and sporadic splats of rain dropped overhead. "Let's make our way over to the lighthouse before it pours hard. It'll be warmer in there."

We shuffled through the woods until the lighthouse's white frontage emerged between the tall trees and dense shrubbery. Branches rustled in the breeze, the ocean crashed, and thunder barked.

After we pushed past the last layer of bush and shrub into the clearing. Shawn's mouth dropped. "No…"

The lighthouse door hung wide open. Papers furling in the air.

THIRTEEN

"No, no, no!" Shawn dropped the duffel and dashed to pick up the drawings. The last time we were here, we'd left in a panic, the window and door wide open to the elements.

I ran over and began to help him. We were as ants when a foot treads upon their carefully built home. Scurrying to-and-fro, frantic, arms reaching in thorny bushes, getting scraped up. Muck soiling our clothes and faces. Burs in our hair. Shawn even scaled up a few trees to remove skewered sheets off branches.

A crack of lightning made me jump and Shawn looked up at the sky again. "We've got to move faster."

"How many loose pages were there?" I called from a distant part of the woods.

"Nine. It's the drawings...I didn't put them back in the tube. Just try to pick up what you can."

"I have two."

It took about ten minutes for the rain to fall hard, pattering against the awnings of leaves. "We gotta get inside the lighthouse before these papers ruin even worse," Shawn hollered over to me, as I spread away some tall grass and leaves to pick out an imbedded page. I pressed the papers close to my body and rushed under large trees for cover making my way back. Drops trickled down my face and arms like tiny streams. The slap of my paces met up with the slap of Shawn's.

I slid against him and inside the lighthouse while he held open the door. I wiped the wet strands of hair away from my face and drew a long breath, leaning against the wall. He slammed the door and said, "Can't believe we forgot to close up last we were here."

A flash of lightning lit up the two windows in the entrance and thunder followed shortly after. "I'm sorry about your stuff."

"You said you found two?" Shawn pointed to my stack.

"I got three now."

"I got four. We're missing two."

"I honestly couldn't see anymore and we covered some good ground," I said wiping a hand over my face.

"Did we shut the window in the keeper's quarters?"

"That room you smoked in? I didn't shut it."

He swore under his breath and kicked the lighthouse's door. "We better go up and see what the damage is there."

When we got in the room, a feather pen and ink had fallen over on the desk. All the small books that sat on it were on the floor, spread out chaotically. A lot of the artifacts had tipped and the loose papers blown to the walls and under furniture. The fiddle stand had fallen back, but there didn't appear to be damage to the instrument. I set my pages down and closed the window.

"Aw, man. Would you look at this place?" Shawn put his papers on top of mine and started picking things up and putting them in their proper place.

I covered a sneeze and then ran my shoe along the floor to collect the fragments of glass into a pile from the lantern, that had also toppled and broke. No sign of the candle.

"Who knows how far those two sheets blew. Could be in the ocean for all we know."

"The weather only got stormy here in recent days," I said. "Maybe they aren't too far." I gathered up the stack and before bringing it over to Shawn, gasped.

"What? What's wrong now?"

"Shawn, the rain…it washed some of the drawings away."

"It's like that damn Reaper's been here. Causing nothing but destruction in his poisoned path."

"No, no." I walked over to Shawn and showed him the top of the stack with the ink bleeding down the page. "See, there's something underneath. Another drawing of something."

Shawn took the sheet and assessed it.

"*To reveal what's underneath, use what you're trying to find,*" I said. "The etching. It's a riddle for water. When Jack said that, he was answering the riddle for me."

"Holy man, you're right. This is remarkable."

"The words are sitting under the tree's roots. It all makes sense now. Roots need water."

"Let's gather some rain and wash the papers in it to see if the ink fades more and reveals what's underneath," Shawn said and further analyzed the area of the one page showing a bit of a picture. "I think under the layer of writing, there's a map."

We both looked at one another, eyes ablaze, and said in unison, "To find the vial."

Shawn almost toppled over in excitement. "O'Sullivan had to make subtle hints toward the map. He didn't want the Grim Reaper getting his grubby hands on it. It's why the pages were separate."

"His drawings were all a disguise for something more," I said.

"It's genius how he did it. The layer of resin, probably from a plant, protected the map underneath all this time." Shawn scraped at the parchment. "Water dissolves the glue."

I scurried to the wash basin and picked up the bowl. "Let's get collecting that rain."

Shawn and I rushed outside, tossed out the old ashy water and remnants of torch from our last visit. We forgot about the rain ponchos, not caring how wet we got now. We sat under the downpour and waited for the bowl to fill.

When we were back upstairs, we took one page at a time and submerged them. Every one seeped black ink, darkening the water so much we kept having to dump it and go back down and collect more rain. We put the artifacts all over the writing desk and on some of the free spaces left on the bookshelves. Gently the soggy pages were laid out to dry in the middle of the floor in their place.

"We have to find the missing ones," Shawn said gently swapping pages out with others (like a puzzle) until satisfied. "We've got most of the island here, but see…there's a middle piece gone, and the bottom right, where I'm guessing the legend is."

"We do have to find them, yes, but Shawn, I'm in awe. You did it. You found the map. The vial isn't out of reach anymore."

"I couldn't have done anything without you."

The lightning flashes, cracks of thunder, and the eureka-moment of uncovering the map created a charged atmosphere between Shawn and me. We looked up and moved toward one another.

Shawn blushed, and said, "The way you talked at the barbeque like you were Wendy. Can you call me Peter Pan again?" He ran his rough hands over my smooth ones, intertwined our fingers, and pulled us chest to chest. I took a deep breath of his smell—a mixture of rain and soap.

"You're Peter Pan. The lost boy of Lunenburg."

He let go of my hands and his warm fingers found their way to my neck. Slowly he drew me in to his full, parted lips. I squeezed his broad shoulders before my fingers explored his wet hair. His kiss was slow and rhythmic, then fast and intense.

My body tingled and burned when he grinded against me, kissing with such fervor. The erotic dreams I'd had returned in full force. When he moaned out a breath, we both almost jumped away from one another. Like me, his ferocious urges wanted to win against any common-sense. "I want you," he rasped.

"I want you, too. But, I'm uh…nervous."

"Same."

I pressed my lips together and asked, "Have you done this before?"

"Uh-uh."

"Me neither."

Shawn exhaled and raked a hand through his hair.

"Truthfully, I imagined being married and doing it then."

"Oh," he said, eyes wide. "Of course. That makes sense."

The pause between us made me uncomfortable. Shawn stared off, down toward the floor.

"Everything okay?"

"Yes, just hold on a sec."

I giggled. "What?"

He waved me off. "Two seconds." Shuffling over to the desk, Shawn browsed the artifacts we'd put there earlier, and pulled a cherry-wood box with a faded, ceramic-tile painting of a crown on the lid from the group. He then asked me to turn around for a moment.

"What are you up to over there?" I asked.

After some clinks and shuffling, he said, "Okay, turn."

He had one knee bent and a beat-up, gold Claddagh ring lifted high toward me. "Jack wore one ring. And it was this one on his ring finger."

"Shawn?" I said, breathless. "Wha—"

"Rebecca Stafford, will you marry me?"

"You... are you serious?"

His eyes were fixed on mine. Not a tremble in his tone. "Sure, why not? I want to make you happy. This would make you happy, right?"

I stared down at the ring and let my vision blur, going into deep thought. This was extremely hasty, maybe even unrealistic. Yet...it was everything I'd secretly wished for, wanted, craved. As unexpected as when I'd first met Shawn at the door. I mean, girls of yore married a lot younger.

A glint of gold brought me out of my rumination. My choice was made up. "It would make me very happy."

"Then you'll marry me?"

I jumped into his arms like they did in movies. "Yes! I'll marry you."

We gave one another a quick kiss, and as Shawn lowered me down, I pulled back and offered him my left hand. He slid the ring on my finger, and though it was big, I cherished it. *This isn't two kids playing make-believe. This is real. Shawn is my fiancé.*

For a moment, I floated. Blissful of my papery form, knowing full well a tether kept me attached to Shawn.

"Now, I can't offer you the big dress and the lavish ceremony. But if you'd oblige me, we can marry right here, right now," Shawn offered.

"Is that even possible?" I twirled the ring around my finger.

"Why not?" He cleared his throat and stood poker straight, chest puffed up. "We gather today to…uh, join two young-lovers in Holy Matrimony," he said in an over-embellished Irish accent, likely trying to impersonate Jack. "Shawn Tyler Barringer an' Rebecca…" he cupped his hand to his mouth at me, "excuse me Colleen, your middle name, if ye please."

"Colleen?"

"That's what the Irish call young girls, I think," Shawn whispered.

"Oh," I smiled, trying to hold back laughter. "It's Leah. After my mom."

"Indeed, it tis. So, Shawn Tyler Barringer an' Rebecca Leah Stafford." He turned to me with a sincere expression, out of Jack's character. "Do you want to do this? I'll understand if this is too weird, too soon, if you want the wedding dress sort of thing."

I shook my head and said, "I don't need the dress. I don't need anything but you."

He jumped right back into being Jack. "Since a ring's been given, ye may continue with yer vows."

I pondered the whole of this romantic gesture. How silly and unorthodox, yet moving and meaningful all the same. And, I believed it.

Shawn took my hand and kissed over the ring. "I, Shawn, take you, Rebecca, to be my wife. To hold onto from this day on. For better or worse. In sickness and health. Until death parts us. If, of course, it does at all."

I took in shaky breaths and in a quivering voice said, "I, Rebecca, take you Shawn, for my husband. To have and to hold from this day on. For better or worse. Richer or poorer. In sickness and health. Until death do us part."

Back to being Jack, Shawn said, "If there be anyone present who objects to this couple bein' joined, let them speak or forever hold their peace." Looking about the room, he shrugged. "Then, I pronounce ye husband an' wife. Ye may kiss yer bride."

Shawn pulled me in at the waist. My husband (it felt great to refer to him as such) brushed my hair behind my ears, held my face, and kissed my lips gently.

All the tears I'd held back burst out. Tears of passion fell as I pressed into him and kissed harder, full of zeal. From there, Shawn swept me up in his arms as if to take me through the threshold and placed me onto the chaise longue.

He removed his clinging, wet shirt and let it fall from his fingers to the floor. I removed mine next. For a moment, he admired me in my bra, and then whispered, "Will you become *one* with me, my dear wife?"

I ran my hand down his stomach. "Yes."

We removed the rest of our clothes, succumbing to the heat of the moment, the devotion, the pain.

FOURTEEN

A visceral, insatiable drive released from inside us. The next day, in between short treks outside in the storm to find the missing pages—this time wearing the rain ponchos—we gave in to one another again on the chaise. His body heat warmed my insides and broke the cold like a mallet on ice. At one point, reason trickled into my brain and I casually mentioned to him how we should be more careful. That although we fiercely loved one another, perhaps on the first trip for supplies, he might want to buy us protection. Until then, there were other ways to be intimate and keep from catching pneumonia.

We slid a nine-cubby bookcase out of the way, nearer to the desk, and pulled off impressionistic paintings—a stormy seascape and one of the Bluenose—that hung above it to dry out our drenched pants and socks over the nails. We'd been defenseless due to the cheap ponchos.

The pot-belly stove that Shawn got going with some dry wood from the shack cozied up the quarters in no time. He then reached into the duffel and pried open a can of clingstone peaches with his Swiss Army knife. We ate them with handfuls of trail mix sitting on the floor in our underwear next to the map. I desired a heartier breakfast, something hot, but didn't dare say anything to Shawn. I knew he didn't want to tarry. Those two pages weren't going to find themselves. So, the moment the last nut of the trail mix slid itself down the bag as Shawn offered it into my hand, I ate it, we dressed, and were out searching again.

The lightning lit up the sky, the rain fell, and the wind whistled. It took little time for our pants to cling and our hair to plaster on our skin as we ran through thickets of trees, the hood of our ponchos blown back. Wild people hunting…for paper. Our tribal-paint became mud splatters up from our shoes against our faces. Our battle cries were hoots and shouts between bushes at one another.

I massaged my temples and around my eye sockets. Staring up, down, all around made my eyes like wood-grain in my skull, no matter how humid the air felt. How long would it take for Phillip or Andy to find us? There was no *if*, the way Shawn chose to believe. To me, there was only *when*. They had to be out searching. The image crawled up my spine in one long shiver.

"You want to go back?" Shawn showed up behind me and caused me to jump.

"No. I'll be okay. We really should keep looking."

He wiped the hair from my eyes and kissed me on the forehead. "You're shivering, Becky. I don't want you to catch your death out here."

"Put your arms around me," I said, teeth chattering.

When he did, his chill became mine for a few seconds before his warmth. "We need this damned rain to quit." Shawn nuzzled my neck. "I'll take you back to the lighthouse. You stoke the fire and keep it alive for the night. Eat a bit of a late lunch while I continue to search. I'll bring the flashlight for when the sun goes down."

"No, Shawn. You could get sick in this rain, too, and I don't want you going it alone."

He swiped a hand in the air. "Don't worry about me."

There was no sense arguing with him. He made his mind up, and we were already heading back to the lighthouse.

Our socks and shoes slapped against the hard floor, echoing as we climbed the stairway. The intense wave of heat off the stove when we entered the room made me fully comprehend how cold it had been outside. I removed my socks, pants, cardigan, shirt and laid them in front of the stove.

Shawn unzipped the duffel, removed the afghan and wrapped it around me. "You sure you don't want to stay with me?" I asked with a flirty inflection.

"Your bare skin is tempting." His hand snuck into the afghan and softly caressed over the lace of my bra.

"But…" I said, sliding his hand away and wrapping tighter in the blanket.

"But I've waited years to find that vial. Now that the chance is there. A *real* chance—"

I turned to face him. "You have to take it."

"Yah," he said eyes down.

"Be safe out there."

"I will." He kissed me quickly and went to grab the flashlight.

The lighthouse instantly felt hollower without Shawn. A ghostly old place of echoes and windy hands grasping around it. I slid the afghan from my shoulders and removed a piece of wood off the pile Shawn had stacked neatly in a triangle by the stove. With a sturdy tug, the door opened and released a charred smell and raw heat that removed any last bit of chill in me. I dropped the log on the embers and blew on them before closing the door. The shadows coming off the curios and furniture brought on a touch of claustrophobia, and the idea of being surrounded by misshapen people.

I passed the time by fiddling with my wedding ring and finishing Peter Pan on the chaise with the smashed hare bell placed at my side. When I positioned myself differently, the scent of

Shawn's sweat invaded my nostrils and made me hunger for him. Worry. Wonder.

The spit and crack of fire interrupted my thoughts here and there. But when even that couldn't rid me of my concerns, I began to eat. I rifled through the duffel and munched on granola bars, fruit leathers, picked out all the Smarties from the trail mixes. Incapable of stopping my current gluttony, I ate and ate, knowing full well I shouldn't be devouring our supply of food.

With a mouth full of Smarties, I murmured O'Sullivan's chant, pacing the floor. Mindful not to step over our delicate map, now dry and rumpled as one would imagine a map of old to be. I stared out the window for minutes on end, hoping to see Shawn moving below. When my eyes got dry and head ached, I went back to the chaise longue and fell asleep.

***

Shawn wasn't back yet.

I woke after almost falling off the chaise in a deep sleep and stared out the window again at night's harsh black visage; a slice of shy moon peered around a cloud, afraid to expose itself. It wasn't pouring anymore. No sound of whipping winds. A stream of light came up from the forest, going side to side.

Something in me roiled. Something wasn't right. I began to panic, dumped all the contents out of the duffel, got dressed into fresh clothes and searched for another flashlight. When there wasn't one, I combed the room for the thick, beeswax candle Shawn used the last time we were here.

When the lantern broke, the candle had rolled under the larger bookcase. I swiped it from under there and snapped a match off the book Shawn set by the pile of wood. I lit it and tucked the rest of the matches under my sweater in my bra. Scuttling down the staircase wrapped in a circle of light, I rushed outdoors.

"Shawn? Shawn!" The tranquil surge of ocean beyond and rhythmic rustle of leaves blown by gentle winds—sick of gusting in full strength—is all that answered. I cupped around the candle to keep it from going out. Moving in the direction of where I saw the light from above, I left the clearing and safety of the lighthouse. My knees knocked together and my voice quivered when I called out, "Shawn!"

Next, I let out a throaty cry. An ugly squawk of withering anxiety. I hated the crunch of twigs beneath me and the crowding, warped branches above. I hated the all-consuming darkness. My feet took me down different paths until I felt certain I was lost. Before cowardice convinced me to turn back in hopes I'd reach the lighthouse again and not pummel down a cliff, I took a deep breath in and hummed the pocket-watch's song. The candle's flame coiled and flitted about with every stride I took.

Fifteen minutes in, my ears began to play tricks on me. Whispers of my name started to drift on the breeze, calling out from side to side, all around. I hummed louder and louder until the woods quieted in a hush.

"Rebecca." A voice from behind spoke my name clear. It made my breath catch in my throat. I stiffened, instantly rooted to the spot. Afraid to turn around, and yet more afraid if I didn't, I rotated my feet as if they were attached like a toy army man.

Jack O'Sullivan hovered over me, eyes mirroring the dancing candlelight. Through heavy mustache and beard, his cheeks inflated and with a concentrated puff of air, he blew out the flame, disappearing with the light. Or had it been my deeply exhaled shriek that blew the candle out? I wasn't certain. But I dropped it and held my heart. Heaving in several gulps of air, my body trembled. Going from stiff to jelly.

My eyes adjusted in the pitch-black. Shafts of light went back and forth between the trees and reflected on high leafy boughs. "Shawn!" I hollered, trying to scrounge for the candle on the ground. When I had it upright between my feet, I pulled the matchbook from out of my bra and tried to relight the wick with unsteady fingers. After a few wasted matches, the flame was revived and I moved back through mucky grasses, sodden wood, sharp twigs scraping my cheeks and tearing at the threads of my knit-sweater. "Can you hear me?"

After thinking it through, I had traveled straight past Shawn's location. If it hadn't been for Jack appearing and blowing out my candle for me to see the flashlight beams, I might've continued in the woods and got even more lost.

"Becky!" Shawn's voice sounded hoarse, labored.

"I'm coming!" I rushed, tripped over a tree root, and crawled my way back to standing. Dirt imbedded in my nails and was all over my jeans and stretched-out, tatty sweater that revealed my elbow and part of my waist. The candle had been forced from my hand, nowhere to be seen. With the shafts of light near enough, I didn't need it. When I found Shawn, he was flat on his back, arms splayed like a bird after hitting a window. The flashlight resting at his side now that I found him. "What happened to you? Are you okay?"

"I fell…from the tree," he groaned. "Trying to get…one of the pages. I worried…to use the flashlight…as a beacon. Didn't want to draw to much attention here."

"Shawn I'm glad you did. I hope someone finds us. We need to get you to the hospital."

"No. I'll be fine." He shot up, leaning on his hands with a grunt. "A few bangs and bruises. What about you? I thought I heard you scream."

"I did. It's nothing to worry about."

"How exactly…did you…find me?"

"Jack showed me the way. That's kind of why I screamed. He just sort of showed up."

"He appeared…again?" Shawn's grin grew to a toothy smile. "Your powers are growing…stronger…than I thought they would."

"You sound awful. Like every word you say hurts." I swept up the flashlight and examined him under its beam. "You could've broken a rib or something. We need to go for help."

Shawn chuckled and rapped a weak fist over his chest. "I'm as fit as Jack's fiddle. Well, maybe a few loose strings." With another grunt, he rolled onto all fours. "Besides, it's late. I need rest, is all. If I can get to the lighthouse, I'll sleep it off."

"Let me help you up." I kneeled next to him and lowered my shoulder. He put his arm over me in a puppet sort of way. Ridged and unnatural-like. "You sure you're alright?"

"Becky, I'm fine. I swear," Shawn said. When we gradually rose, he let out a few moans and sounds through his teeth. "Good to be back upright."

"How long were you lying here?"

"Half-hour or so."

The idea of him there alone while I slept made me ill. If I hadn't woken until morning, would he have attempted to crawl his way back? And if he couldn't make it the whole way, what then? I kissed his floppy hand over my shoulder. "I'm glad I found you."

"Never read that in the ol' story," he said.

"Read what in which story?" I asked as we hobbled together through the night, the flashlight leading the way back.

"Wendy saving Pan."

"She saved him in different ways."

Shawn looked up at the sky, a few stars twinkling down on us. "Well, I like the way you save me."

FIFTEEN

The night turned out to be a restless one for me. I kept the fire stoked and watched over Shawn as he slept under the afghan. I sat on the floor next to the chaise, my hands combed through his hair. As his chest rose and fell, I timed his breaths, making sure everything appeared normal.

"How'd you sleep?" he asked me in the morning when he opened his eyes to me resting my head against the edge.

"A little choppy, to be honest. But I'm well rested," I lied. "How about you? How do you feel?"

"Bruised like a black banana," Shawn said and then laughed. "Ugh! I shouldn't laugh."

When I got up from the floor, knees creaking, he tossed the blanket off and then lifted his shirt. Bright red and purple streaks stained his sides.

"Shawn, that's terrible."

"It looks worse, trust me. Nothing a bit of ice won't fix."

I folded my hands over my chest. "Yah, but that's all the way in the cooler at the caves. You need to rest, not go trekking off again."

He felt along each rib and clicked his tongue, "No breaks. That's a relief."

"Let me get you something to eat." I sat and pulled a few cans of food from the duffel, amidst the empty bags and fruit leather wrappers. Then I remembered my pathetic feast on almost all our snacks. Shawn moved from the chaise longue and stood next to me. "Cans of corn bits, diced pears, apple sauce. Not too much else. What happened to our snacks?"

I zipped up the duffel to hide the evidence, cornered by my shame. "You were gone for so long. I worried and ate."

"That much?"

"There wasn't a ton of stuff, Shawn," I spat. "You were in such a rush, you barely packed enough to get us through a day."

"Woah, no need to *bite* my head off. Didn't you have enough to eat last night?" he teased with a hint of ridicule.

I threw the last bag of remaining trail mix at him. "That's not funny."

"Hey, I'm wounded here," he said catching it in his arms. "No throwing things at the invalid."

"You're as fit as a fiddle, remember?"

Shawn rustled the bag around, reached in and jostled the contents. "Hey, did you eat all the smarties out of here? Those are my favorite."

"They're my favorite, too," I griped. "How was I supposed to know?"

Shawn dropped the bag on the floor next to me, a few pieces of dried fruit and almonds spilled out. "Everyone loves the Smarties."

"Have some apple sauce. It's healthier for you anyway."

He reached under the desk, pulled out a small stool, and peeled off his crusty socks. "You sound like my mother."

"I'll take that as a compliment." Cracking open a bottle of water, I got up and drank it while leaning next to the window. I missed my own bed. I wanted a decent meal. With the other hand, I played with the frays of my sweater.

"Well, looks like I'm going to have to make the journey to the cooler after all," Shawn said.

"It was a few snacks, not the whole world's supply. Sheesh." I turned to him and saw his usual snarky grin. He suppressed laughter. Part of me wanted to wipe the look off his face and say, *"Be serious for once"*, but the other part wanted his lips, reveling in the fact we argued like real married people.

He pressed his hands on his knees, got off the stool, and resigned himself to a can of apple sauce. He knelt at the duffel, took out his Swiss Army knife, and pried the top open with an exerting groan. Before he made his way back to the stool, I tugged on the collar of his shirt and planted a kiss on him. The can of sauce spun in the air and splattered all over us as we firmly embraced.

"The chaise?" he asked, wiping apple sauce off my cheek with his thumb and tasting it.

"We can't," I said. Being the voice of reason in this situation felt tedious, but necessary. "We need protection."

His eyes almost rolled back in his head. "I know..."

"Let's wipe the rest of the sauce off us and go get that cooler together."

Shawn kissed me once more and said, "Spoilsport."

I half-grinned and took off my sweater, deciding to dress in the t-shirt and cardigan I had drying on the nails from the other day.

"Maybe it's the right time to go into town. The storm passed. I can stock up on supplies."

"I'm coming with you."

Shawn unzipped the duffel, threw on a ball-cap and stuffed sunglasses in his jean pocket. He found his hooded sweater and slid it over his head slowly, so as not to aggravate his battered sides. "You'd have to stay in the boat when we get to shore, otherwise people are going to know it's you and me sneaking around." He reached back and pulled the hood over his ball-cap.

"That's easy enough. I'm just not okay with leaving you again."

"I really worried you, huh?" He took both my shoulders.

I wanted to explain how our paper-doll selves were linked now. How I no longer blew about, wandering in uncertain air. How he made my dreams come true by marrying me. How he saved me. But I said, "Shawn, I need you. This world needs you. If anything were to happen—" I didn't complete the sentence. "All I know is there would be no magic anymore."

"The page is still stuck in that tree I fell from. But I think it's the legend. That'll get us a long way before we need the other. And hey, maybe we'll stumble across it as we follow the map," Shawn said. "I'll heal up and then give the climb another try."

"Let me go get it." The vial began to be as important to find for me as it was for him. It didn't mean he'd never get hurt, but if it gave us long life…a taste of immortality, I wanted that.

"It's pretty high up."

"I'm not afraid," I said, "Shawn, we have to get that page."

"Okay…" He hugged me in a determined way, and I took caution embracing his ribs. "Once we're done getting supplies, if you still want to go up and get it…"

"I'm not changing my mind," I said.

We emptied the duffel and stuck in a few bottles of water along with the flashlight. It took Shawn forever to agree to let me carry the damned thing. But just as I suspected, it wasn't heavy with the few items inside. The gloomy sun, peeking behind the overcast sky, appeared out of the windows while we made our way downstairs. Dust motes glittered in the dull light. At least the rain and storming ceased. A good day compared to the others.

Out of the woods and at the top of the cliff-face, the caves positioned directly below us, ocean rushed in them and hammered against stone. As enticing as the food inside the cooler sounded, both of us didn't move a muscle to make the decline. Phillip's fishing trolley and a larger boat (one Shawn confirmed belonged to the Coast Guard) broke over the waves toward the island.

"We have to grab that cooler now and get to Hangman's Tree," Shawn shouted like we weren't near one another.

"What about the lighthouse?" I said just as loud.

"No. They'll be heading there." Shawn waved me forward and stomped down the trail, holding his sides. I threw the duffel's straps over my shoulder, squeezed it under my elbow, and hurried down as well, skidding against rocks and doing goat-leaps over larger ones. The water bottles smacked against the flashlight. *Glack, glack, glack.* I turned to see I'd passed Shawn, who had his hands on his thighs and face scrunched in agony.

"This is too much. You're going to wreck yourself more," I said rushing over and rubbing up and down his back.

"I hate to say it…we'll have to forget the cooler. But don't worry, I'll figure something else out."

"I can get it myself. Shawn, you need that ice."

"No. It's such a bugger to cart around, and you've got the duffel. I'll be okay."

"You keep saying that, but look at you all hunched over."

"We have to go, Becky."

Shawn wrapped his arms around himself in a tight hug (the movement of running hard probably rattled his ribs) and led us back into the sanctuary of the woods.

The duffel lashed right and left against my back. Leaving the cooler behind made perfect sense even though my mouth watered at the idea of eating the cold, crisp contents inside. If we couldn't get back to the lighthouse, that meant the leftovers from our snacks and canned goods were out of the question, as well.

The mind…such a frustrating thing, working against you at your worst. Right now, every fast food commercial I'd ever seen came as flashes in my head. Burgers, fries, fried-chicken, milkshakes, Eggo waffles.

Shawn will figure something out, don't worry. No matter how much I made that my mantra, it didn't stop me from realizing this plan sucked. Coming to the island, living here. A daydream. A fool's paradise.

Andy's scolding didn't seem so idiotic anymore, as much as I hated to admit. *It's high-time you take life seriously.* I looked over at Shawn, dark circles under his darting eyes, that crazed tic at the edge of his mouth. Someone had to be the logical one.

Birds (and probably every other creature) took off in alarm as we trudged our way over to Hangman's Tree, interrupted of their solitude and slumber. Once inside, Shawn took off his ball-cap and fell on the pillows in the corner, gasping and hollering through grit teeth.

Happy to be rid of the duffel, I threw it by the entryway, and went over to him. "What can I do? How can I help?"

"Don't want...to talk...right now."

"I understand." I shuffled next to him, and listened to his hoarse lungs. The next time I looked over, Shawn's eyes were shut and a few snores came out of his wide-open mouth.

Hunger and the prospect of being captured brought forth an alertness. The same alertness deer have during hunting season. Something was in the air. Something alarming and thick. In places our eyes can't reach, someone waited. Prowled. *I must be on guard. Watchful.* The walls closed in.

When it felt like hours had gone by, I stood up and hovered over Shawn's body, slapped over those pillows like a sack of potatoes. *How can he sleep?* Sure, a body needed to heal and all that, but it still baffled me. Maybe the smooth, slack way his jaw hung made him seem too relaxed, not the I'm-so-exhausted, passed-out look one would expect. I guessed it had to be one or two in the afternoon. When would we eat again?

Part of me considered Shawn saw this as a game, just as Peter enjoyed his rivalry with Hook. *To die will be an awfully big adventure.* Sure, Peter. Maybe for you. Maybe survival is a gamble to you. Flower petals to be plucked. *I live, I die, I live, I die. Oh, I live. But tomorrow, we shall see.* No! I wanted to live, no questions asked.

I shook Shawn's shoulder. "Wake up."

"Mmmfff?" His eyelids fluttered and shut.

"Wake up."

"Huh? Becky?" Shawn opened his eyes and yawned. "Ack!"

"What? What?" I asked. "Your ribs?"

"Dammit. They still feel so raw. I figured a bit of rest might help."

My eyes surveyed the room. I held my aching stomach. "Look, I know you're battered. But we need something to eat. You need to eat…to heal and keep your strength."

"Man, I am hungry. You're right."

"What was the plan? What did you have in mind?"

"Have in mind?"

"Yah," I said trying to keep my tone from sounding frantic. "You said you'd figure something out for us."

Shawn eased himself off the pillows and stood when I did. He put his hands over my temples and kissed my ratty hair. "I think I know just the thing." After letting me go, he got on all fours near the exit and slowly descended the steps of the tree.

"Wait," I hollered from above before following after him. "Where are you going?"

At the foot of the tree, Shawn took out his Swiss Army knife. "I'm going to make a spear."

"What?" I asked. "You're not going to skewer us a squirrel, are you?"

"No, no. Nothing like that. Not much meat, and I figure way too strong." He winked when I stuck out my tongue. "I'm using it to catch us a fish."

"But how?"

"There's a shallow lagoon on the island I've fished from before. About twenty minutes hike from here. A few Bluefish get trapped in there when the tide is lower. It might be our only chance." He broke a sturdy and straight branch from a nearby tree and fashioned the end into two, thick points—one point longer than the other. Running his thumb over them, he said, "Perfect."

"We won't be able to cook it. The smoke will give away our location."

"Becky. Let me provide. I can do this." Shawn made a few jab gestures in the air with the spear. I could tell the motion caused discomfort for him, but he hid it behind stiff lips and hard blinks. "We'll make a small fire, just enough to heat up the fish," he said.

"If that's the best solution we've got to get some food in us..."

Shawn held the spear in one hand, proud. He knelt and with the other, dug his fingers into the moist ground streaking two lines of mud under each eye and one line down his forehead. "Get us big fish."

"Alright Chief Barringer, this isn't some game. I'm hungry."

"I know it's not a game, but come on. Sometimes when things are dire, you gotta laugh about it."

"Har, har," I mocked. "Now let's get to that lagoon."

Shawn shrugged and traipsed ahead, using the butt of the spear as a walking stick. Perhaps he knew a thing or two about spearing fish, he did carve the stick a certain way I would've never considered. Still, I doubted the task to be easy. I too often mistook the aura around him for wisdom with a hint of whimsy, now I saw it might be nothing more than sheer cockiness.

The forest dwindled on our trip down the island, which began to slope on quite a decline. Unlike the lighthouse, which sat propped on a rocky cliff, the land became a flat, rock-strewn sandy clearing with patches of grass sticking out and a gaping view of the ocean.

"Shawn, this isn't smart. We're too exposed." I was ready for the Coast Guard or our parents to sail by and spot us at any moment.

"Hide behind one of those bigger rocks and let me go to the water on my own. I'll be stealthy."

I didn't argue and scurried behind a pale rock, like a timid crab ducking for cover in its shell.

Shawn rolled up his jeans to his knees and army-crawled over the rocky sand. Keeping a close eye on his surroundings, he used the taller grasses to hide for a time before continuing to the lagoon.

In a low crouch, he lifted the spear to strike. This pose he seemed frozen in, waiting for the right time, blurred my wits. Such an untamed handsomeness. He made me forget I wanted food, and made me thirst for how warm he made my blood every time those rough hands were on my body.

Not long after, my hunger returned when Shawn jabbed the stick in the water. I cringed at the loud slap, worried the sound somehow reached Andy or Phillip's ears. When he brought the stick up with nothing, I ground my scaly teeth that hadn't had a proper brushing in days.

Several times, Shawn went back to the-crouch-and-wait-to-strike pose after failed attempts to stab anything. Every slap from the lagoon made my skin crawl, and my jaw pained me so much I developed a throbbing headache.

"Come on, come on," I whispered out coaxes as if it would help. "You can do it."

On what had to be the thirteenth strike, Shawn lifted the spear with that glistening, silvery-blue flapping fish and gave a triumphant rooster crow toward the sky. I wanted to hush him up, but got carried away in the moment, too.

"Woo!" I hooted raising a fist.

He ran back to me. "I got him. I got him. Ah ha ha!" The fish wriggled and oily juices splashed against his mud-painted face.

"Oh, Shawn…you did it! Let's get out of here and find a place in the woods to fry that thing," I said patting him on the back, approving the animal he'd become. This fearless, and albeit, self-assured side of him did get us dinner, after all.

"First things first." He bent and picked up a fist-sized stone. "Turn away. I don't think you want to see this."

"You're going to—"

"Put him out of his misery," he cut in.

I turned and covered my ears after the first *thunk*.

Scuttling ourselves back to the blessed cover of trees after killing the fish, we found a miniature clearing. The best spot to fry fish over a fire and try not to get caught.

"Grab the spear. I've got to make a fire by hand," Shawn said offering it to me.

"We forgot the matches, didn't we?"

"I stuck some in my pocket but after so many days of rain, they're ruined." He scraped at the ground to get rid of the grass, made a dirt pit, and then gathered the driest branches he could find for kindling.

Browsing around the clearing, Shawn collected some grass in his hands. "I need better tinder than this. It's not the driest. What's your sweater made of?"

I looked down at my cardigan. "Cotton. Why?"

"That'll work. Can I cut a piece of it off?"

"I guess so."

He flicked the blade of his Swiss Army knife and stretched out the bottom of my cardigan and sliced a portion off. After tearing it into threads he made a nest along with the collected grasses and put it under the teepee of kindling.

"You're very skilled at all of this, Shawn."

"Learnt from Grandpa Barringer and my pop. Basic survival skills," he said. "I'll take you through it step-by-step, in case you ever need to do it yourself."

Shawn explained how to create a fireboard out of a thick branch. He then used his knife to carve a hole in it. Then, he took a small stick, set it in the hole, and positioned the nest of tinder close by.

"Now, see how I roll this stick inside the fireboard to create friction? Go ahead and blow lightly on that to help it catch."

As I did, I thought, *maybe Shawn can take care of me out here. Once we eat this fish, all will be well again.*

When a spark erupted against the wood, butterflies flitted inside my hollow stomach. I blew steadily until a thread of cardigan took. The flame ran down like a stick of dynamite from the cartoons. It ignited the rest of the nest and we had the beginnings of a fire.

Shawn wiped his blade on the thigh of his jeans and then took the spear back, "I've got to clean out the fish."

After the greasy innards littered the ground, he skewered the gutted fish lower down the middle of the spear, and propped it over the teepee to cook. Filled with gleeful relief that we were finally going to have hot food, I took him by the cheeks and planted my lips on his.

"You sure you want to kiss this face?" He pulled away. "I'm filthy. Should've washed in the lagoon."

"I'm not fresh as a daisy, myself." I giggled. "I just can't thank you enough for all you've done. Especially in your condition. How are your ribs feeling?"

"They ached lots before, but the adrenaline from the catch and getting this fire going has me on a high."

"Rest now, dear husband. I'll rotate the fish on the fire."

"You sure?"

"You kidding? It's the least I can do." I grabbed the spear and turned the fish around, the smoke caused by the fish's oil billowed up. I tried to disperse it by waving and flapping my arms.

Shawn sat down and leaned against a tree.

"How long does this thing take to cook?" When I looked back at him, his eyes were already shut and arms slack over his chest. I shrugged and figured I'd just poke at the cut underneath the fish after five minutes and see if any meat flaked off.

The sky above grew to a darker grey as I continued to rotate the fish over the growing flame. No matter how hard I tried to keep the smoke at bay, the oil was no match for me.

A distant crack echoed in the woods, my hand tensed on the spear.

SIXTEEN

I lowered the spear down over the fire, and quickly released my hand off of it. The blood returned to my knuckles in a prickly flow. "Shawn someone's coming."

This time he didn't need shaking to wake. He got up from the ground and stood next to me. "I thought I dreamt it. What did you hear?"

"Branches breaking."

"Me too." Shawn stared blankly ahead, tilted his head to one side, and perked an ear. Several more snaps and cracks straightened him up. "They aren't far. We have to run, right now."

"But what about the fish?"

"Leave it. There's no time."

"You can't ask me to leave the only thing we have to eat."

Shawn strode head. "Becky, come on."

I whimpered at the shuffling movement in the forest straight ahead.

"The smoke is coming from over there," a strange man—likely, a Coast Guard officer—said.

Desperate, I kicked the spear off the fire and dug out a sizzling hot chunk from the fish's belly. I juggled the piece in my hand while running, blowing on it intermittently. The flesh of my palm bubbled and I didn't care. The only thing I regretted...not grabbing more.

Trying to dodge low-lying bush and branches above, I nibbled the bit of hot fish, burning my tongue in the process. I breathed through my teeth, trying to soothe the scald. I ran, ate, burned, and felt slightly insane over the whole thing.

Shawn remained steps ahead. Part of me thought to save him some of the chunk of fish, but intense hunger entertained selfishness. *It's all mine. I thought to grab it. My hand and mouth have scorched for this.* Not once did my brain remind me that Shawn made all the effort to catch the thing, bruised ribs and all. After taking another bite, flakes falling off my lips, I tucked the remaining hunk inside the pocket of my cardigan for safe keeping.

Everything looked the same on O'Sullivan Island after a while. Every tree was a repetition of the tree prior. Every stump, shrub, plant, animal. It didn't matter. But, when I felt sure we were going in the direction of the lighthouse I called for Shawn to stop. But he told me we didn't have time for that, the Coast Guard would be closing in on us.

It seemed an eternity before he stopped at a tree and leaned against it, out of breath and groaning.

"Shawn, you're never going to heal at this rate."

"The page."

"What page?" I asked, shrill and unable to think straight.

"Climb...this tree...the missing page...it's up there."

I pointed behind us. "The guards are coming."

"Get that page. Hide up there and...I'll head them off at the pass."

"Come up with me."

"You know I can't." He kissed me quickly and said, "Now get up there."

I heaved myself up the lowest branch and took to the others, my inner child remembering the skill of it well. My strength surprised me and I recalled Shawn talking about the adrenaline he felt while fishing. I attributed my newfound pep to that.

While straddling the tallest branch I could climb—tree-sap marking my clothes, strands of hair, and face—I wrapped one arm around the tree's trunk and looked to see if the page was anywhere in sight. I'd been so involved in climbing, I didn't bother keeping an eye out for it.

Voices blended and boomed below. I looked down between the barky arms of leaves and spotted a crew of five male Coast Guard officers, wearing pale-blue shirts and orange reflective vests, surrounding Shawn. I dug into the pocket of my cardigan and removed the last bit of fish—a hint of bitter sap tainting the taste. As if it were popcorn, I ate and observed as Peter Pan and the Indians talked it out.

One of the fifty-something men tried calmly speaking to Shawn. "You know this area is restricted. You've got a pretty worried father who wants to take you home. Best come with us." In my mind the conversation turned to, "*This land is restricted. Even for the Great White Father who tries calling it home. Leave now, pale one.*"

I expected a corny line from Shawn like, "You'll never take me alive!" All he did was shake his head. He hardly seemed afraid of anything, like Peter. But not so this time. It made the movie reel in my head disappear.

"Come on, boy. Let's not make things difficult."

The other four remained in their positions, no doubt hoping for the best-case scenario where Shawn goes along with them no muss, no fuss.

"Where's the girl you're with?" The guy with the receding hairline stepped closer to Shawn who was beginning to look like a cat cornered in an alley, back arched and hair on end. "Is she okay?"

Silence alone answered the man. "Fine. I'm sure she is fine. Just come along with us, alright?" In a swift lunge, the balding man had Shawn by the wrist, who writhed worse than the fish did impaled on the spear from out of the water. On that note, I shoveled the last, tasty morsel of fish in my mouth while my heart raced watching Shawn bite the man right on the wrist and wound between the others. What an escape. *Run, Shawn! Run!*

"He bit me!" The balding man screeched. "He bloody bit me!" He took off after Shawn with his comrades in tow.

The scene, in all its realness, ended in a way that made me want to clap. Instead, I wiped my greasy hands on my pants and climbed up higher in search for the page that I promised my brave and self-sacrificing husband I'd get.

Fluttering back and forth, pinned against the trunk by thick fingers of leaves, the page waited for me close to the top. (Shawn wasn't kidding when he said it was up high). I gathered up more courage and kept going. My arms buzzed, unused muscle throbbed and worked as hard as possible to keep from tiring out. Once I had the page folded carefully and put in my fish-soiled pocket, I collected my breath and made the descent.

Before reaching the bottom and risk getting spotted, I waited and listened. Brisk crunches of forest floor made me recoil behind a veil of green.

"Becky? Becky?"

I peeked my head out and stared down at the bottom of the tree to see Shawn staring up at me.

"Come down," he said in between heavy breathing. "It's safe. I wound them around the woods. We have time to make it back to Hangman's Tree."

I crept my way to a branch I felt capable of jumping from, and then dropped down to the ground.

"Did you get the page?"

I removed it from my pocket. "Would I let you down?"

Shawn feigned a smile and removed a twig from my hair.

"You look paler than *Old Broken Down's* new paint. Let's just take a breather, right here."

"All this running and horsing around...I'm beat." Shawn

wiped a hand over his face and fell back against the tree. "But now's not the time to take a rest. We can't risk them finding their way back here."

"If you say so."

The way he slouched and hobbled made me wonder if he'd twisted an ankle trying to outrun the Coast Guard. But it might've been just the fact his ribs were that sore. I could almost feel the adrenaline fade from him bit by bit, inviting more pain into his body. The trees reached at him, waiting for him to faint.

I shouldn't have eaten the last piece of fish. What kind of a wife am I? Look at him. He needed it more than me.

We made it to Hangman's Tree without anyone following us. I prompted Shawn to make the climb first. I wanted to be below him in case he lost strength in his grip. He crawled over to the pile of pillows when we were inside. I removed my cardigan and began tearing it in long strips.

"What are you doing?" Shawn inquired.

"I'm going to use these pieces to wrap your ribs. I should've thought of it sooner. It'll keep things together, instead of wobbling around whenever you move."

"Shucks, I should've even thought of that," he said and collapsed on the pillows. "But how does anyone think straight without food? I keep thinking about that fish. The gulls or some animal probably got to it already."

"Yah..." I kept tearing and piling the strips on the treehouse's floor. "Shawn, I've got to be honest. Before we ran, I nabbed some fish and I ate it. I should've offered you some, and I didn't. It's like you said. I wasn't thinking straight."

He propped up on his elbows. "Hey, it's okay. I understand. And you know what, I said to leave it behind. If you were able to grab some, you deserve it."

"I've been riddled with guilt this entire time. I ate the snacks and then deny you the fish."

"Don't worry yourself about it. I'm thinking I can sneak to the lighthouse later, when the folks are sure to have gone back to the boats to catch some rest. Gather the remnants of food there."

"I don't know if that's a good idea, Shawn."

"I have to try. We don't have a better option. Besides, I haven't been caught yet. I'll paint myself up with mud and go even more unseen."

I collected all the strips in my hands and brought them over to him. Kneeling, I said, "Sit up more and remove your t-shirt."

When he did, I picked up the first strip and slid it around him. "It has give…but I don't want to tie it too tightly."

"Do what you have to. I can take it."

"I'll tighten it on the count of three. One, two, three." I pulled and Shawn grunted while I tied it. "There. How's that?" I touched the binding gently and swept over parts of his warm, bare skin.

"It's good," he reassured.

With the rest, I wound, wrapped, and tied until Shawn's midsection looked like an ancient Egyptian mummy's. "How's your breathing?"

"The bandages have stretch to them, like you said. I can take in breaths. In fact, this feels amazing," he said rotating his back.

Sweeping me over his lap, he cupped the back of my neck and then kissed me with forceful intention. As if the cardigan wraps gave him a new lease on things, and restored his strength.

His touch held such direction…a plan. Mapping out my body just like the island; the one he longed to remain on for an unbeknownst amount of days, while I envisioned our life off this piece of land. Surely, we couldn't get away with staying here much longer.

We'd graduate school as husband and wife. Then, the house we'd buy would be close to the ocean so Shawn could fish and boat as much as he wanted. All the places I hadn't been to around Lunenburg that all the tourists spoke of, we'd visit time and again. Aaron—finished university and moved back—would stop over often to share a meal with us at the table. Eventually, we'd have two children. Shawn would teach them all about the legends of O'Sullivan. We'd save some special water (once we found it) just for them, and all live long lives, together.

We laid side by side, the reserves of our energy sapped from our romantic interlude. Shawn's arm wrapped around me.

While his head likely stayed busy browsing through ways of prolonging our stay here on this unrealistic plot of land, mine remained on *home*.

SEVENTEEN

After Shawn woke me with a gentle rub on the shoulder, we took off from Hangman's Tree toward the lighthouse in the pitch-black night, duffel bag in tow. We hid ourselves in the trees, just on the outskirts of the lighthouse's clearing.

I directed the flashlight at him while he tore at the ground and slathered mud all over his face and arms. "So, what's the plan?" I asked.

Shawn pulled back some branches and looked out. "Don't need a plan. Looks pretty deserted out there to me. No tents, no lights, no noise. I'm going to sneak on the ground like I did at the lagoon. I'll get inside the lighthouse, stuff the food in the duffel, and meet you back here. Easy-peasy."

I handed Shawn the flashlight. He turned off the switch, threw it in the duffel, and without another word, hunched down on all fours, slunk out from the safety of the trees, and then army-crawled on his belly toward the lighthouse. Its white exterior stuck out against the contrasting dark. A good thing, too. It made an easy target for Shawn to see. Even with well-adjusted eyes, I found it tough to spot him until he stood up at the door. My breath faltered in my throat when he opened it and stepped inside. Even more so when lights beamed from the doorway and raised voices vibrated inside, and finally back out. Phillip held Shawn by the collar of his shirt. Andy appeared holding an oil-lantern from behind.

"Get ahold of yourself, boy. You're acting like a wild animal," Phillip said. "Look at you. Full of mud, sticks in your hair, and God knows what else."

"Let go of me," Shawn hollered, swinging his arms at his father like he didn't know him anymore.

"Andy, a bit of help here."

Andy set the lantern down and wrestled Shawn's arms behind his back while Phillip continued scolding. "You've worried your Mom sick with all this foolishness. Taking my boat, not telling a soul. Biting one of the Coast Guards. What's wrong with you?"

"You wouldn't understand," Shawn hissed.

"Stop acting like a fricken barbarian, and talk to me like a human being; your pop," Phillip roared. "I've let some of this go over the years, these fixations with legends…"

"No, you haven't," Shawn rebutted. "The only times you've let a few things slide is because of Mom."

"Do you blame me? Look what's become of you on account of it." Phillip waved his hands wildly in front of Shawn.

Shawn wriggled in Andy's grasp. "You forced our hand. You said we couldn't be together. We love each other."

"If you truly loved that young woman you wouldn't do something so careless. You'd act responsible. I'd never in my wildest dreams put your Mom through this. What were you planning to do? Live out here?"'

"I could do it."

"That's nonsense, Shawn. I taught you better. Stop thinking about what you want and consider Rebecca's needs."

"We're in this together."

"Yah? Did you even ask her?"

"I don't have to ask her. I know what she'd say. She wants to be with me, too."

"You sound pretty confident. Or is it that you're being selfish?

Assuming she wants exactly what you want."

Shawn stopped struggling and lowered his head. If I didn't know any better, what Phillip said started to whittle down his sureness. In broken squawks, he replied, "Aw, and you probably wouldn't have gotten so upset if Mom ate all the Smarties in the trail mix, either."

"That's right, son, I wouldn't have gotten upset over Mom eating...wait, what?"

I laughed to myself.

"Where's Rebecca?" Andy piped in. "Tell me where my daughter is."

Viewing Andy, even from a distance, covered in orange light from the lantern, I could see he had a cleaned-shaved face and hair neat. I shifted in my position. His plaid button-down shirt tucked into stain-free jeans. Healthy, full stomach just on the cusp of falling over his belt. The embodiment of home, safety. I looked around at the shadows and uncertainty surrounding me and felt confined. I needed out. Andy became the way out.

I rushed out of the bushes, sobbing over-dramatically. Andy immediately released Shawn and we embraced. He looked down at me in awe. The last time I hugged him in such a way was the moment he'd arrived at my door after Mom passed.

"Becky...so, this really wasn't what you wanted. Pop was right?" Shawn—thrown to the ground on all fours—stared at me with doleful eyes.

"I'm so sorry, Shawn," I sobbed. "I love you. I do. But I can't live savage like this anymore. I thought I could. But I want my bed, a hot shower. I want to eat comfort food." I buried my head into Andy's chest.

Andy put a hand over my scraggly hair. The touch was awkward as usual. "Okay, alright. There, there."

"You're like the others," Shawn accused. "You think I should grow up."

"No, it's not that. I—" There was nothing I could say that

would make this better. So, I stopped.

Phillip offered Shawn his hand and said, "Son, own this like a man and admit you acted on a whim. This couldn't have carried on, even if you wanted it to."

While we were led away into the dark toward the caves, a palpable sensation of regret exuded from Shawn. Bits of fairy dust, once covering him from top to bottom, slowly fell away into the void. The boy in him had learned a hard lesson. When the man decides to emerge within, the boy is often left with no weapon in his arsenal save for bitterness against the harsh truths the man comes wielding. At some point, the boy must give up and surrender to the man.

This apparent fight worried me. I wanted the man, but I wasn't ready to completely say goodbye to the boy. The boy believed in me, made me feel alive. If the man came around and snuffed out all the adventure, who would Shawn truly be? Did I make a mistake by running into Andy's arms? Did Shawn see this as a betrayal? We'd gone through so much to stay on O'Sullivan Island. We found one of the last two pages of the map. The vial practically in our grasp. I think that's what bothered him the most.

If only he understood that during these desperate circumstances pragmatic thinking was required.

After Phillip hitched up *Old Broken Down* to his fishing boat, we departed the island with the Coast Guard ushering us against the bitter ocean breeze, under a sheet of stars. Shawn sat by himself with his head in his hand. He wouldn't look at me.

As his wife, I probably should've stood by him. For better or worse. Instead, I let him down. I should've detected the subtle pulling away of our paper-doll hands. Unfortunately, satisfying my hunger and sleeping under thick blankets dominated my every thought.

EIGHTEEN

The rainstorms returned to the town and forced their way indoors through Andy. More appropriately, Hurricane Andy. Ever since arriving back from the island yesterday, he never stopped thundering words about my irresponsibility. Though it was Monday, school and work were put on hold due to my shenanigans.

I stayed locked in my room shoveling down leftovers and snacks of all kinds, wrapped in the embrace of my thickest pajamas after another abnormally long shower. My incessant gluttony and craving for comfort made all the words he shouted incomprehensible.

That evening, once satisfied with the amount of food eaten and sleep I'd caught up on, I dressed in actual clothes and carelessly moseyed downstairs into the kitchen to grab a drink.

Andy sat at the table with a tumbler and a bottle of Scotch, a frown creased his brow as I slunk to the cupboard and grabbed a glass. As I opened the fridge and filled it with orange juice, a creeping sensation curled down my spine. A clap of thunder rattled the dishes in the cupboards and made me jump a bit. When I closed the fridge, Andy stood right in my face. I fumbled my glass and nearly dropped it.

"Don't just appear like that."

"You're going to park your butt on one of those chairs by the table and you and I are going to talk whether you want to or not."

"You mean fight, not talk," I said recoiling at his alcoholic breath. "How much have you had? Maybe we should wait until you're sober."

"Sit your ass down!" Andy stomped a foot and pointed toward the table. Lightning lit up the dim kitchen and another heavy rumble of thunder followed.

I hurried to a seat and sat with my head down, eyeing my swirling juice.

"You're one selfish brat, you know that?" he started. "You fill your mouth enough? Get enough sleep?"

I stayed silent.

"Good! I'm happy for you. At least one of us got to do those things over the past few days." He took a swig from his glass and set it down. "You take off from school without so much as a word to anyone where you're going. I came home that evening…and time just kept passing until Margaret and Phillip knock at my door and ask if I've seen Shawn. Then, I knew. So did Phillip."

"You told the principal to keep us separated," I piped in. "I was told I had to join programs. Not even get to eat lunch. It's like everyone's watching my every move. Telling me who I should spend my time with. It's oppression."

"Maybe that's because you haven't proven to be trustworthy. Every time you go off with Shawn you get into trouble."

"People say Shawn's trouble because he believes in something they don't. He's pursuing what they deem as a lost cause. He marches to his own drum and doesn't need anyone's approval. Not even mine. He's taught me a lot about being true to myself."

"You're only buying into his bologna because you're infatuated with him."

"You just hate that he and I are close in a way you and I will never be. But who's to blame for that? It isn't me. I wanted you in my life years ago. That didn't seem to matter to you then, and I sure as heck know it doesn't now."

"You don't know anything about anything, kid," he spat and dropped into his chair.

"That's your rebuttal to everything I say. *You don't know anything. You've got rocks in your head. You're clueless about life.*" I flicked a crumb off the table. "Why don't you take one of your happy pills and leave me alone."

Andy drank the rest of what sat in his tumbler and let only the thunder talk for a while.

"I'll never be the father you want me to be," he said minutes later. "You'll forever hold the past over my head."

"It's what you deserve."

"And maybe I do, but what the hell, Rebecca? Don't you have any respect for yourself. Everything that boy says, you do. He walks all over you. You've stayed nights with him."

"Yah, so?"

"You're only sixteen," Andy barked.

"Being sixteen doesn't make my life less my own."

"You probably crawled right into bed with him and gave it all away, didn't you?"

I stood from my chair. "Ugh. We're through having this conversation. It's none of your business."

Andy poked at his temple. "He's right in there. Always there in your head, manipulating you. You're too obsessed with him to see he only wants what's good for himself. You're just a bonus."

"Don't you dare judge him. Shawn and I are dreamers and we're in love." I stormed out of the kitchen, on my way to the stairs when Andy blocked me.

"You're not running away this time. We are going to settle this between us once and for all," he said.

"Fine. Let's settle it."

"Make friends with some girls your age. Be a kid. There's so much time to date and all that later. Let Shawn go."

"No. I'll never do that."

"Phillip agrees that you and Shawn need to find others to spend your time with. What you two have isn't love. It's unhealthy."

"It is love, no matter what anyone says."

"If you love him, then let him go. If it's meant to be, you two will come together later when you're mature enough to handle a relationship."

"I'm not turning my back on my husband!" I screeched.

"Your...your what?" Andy stumbled back with a crooked grimace.

I lifted my hand and showed Andy my over-sized ring. "He asked me to marry him at the lighthouse. I said yes."

"Newsflash. That means he's your fiancé, not your husband."

"We performed a quick ceremony there, too. We're married."

"This...this is ludicrous," Andy said and slapped his forehead. "I can't believe you honestly think the words coming out of your mouth are factual. You're further gone than I thought."

"Yah, and you're a marriage expert."

He squeezed the bridge of his nose, took in a deep breath and said, "Just because you do some hokey ceremony together doesn't make the marriage legitimate. There's no legally binding document."

I pushed past him and into the living-room. "Binding! Ha! Like some stupid document means anything nowadays. You and mom were once married with a legally binding document to prove your union, and what did that do? You left her. You divorced. A paper is exactly what it is, a dead tree ground up with some legalistic words spewed on it. Man-made, holding no merit. Shawn and I were married with our deep love as our *binding* document. So, to hell with your reasoning."

Andy stomped over and rose an eyebrow. "You *wouldn't* sleep with him. That's what this is about. You wouldn't have sex with him and that's why he asked you to marry him on some ridiculous whim."

"Shut up! That isn't why. He asked me to marry him because he loves me as much as I love him. He respects me. We had sex because I wanted him. I want every part of him. Even if he didn't ask me to marry him I would've. There. Chew on that."

Andy took me by the shoulders and gave me a sturdy shaking. "You are not married and you'll never see that boy again even if I have to move us back to Ontario."

"Let me go." I squirmed, lifted one knee and came down hard on Andy's big toe with my heel.

"Ow, son-of-a…mmmffff." He released me, but within that split-second wound back and slapped me against the cheek.

I curled in, clutching my face. It tingled, heated up, and felt swollen under my palm. My eyes watered.

"Uh…" Is all I heard weasel out of Andy.

My ears went hot when I uncurled, still holding my face. I scowled at his stupidly neat hair, the bags under his round, dumbfounded eyes. The deep crinkles in his cheeks as his lips drooped. *Everything's your fault. You and your façade of comfort. You lured me in. You made me betray Shawn.*

How could I have been so naïve? Wherever Shawn resided, that's where home was. Not Andy. Never Andy. I promised myself to never forget that again, and to do whatever it took to recover the loss of Shawn's fairy dust.

"Rebecca, I'm so sorry…"

His shaking hand reached for me and I moved away. "Don't you touch me. You're a terrible person. And you'll never be my father. I hate you."

I could almost hear Andy crack. At any moment, I expected a crooked line to appear, traveling down the middle of his body, breaking him apart like the shell of an egg. And, I didn't care in the least. I wanted him to feel guilt. Shame.

"I didn't mean to hit you. I would never do something like that. I got out of hand. I screwed-up. See, I never should've drank.

I haven't touched a drop ever since your mom...and I'm terrible with words, with relationships. It's why I work all the time. It's the only thing I know how to do right."

"Save it. I don't want to listen to another excuse." I hurried to the door, grabbed my raincoat, slid on some shoes, and slammed the door in Andy's face. "And don't you come looking for me!" I screamed.

Steely rain came down on my head when I stepped off the second step into the gloom. I threw the hood of the raincoat over my head and made for Shawn's backyard.

I located where his window would be upstairs. There was a faint light on in the bedroom, his window was open a crack and I heard him playing guitar. A somber, slowly strummed tune. No lights were on in the Barringer's kitchen, but I knew I couldn't shout out to Shawn in fear his parents might hear.

Dripping wet, I paced his yard searching for something— anything—to throw at his window to get his attention. *The plastic watering can near the garden.* I picked it up and with every ounce of strength, aimed it at Shawn's window and threw. The hollow interior filled with wind, thwarting my aim, and the watering can was hurled across the backyard.

"Dammit."

I began looking for anything else I could throw—something heavier. Finally, I removed one of my shoes, dropping my socked foot onto the mushy ground. The thud against Shawn's window made me cringe. *No shattering glass—that's a relief.* Waiting now was almost more unbearable than how cold I felt from head to toe. The blinds rose and then the window slid all the way up with a swish. Shawn called down to me in a loud whisper. "Becky, is that you out there?"

Just looking at him brightened my spirits. "Yes. Come down here, I have to talk to you."

"What the heck are you doing out in this flood? You're gonna get sick."

"We don't have time for that. Meet me outside."

"What's going on? You okay?"

"Just get down here."

Shawn closed his window and in seconds the light in his room went out. I hid under the small ledge of the garage's roof, barely shielded from the deluge. The kitchen light turned on, a few minutes later the back door of the house slowly opened, and Shawn appeared wearing a bright-yellow rain jacket. I wrung my hands together, and blew into them. I couldn't wait to be with him after what happened, that I left the garage and met him halfway in the yard.

He took me in his arms and kissed me. "Becky...you're soaked and freezing cold. We need to get you inside."

"Andy and I got into a huge fight. He slapped me." Rain bubbled past my lips as I spoke.

Shawn took a step back. "Should I call the police?"

"No police," I said.

Wiping the stuck strands of hair from my face, Shawn frowned at the redness on my cheek.

"He wants to stop us from being together, he threatened to move me back to Ontario. I told him I'd never let you go."

"Come on, let's get out of this storm." Shawn gently tugged me on and we stepped into the dry, grubby confines of the garage.

"We have to leave," I said. "You and me. Take the truck, take a bus. We need to run away." My teeth chattered. "I can't live like this."

He pulled me in and I rested my head on his chest and cried. All the suppressed tears from the argument I had with Andy poured out. "I let you down when I gave up on the island. And I'm sorry. I made a mistake."

"Don't worry about that," Shawn said. "You didn't let me down for one second. The truth is, what my pop said stung. It was wrong of me to tangle you up in all this mess about legends. Not letting it be your choice. I got excited about your visions..."

"No, Shawn. I want to fulfill that legend as much as you. If it means getting more than a lifetime with you, then I want it. Okay? I took off with you to the island because I want to be where you are. You didn't make me do anything. I believe what you believe. We're in this together. Husband and wife."

The fairy dust he'd lost returned. He took my hand and squeezed a little. "Then let's take *Old Broken Down* to the island. The weather guy said the light-show and the rains should blow over soon. We'll sleep in the lighthouse until morning comes. From there we'll add that page to our map and go out and find the vial…and then sail to Mahone Bay, Halifax, anywhere. The world's our oyster."

"Is it safe to boat out right now?" A flash broke through the grimy windows and emphasized the wet places on me and Shawn's face. Thunder collided above us. "See what I mean?"

"We can wait it out in here for a bit," he said.

I let out a deep breath. "But for how long? Andy's probably on the phone with your parents right now."

"You're right." Shawn kissed my forehead. "So, I guess the only thing left to ask is, how much do you trust me?"

"I trust you with all I have."

"Then trust me when I say, I am confident with my sailing abilities even in a small storm. We can do this."

"You think so?"

"I know we can."

"Okay then, Captain Shawn Barringer," I said, "get me out of here."

Shawn removed an oil-lantern from a shelf, lit it, and we left the garage. When we reached the weathered stairs, we rushed down the slippery boards. After trudging across the pebbles, we stood in front of the dock and looked out at the ocean to see some waves coming in, churning and choppy with the occasional large one now and then in the distance.

I looked up and said, "It does seem like the storm clouds are breaking up. How do you feel about those waves?"

I turned to see Shawn no longer beside me. He ran down the dock to *Old Broken Down* and pulled off the tarp.

After one step in his direction, I stopped for a beat, face expressionless. My heart thrumming, giving me minor chest pains.

"Shawn?" Phillip Barringer hollered out from their house. "You out there?"

"Becky, come on," Shawn said. "There's no time to lose."

I looked in the direction of his father's shouting and then shuffled down the rest of the dock and got inside the boat.

We both began to move with urgency. "Here, put this on tight," Shawn said, handing me a lifejacket. He hung up the lantern on the rod and then untied the boat from the dock.

It felt like just seconds later that Shawn tried to steady *Old Broken Down* over the rolling swells, some of which closed out and broke with a crash against themselves. When we could barely see Lunenburg anymore, he handed me an empty tin pail. I looked blankly at him.

"You might need to use this for bailing," he explained. I took it from his clammy hands, wondering if he could feel how badly mine trembled.

O'Sullivan Island never felt so far away. The waves piled over each other, thrashing around the boat, spraying cold seawater up at us and down our necks. I bailed as efficiently as possible, watching Shawn work to paddle us through. Every vein in his face forced its way to the surface of his skin. The lantern spinning and clattering against the rod. A premonition of doom sat heavily upon my shoulders. The storm grew stronger, and we weren't getting closer to the island—in fact, we weren't getting closer to anything. We were being forced further out to sea.

I imagined that great expanse of endless water and started to lose my nerve. I recalled the dream where mom stepped in front of me on the dock, warning of Shawn or perhaps, now I thought of it, warning of the ocean. Warning of this moment. *I shouldn't have gotten into Old Broken Down. I shouldn't have agreed to this.*

Smearing away strands of salt-streaked hair the wind pasted over my mouth and eyes, I continued to bail water. Shawn craned his neck to remain looking back as he paddled, unable to see I stood up. Not thinking, I figured this would help me bail more efficiently. A roaring, wild wave hit, climbing out of the sea so fast I didn't have time to react. It pummeled me overboard and I hit my head on the edge of the boat.

Water filled my lungs as I went under. Seconds later, my head bobbed up, breaking the surface. I hacked and coughed, cradling my head in my hands from the agonizing pain. When I brought my hands to my face, I saw the blood. I looked up at Shawn, a blurred smudge hovering over the side of the boat with a halo of light from the lantern behind him. More waves crashed down on me, as I fought to stay on the surface. I made out Shawn's hand reaching out to me. His panicked shouting sounded far away through the water trapped in my ears. "Grab my hand!" he kept saying.

I tried to speak only to suck more water into my lungs, my throat raw, burning, suffocating.

"I've got you!" Grunting, he pulled me back into the boat. I fell into the bottom of it, dead weight, hyperventilating and gagging. Shawn took off his lifejacket and placed it under my head to cushion me from the cold floor of the boat. He turned me on my side and gave a few quick thrusts to my back to help me clear the water. When he turned me on my back again he said, "Becky, look at me. Breathe. Come on."

I coughed and inhaled a tortuous breath of razor blades. "Shawn," I said, hoarse. His quivering body surrounded mine. "You're going to be okay," he said, kissing my head. "I'm going to get you out of here." He pulled off his rain jacket, tucked it around my body, and then resumed his task at the oars.

The ocean's surface grew to a tumultuous rage under the storm's spell, despite the claims of the weatherman.

I tasted metal in my mouth as I lay in a half-foot of water that had spilled in over the sides of the boat. I hardly sensed my own existence anymore. My eyes were the only thing that still moved as I tried to keep Shawn in sight. He remained determined. His fingers were probably blistered, his arms numb from the cold like mine, yet he didn't stop paddling. Every one of his neck muscles strained like tightropes as he paddled against the current. Sadly, this arduous fight proved futile. The unrelenting whitecaps forced us further still.

Shawn shouted at the sky, an animalistic growl, his eyes darting around. "No!" He released the oars and his eyes gave way to weariness. His purple-red hands flew to his face in defeat. I never heard a man weep as hard as he did at that moment. Sidling up next to me, he said something through crying. Things I couldn't hear.

I wanted to tell Shawn sometimes things are bigger than us. I wanted to declare my love for him more than ever. With the last bit of strength in me, I moved my feeble hand to touch his ankle—the only part of him close enough to reach. I hoped, somehow, I could transfer all my love and thankfulness I had for him in that one touch. But before I had the chance, a loud wooden crack forced my hand away. Glass shattered and kerosene from the lantern splattered across my face, leaving me no time to scream.

NINETEEN

My eyelids were swollen and heavy as bricks when I tried opening them. I felt warmth tucked around me. *Being out in the storm must have been a nightmare. I'm at home in bed.* But then why did my entire body ache? I felt the squeezing pressure of a hand in mine. Because I couldn't turn my head, I rolled my eyes to the right, straining to see whose hand it was.

Andy. Or so I thought. This man had far more wrinkles than normal, haggard, seemingly years older. It wasn't until I looked up and saw a tall silver stand with a clear bag of fluid attached to it that I realized, *I'm in a hospital room.* My heart jumped.

"Where's Shawn?" I said, mustering the little strength I had to get the subtle, barely audible words out. My throat felt scorched dry. My lips were broken, the subtle tang of blood seeping through cracks and onto my tongue.

Andy turned to face me, his bloodshot eyes hope-filled. The aged look he carried fell away as nothing more than tiredness with the disquieting smile he gave. "You're awake? Thank, God!" With hard lips, he kissed my hand and then pressed it to his cool cheek. I couldn't move my hand from him for the life of me, helpless in my own body.

"What . . . happened? Where's Shawn?"

"Fishermen found you floating in the Atlantic almost eight miles away from shore," Andy said, choking up. "You've been in the hospital for four days. The doctor said when you first arrived, you were suffering heavy bruising, shock, and hypothermia. They've been coming in and out to check your vitals and…"

My lips stiffened and I swallowed hard. Memories flashed like slides in my mind: three blurred, unfamiliar faces stared down at me—men with beards, in bright-orange hooded raincoats and knit hats; their lips moving vigorously, sharp ringing in my ears, their alarmed expressions while wrapping me in a foil blanket.

Andy's eyes looked like glassy grey pools. "I haven't had a wink of sleep these past three days wondering if you were going to make it." Finally, the barrier that kept Andy from crying broke. "I'm sorry for fighting. For laying a hand on you. When I came looking for you at the Barringers' and you weren't there…" His head sagged onto the mattress. His shoulders shuddered from silent, heaving cries. "You're alive. You're alive. Forgive me. I'm so…sorry."

Still, he wasn't answering the most important question. "Where's Shawn?"

Andy's face lost color. Another tear built up in the corner of his eye, and then I blacked out.

***

The next time I woke, I opened my eyes without effort. "Shawn?" The skin on my face felt tight from dried streaks of tears. Still in a hospital bed with an IV in my wrist, I had no idea the time or day. The lights were out in the room and the privacy curtain pulled part way around. Andy snored in a chair beside my bed, his jean-jacket draped over him.

I remembered getting a needle at one point. A blue-gloved hand stuck it in my wrist. "No signs of necrosis," someone had said. My skin was gray, and I'd seen the needle go in, but I couldn't feel anything. I wondered then if I was dying. The doctor said he gave me morphine and it would ease my pain.

Now, as I laid here, I looked down in horror at the bottom edge of the privacy curtain. Black water flowed swiftly under it. I tried to find the button to call the nurse but couldn't feel it anywhere nearby. The water continued rising toward the top of the hospital bed. Part of me figured, *I'm stuck at sea in that wretched dory again.* I scooted the dead weight of my body to the edge and looked over. Through the murky ripples and darkness, I saw Shawn's face appear. His eyes wide with terror and bubbles expelling out of his screaming lips. I hollered and jerked back. My throat went raw and the sudden movement made my body crumple in pain. I began to cry.

Suddenly wide awake, Andy threw his jacket off and rushed to my side. He took my shoulders gently. "It's okay, Leah," he said. He kissed my perspiring forehead and helped me lie down properly in the middle of the bed, making sure I hadn't pinched off my IV. "I love you. I'm here."

Leah. Why is he calling me by my mother's name?

Had my being in the hospital brought Andy back to some suppressed, horrific memory of my mom? But why? He mentioned quitting alcohol after mom. Had he done something to harm her, or could it be something else? Questions swam through my already tired mind. I turned my head enough to see he'd already fallen back asleep, no doubt from a state of delirious exhaustion. I sighed heavily and lowered my eyelids.

***

Warm shafts of sun spilled into my room and woke me. The privacy curtain had been opened and the pastel yellow curtains at the windows tied back. A table to my right overflowed with gifts and flowers. A second window by the door had its blinds open, staff and visitors bustled past and down the halls with purpose. Staticky voices came over the intercom and interrupted Margaret, Phillip, and Andy, who stood in the doorway, speaking to who I assumed to be the doctor—a tall, black man wearing square glasses, and a button-down shirt with beige slacks. Everyone looked as if they'd been up for ages. The doctor's hands rose to stop the chatter and in a low voice said, "I stand by what I said. It's far too soon." With a nod, he left. The parents kept talking over one another, their words jumbling together so I couldn't make out what they discussed. Finally, Andy's voice rose above the Barringers'. "I'm with the doc. It's unfair to put her through it all over again. She's still having night terrors and shouldn't be put under further stress in her condition."

Margaret's eyes squinted and she began to sob uncontrollably. "But time is passing," she said, "and Shawn still hasn't been found. We need to try. Please...from one parent to another."

Andy's lips pressed into a compassionate line. He made his way over to me and sat on the bed. "You're up." He tucked the blankets in around my feet. "Didn't know you were up. How are you feeling?"

"Shawn still hasn't been found." I repeated these words to myself.

Andy glanced at the Barringers, who inched closer toward us arm in arm, looking intently in my eyes. He turned back to me and patted my hand gently. "Yes. It turns out that we need your help. It's been nearly a week now and...the police and the Coast Guard haven't found Shawn. Any information you remember may be valuable in finding him."

I heard the gasps from Margaret trying to stifle her crying in the background.

"O'Sullivan Island."

"That's the place with the lighthouse? They checked there," Andy said.

Out of the corner of my eye, someone moved slowly by the window close to the door. I looked over and my mouth fell open. The way the wet hair fell over his eyes, the strong cheekbone and aquiline nose. I shook Andy's arm wildly. "He walked by the room just now. Seconds ago. Listen, can you hear that?"

We all went quiet. The sound of waterlogged shoes slowly

slapped down the hall.

Everyone's faces were confused. They looked back at me.

"What are we listening for, Rebecca?" Andy asked.

"What do you mean?" I said, pointing. I grabbed his face and turned it back in the direction of the door. "Shawn walked by with wet shoes. The slap sounds. You didn't hear it? I think he might be looking for us. His face…it's like he was in pain. He needs help."

Andy removed my hands from his face. "Are you sure it was him?"

"He needs to know where we are," I said. Before I shuffled all the way to the edge of the bed to go searching for him, Andy put a hand on my shoulder. "You can't leave your bed, Rebecca."

Phillip joined Margaret who, with a glimmer of hope, bolted from the room and asked a few nurses close by if they'd seen a boy around with wet shoes. She described him, gave his full name, and asked if they might inquire at the front desk to see if he'd checked in.

When Phillip escorted Margaret back in the room, we waited in anticipation. My stare stayed fixed on the door. Andy got up and crossed his arms over his chest, his eyes directed to the floor. He didn't believe me.

One of the nurses returned, just peeking her head in the door. "I'm sorry, Mam. We haven't seen a boy around by the description you gave, and no one by his name has registered."

Margaret threw her hand over her mouth and buried her head into Phillip's chest, sobbing.

"I'm sorry," the nurse whispered and disappeared from the door.

"That doesn't mean anything," I said. "I saw him. He's out there."

"Rebecca!" Andy's voice rose. He eyed Margaret and then me, "That's enough."

"He needs to know where we are. I'm going to him." I kicked my legs to pull the sheets and blanket off me.

"No, Rebecca. Stop," Andy said.

When I hadn't the strength enough to get off the bed after exerting so much energy, howling cries burst out.

Andy put his hands to his ears. "I'm getting the doctor."

"Let us," Phillip offered. "Stay here with your daughter."

Before anybody could leave, the doctor and a rotund nurse entered. The nurse asked Phillip and Margaret to kindly move out of the way while the doctor hovered over me with a reassuring smile. "Rebecca, I'm going to need you to calm down. How about some nice big breaths for me? I'll count with you."

I took the first shallow breath in between heaving jolts in my chest.

"That's one," the doctor said and waited until I finished my next. "Two. Hey, that one sounds better already."

I took a third breath and calmed myself back onto the pillow.

"Three. Perfect. Okay…I've got that little light here. You remember it, right?" The doctor pulled what looked like a pen from his shirt pocket and clicked it. "Can you follow it for me with your eyes?"

"That's it now, right and left. Up and down. There you go," he said and then clicked it off and stowed it back. "Your breathing sounds better. How does it feel to you?"

The heaving jolts in my chest subsided, but a heaviness in my heart weighed me down. I shrugged.

"Being here is tough. We understand. Especially after going through so much. If there is anything we can do to make you more comfortable, let us know how we…"

"My daughter's hallucinating," Andy said, frantically, cutting the doctor off and me from wanting to shout, "Just go and find Shawn! That's all I want." He whispered the next part, but I overheard. "She saw their lost son in the doorway. That drug she's on is making her see things."

"Mr. Stafford," the doctor said sympathetically, "perhaps we can discuss this in the hall? Your daughter needs rest."

Andy paced the room a few times, taking in his own deep breaths. "Okay."

"We shouldn't have come," Margaret cried. "I'm sorry." Phillip escorted her out of the room. Andy waved while they were on their way out. "I'll be in touch."

"Come on," the doctor said, patting Andy lightly on the shoulder.

"I'll grab you some water, Rebecca," Andy said tucking a sheet over me.

As they walked out together, the doctor continued, "I'll speak with the nurses and make a note to give Rebecca something other than morphine. There are some patients who do have strange reactions to it."

"Thank you—I appreciate that."

I tucked the bed sheet up over my face, feeling the cool damp spots my tears made on it. When I lifted it off for some air, the sun had disappeared and the room was bathed in darkness. Shawn sat on the edge of the hospital bed with his back turned, his clothing ragged, drenched, and salt stained. I held my hand over my chest, startled. "Shawn, I knew you were here. Are you okay?" I moved through the pain to reach him with my hand. I just needed to touch him. He turned to me with anguish in his eyes and when he tried to speak, so much water poured from his lips; too much. I withdrew my hand, screaming.

Andy clambered in and practically threw the pitcher onto the edge of the counter. It slid off and hit the floor with a thud, spreading water like shattered glass across the tiles. Shattered glass. The lantern. I licked my lips, sure I tasted kerosene. *Too much water, there's too much water.* When Andy wrapped his arms around me the room turned back to sunshine and Shawn no longer sat on the bed.

"I'm here, I'm here. What's the matter?" he asked.

"I don't know what's happening to me!"

***

"Wake up."

"Hmm?" I roused and rubbed at one eye, my head heavily fogged from being interrupted out of deep sleep. Rays of moonlight from the window made it possible to see in the hospital room, but just barely. I leaned up and looked to my right and could make out Andy asleep, snoring softly, on a cot the nursing staff brought in for him. My skin crawled and heart pounded. Who called for me? Could it be?

Throwing my legs over, I slid out of bed. My bare feet hit the floor with a quiet slap. I tied my hospital gown tighter and pulled the IV out.

With cautious and quiet steps, I made my way over to the partly open door. I peered right and left down the halls. Oddly quiet. Then again, patients were sleeping and no doubt the staff were minimal these hours. Slinking out, I put my hand on the railing along the wall. A trail of blood seeped out from under the tape the IV had been fastened down with.

"Come find me," the faint, familiar voice said.

"I'm trying to," I answered in a murmur.

I stopped abruptly and looked behind me. The fluorescent lights above turned dull and began to flicker. *Tsst, tsst, tsst.* The longer breaths I took in were filled with fumes of antiseptics. Had my eyes begun to play tricks on me? The shadows around corners and different halls began to spread as ink stretches upon paper. I continued forward, regardless. The desk to sign in for emergencies was vacant with papers stacked beside an old computer. A pen rolled along the desk and stopped beside a coffee mug like someone had just left. In the back, in a room, muffled voices chattered. A few laughs. The nurses and doctor might've been having a break.

"You're getting closer."

"Shawn?" I pressed my back against the wall, my nostrils flaring.

Forgetting how to get back to my room, I pushed past a set of heavy doors and began to rush down a forlorn wing. When I hit the end of it, I angled right and kept on going down another.

Shawn stood at the far end in front of a window, arms heavy at his sides. Eyes blank, repeating over and over, "Solemn things, solemn things, solemn things."

"Shawn, stop this," I shouted, gaining momentum. "This isn't a game. You're scaring me."

An ear-piercing crack rattled the hall and froze me out of my run. The glass behind him, turned to a spider-web of lines, shattered into a million pieces and brought a mass of ocean flooding in, sweeping Shawn up into it, coming for me. I slipped while turning, got back up, and dashed down the hall shrieking.

A tall, thin woman in floral scrubs came around the corner. "Woah!"

I felt my knees buckle when we collided full-tilt. "What in the name of all that's Holy is going on?" she asked, rubbing her hip after falling directly on her bottom.

The ice-cold floor and bits of dirt pressed against my forehead, my eyelids fluttered and blackness came.

***

"She went unconscious after running into Gladys, one of the cleaning ladies," A nurse explained to Andy. I listened, slightly coherent, back in my assigned hospital room. "It looks like she got up out of bed and from there we don't know. Gladys claims she looked pale and afraid."

Andy put his hand on top of my head for a second. "Could she still be having latent reactions to the morphine? She just recently got off it, and they're giving her something else. Toradol, I believe."

"Let me speak with the doctor about all this and see what he wants to do."

When the nurse left, my eyes opened and Andy peered down at me. "Do you remember you got out of bed? Took out your IV?"

A shiver passed through me. A grim sensation. *Grim.* I pondered O'Sullivan and the concept of the Grim Reaper. A hospital often symbolized the last place people go to pass away. I felt trapped and surrounded by the ugly shadow of death lurking around me. I needed to get out of here. Get away from the horrible images involving Shawn that were lies...all lies, meant to sweep me up in their torment and break me. The last place he'd be found was in this forsaken stack of stones. I'd been here long enough. Time to heal and find him.

"Rebecca, please answer me," Andy implored. "You could've been badly hurt. What got into you?"

He didn't say it in his usual *Andy* way, purposefully condescending. A lone tear straggled down my cheek. "Solemn things."

TWENTY

With the morphine well out of my body after five, full days, I didn't seem to be having any more episodes and had stable vitals. They released me from the hospital, and unknowingly the clutches of the Grim Reaper. I didn't remember details from the horrid hallucinations—or rather, death's cruel tricks—trying desperately to stow them away in a box and ship it somewhere far out of my subconscious.

The homecare instructions from the doctor consisted of exercising caution when going out into the cold, as I'd be more sensitive to it and susceptible to getting sick again. Andy unpacked one of my cable-knit sweaters to pull over what I already wore. He swung a winter jacket over my shoulders when we walked out of the automatic doors of the building and stuck a black knit hat over my head as if it were mid-winter.

The other bit of homecare involved putting consideration toward speaking to a therapist about my experience. He called it Post Traumatic Stress Disorder. I didn't want to talk to a Shrink. There was much to do in looking for Shawn.

The official search for him had been called off a day before my release. They pronounced him dead. This news wrenched my gut and I'd gotten sick all over the hospital floor. Phillip and

Margaret prepared a memorial service for tomorrow afternoon.

"The staff gave this back," Andy said handing me my wedding ring at the truck. "Had to take it off you for some of the procedures."

I plucked it out of his fingers, and after sliding it back on, felt a small sense of ease.

My breath fogged up the truck window. Life continued; cars drove past, people talked and laughed on the street, an old woman pulled weeds and shriveled plants from her garden. Motion. But I felt none of the momentum. My paper hand stayed firm in Shawn's; stuck in stillness somewhere. Not quite limbo, as I knew he was alive. If I survived, surely he did.

How could the authorities quit the search?

I didn't know at what point I fell asleep on the short drive home. When Andy parked the truck in front of our house, I stirred. Subtle guitar music reached my ears through the glass. "Shawn?"

"Uh," Andy coughed. "We're home." He removed his seatbelt, opened his door, and got out. After removing the small suitcase out of the truck bed, he opened my door to help me out.

The tuneful strumming drew my steps and pulled my heart strings in the direction of the Barringers' house. Somewhere in between yesterday and now, Shawn found his way home. I knew the sound of his playing.

"Rebecca," Andy snapped me back to reality.

"Huh?"

"Coming in?"

"You have some nerve. Why didn't you tell me?" I frowned.

"What do you mean?" Andy took care to word things gently so as not to set me off. To him, I must've been a ticking clock on a bomb, a constant worry…like Hook's dreaded alligator. *Tick-tock.* Any moment I may snap. Devour the silly fool who dared test me.

"The music. The guitar music coming from the Barringers' backyard. Shawn's home and you said nothing."

"I'd never do that," Andy answered. "Of course, I'd tell you.

That's Aaron. You remember Shawn's older brother? He came home yesterday...for the mem—"

"Don't say it," I hissed. "Don't you dare say it, as if you believe him to be dead, too."

Andy bit his lower lip and then nodded. "Okay. I'm sorry. Why don't you come inside? I'll make a drink to warm us. Hot chocolate or something."

"I don't want anything to drink." I said before walking into the house. It felt like ages since I stepped on our floor and heard the creaking of the staircase up to my room.

Andy followed behind with the suitcase. I stood in the hall and then followed him into his bedroom, robotically. My steps didn't feel like my own.

"My boss said I can take as much time off work as needed...to be here for you," Andy said, throwing the case into the closet to be unpacked at a later time. He checked the phone that rested on the tan Ikea end-table next to his bed before sitting down. "Phillip and Margaret called a few times. I should let them know we're home now."

I scowled, twirling the wedding ring around my finger. "How can his own parents give up like this? The whole memorial is a slap in the face. He's not dead!"

Andy closed his eyes and lowered his head. When he looked back up, I expected a better answer than, "They've done everything."

"No," I protested. "They haven't found a body, and until then nobody can be absolutely certain." The corner of my left eye started to twitch in agitation.

Andy sighed. "It's true they haven't found anything, but it's the ocean. Trained professionals searched day and night, thoroughly, as much as humanly possible. They even prolonged the search. It's over ten days since the fishermen found you. Phillip and Margaret want their son to be alive, they probably wanted the Coast Guard to look forever, but a person can only hang on for so long before needing closure. Otherwise, they're stuck in limbo, waiting for something that may never happen. It just isn't healthy."

"Limbo is letting go." I turned to walk away and paused. "You of all people should know that."

"What's that supposed to mean?"

I looked back at him. "You say I don't know anything about how you feel. But I see how much you're drifting in this life. You have no one to hold onto. Your hands are searching. You let Mom go. And you had me. *Had*," I said in between holding back tears. "What you're in right now, this day-to-day mundanity of going to work, eating, sleeping, and doing it all over again to escape that gnawing ache within...*that's* limbo." Hot tears rushed down my cheeks, neck, and pooled into the small crevices of my collar bone.

Andy appeared at a loss for words. He stared down at the floor with unblinking eyes.

"Shawn...he took my hand when you wouldn't. He keeps me from the hell you're currently facing. So, tell me again how you think people need closure by letting go. Is this what you tell yourself to feel better for deserting your family?"

"Rebecca," Andy said, voice breaking.

"Well, what then? Why'd you do it? Did you hurt Mom drinking too much one night? That why you left?"

Andy sat on the edge of the unmade bed (a goose-down comforter and sheets all helter-skelter, like my mind) and hid his face against his shoulder. He cried silently, his back trembling.

I waited for answers and when none came, I said, "You did, didn't you? That's why you called me by her name in the hospital that one night? It brought you back to a terrible memory."

Andy wiped his eyes over his shirt sleeve. "What? I called you by—"

"You did," I interrupted. "You settled me down after I got frightened during a hallucination, or whatever those were, and you called me Leah."

Andy swallowed hard and let the tears crawl from his grey

eyes that turned them a miserable shade of blue. "I never laid a hand on your mom." He slouched and rested his elbows on his knees. "But the hospital may have reminded me of a terrible memory. Yes."

"What was it then?"

"Hospital records had me down as a contact for your Mom, even after all these years. She knew my number. So, they called me when she got into the car accident and told me to get to Emergency as soon as I could." Andy wiped a hand over his glistening, wet face. "I never stopped loving her, you know. Or you." His head hung lower. "I got to the hospital and she...they...they tried to keep her with us. Seeing her in that condition is a horror I want to forget. I let her know I was there...how sorry I was for all the mistakes I made."

My heartbeat rattled out of control, and an upsurge of nausea struck. "You were there when—?"

"When she died," Andy said. "And then I thought of how I'd let you down. I left you both because I got scared. Took the coward's way out. I didn't know anything about being a father. I still felt young. Would I be a good at it? Fail? The stress of the pregnancy came heavy, like a punch to the chest. I started to spend money foolishly at the bar, come home indecent hours."

I lowered slowly to the floor and sat, afraid to hear more and hungry to hear more at the same time. The walls of my world shook, dust and debris coming down on my head. Turned on its axis. Askew like the blinds over Andy's window.

"After you were born...your mom and I had a bad fight when I came home late one night. Nothing physical, but words...and well, they can do damage, too. Sometimes irreparable damage. The shouting scared you and you started to cry. Such a beautiful, tiny thing swaddled in your mom's arms. I just took off. I couldn't handle how pathetic I'd become. How I became the dead-beat Dad I'd feared to be."

Andy removed a tissue from his jean's pocket and blew his

nose. He crumpled it, got up, tossed it in the garbage-bin by the dresser, and sat back down. "Even after I got off alcohol, your Mom didn't want me back. I'd betrayed her trust and she doubted my changes. So, I kept myself buried in work. I mailed gifts for you on your birthdays, in hopes to still be part of your life in some small way. Your mom figured I should stop. That it might confuse and hurt you."

"If you were there when she died, how come it took forever for family to find you?"

"I'm a low-life, coward, Rebecca. The only thing I knew how to do was run. I knew they'd come looking for me, so I packed up and hopped a train to Winnipeg, where I've been living all this time. Figured you'd be better off without me. But then out of the blue, that call came. I couldn't hide anymore. I had to face myself. Face you, warts and all."

"Why tell me this now? Why not before?" I said, eyes swollen and lips trembling. I didn't know if I liked this side of Andy; real, emotional, an open book as compared to his usual cold, closed self. The gap between us seemed to be thinning out and I wasn't sure how to deal with that.

"Because of all this going on with Shawn. I don't want you to feel alone."

"I'm not alone," I said, moving to stand. "He's out there."

And I'm going to find him if no one else will. That became my resolve. When Andy got busy doing something, I'd sneak out. If I knew Shawn, he'd have found his way back to O'Sullivan Island somehow and be out looking for that last page, or already in search of the vial. The Coast Guard, police, search-parties, they probably bypassed him without knowing it.

I left Andy's room and went to lean on the banister of the stairs. Dazed. Though clocks ticked in the house, Father Time had disappeared leaving me no way to keep track. Seconds, minutes, hours...they all jumbled into nothingness, disbelief. It didn't matter, really. A moment to get outside is all I needed. Pushing off the railing, I turned and padded toward the bathroom.

"What are you doing? You feeling alright?" Andy interrupted, directly in front of me, one hand leaned against the wall.

"Uh…I'm not ill if that's what you're wondering."

I closed the door, locked it, and flicked the cold faucet on. The rushing discordance of water forced me back against the wall in terror, my hand slid down over the light switch. With every blink, I saw different things. Giant waves, fishermen's faces, Shawn struggling. Darkness consumed me. I scrambled, frantic fingers reaching for the faucet. Once I turned it to a pathetic drizzle, I searched for the switch, heart rapid.

When I turned the lights back on, Jack O'Sullivan stood before me. The sharp gasping inhale I took in stole my ability to scream. I crumpled to the floor.

Andy knocked. "Rebecca, what's all that ruckus? You okay?"

"Mm hmm." I squinted up at the lofty Irishman.

"Go on now and send yer oul fella away," Jack said, quietly.

"Can you give me my privacy?" I said, brisk.

"Sorry, yah. Of course," Andy answered.

I crawled to the door and pressed an ear against it. Each stair creaked as he descended them. "He's gone. Wh…what are you doing here?" I rose warily, joints moving in slow-motion, with eyes still fixed on Jack—who took a seat on the tub's edge, bent a knee and laid a lazy arm over it. His bucket boots were scuffed, the leather coming away in places and the wool, long-coat he wore piled over the sides of the tub, buttoned down to reveal a salt-mottled grey shirt, a beat-up ankh on a leather tie around his neck, and a huge belt over his trousers.

He ran a hand over his beard. "Why, I'm here because ye've been putting it on the long finger finding me boy."

"No, I haven't."

He cocked an eyebrow, olive-colored eyes lustrous. "Aye…ye have. And just how do you suppose yer going to face the Atlantic when tap-water alone is enough to get ye shook?"

"It's a mind-over-matter thing. I can do it. And, I will," I said.

"Then quit foostering around and get to it, then."

"It's not that easy, otherwise I'd be gone by now." I tightened the faucet to stop the dripping and tilted my head toward the door. "Andy's going to be watching me like a hawk. You heard him at the door."

"Aye," Jack said tucking his lips in, mustache protruding. "But there are ways to keep yer business yer own, love. The oul fella sleeps deeply on occasion when he carries around a tiny bottle of some kind."

"Ativan?" I said, mostly to myself. "I could give him some. Put it in a drink, his supper, or something."

Jack tapped his temple. "Now that's using the ol' noggin, love."

I pulled open the mirror to get into the medicine cabinet. It sat right in plain sight, as if coaxing me to take it. After pulling it off the second shelf, I closed the cabinet and saw Jack had gone.

After unlocking the door, I made for my room. A minute or two later, who else but Andy joined me.

"Can I make you something for lunch? You really need to eat and keep your strength up."

I slid the pill bottle under my pillow discreetly. Food disgusted me. The idea of biting down on anything brought bile to my throat. But, if it got Andy out of my hair for a while, the pills might not be needed...

A flicker of hope. "A burger might be okay. Not a fast-food one."

Andy stared off, thoughtfully. "I think I know a place. Guys at work talk about The Knot Pub. Says they put together a nice patty."

"Whatever. Sounds good," I shrugged and fell on my bed.

"I'll order for both of us and then call one of them from work to drive it over here for me."

I shot up. "You're not going to get it? Why trouble them?"

"Are you kidding? They won't mind."

When he left to call in the order and wait for it in the living room, I exhaled a big breath. "Why are you making me do this to you?" I fell back on the bed and reached under the pillow behind my head to grab the Ativan. I read his prescription: *Lorazepam, dissolve 1 tablet under tongue, once daily.*

The pills themselves were 1 mg of medication. How much would be too much? I spun and popped the top off the bottle and sprinkled two into the palm of my hand. *No. I can't do two. What if it hurts him?* Tucking the one in, I closed the bottle and stowed it under the pillow.

I thought about keeping a few pills for myself before putting them back in the cabinet. Might come in handy. How long would Shawn take to find the vial? It shouldn't be long with the map practically complete. Surely, he'd come back for me if he found it. He spoke of both of us using it and taking off somewhere together. Would running away be necessary anymore? I doubted that our parents would try to prevent us from spending time together if Shawn came back.

That is, if the Barringers hadn't already convinced themselves of his death with the memorial. I didn't get it. Wouldn't a parent spend their lifetime waiting? Sure, it sounded unhealthy. But how awful to go through all the ceremonial duties when he winds up appearing at the door, alive and well.

I turned on my side, yawned, and fell asleep woken eventually by Andy coming in and saying, "Soups on."

"Soup?" I sat up and checked my hand to make sure I still held the small white pill. "Thought you got us burgers."

"It's an old saying," Andy said putting the brown, paper bag on the bed before sliding the drink tray holding two fizzy pops on the nightstand. "Hope you don't mind if I eat with you."

While he unpacked our burger containers from the bag, I slid off the bed and stood in front of the nightstand. "Which pop is mine?"

"Got us both Pepsi. That okay?"

I lifted part of the lid off one and slipped the pill inside. "Yah, it's good. Here you go." I sealed the lid, turned around and handed him the one with the Ativan.

"Thanks."

He took a sip. We ate, or rather, I forced greasy beef down my throat…and then I waited.

TWENTY ONE

While Andy snoozed on the sofa, I threw on a jacket and went out to sit on the front step to tie my shoe. A brown wren skipped along the sidewalk and onto the lawn, watching me with dubious eyes. It pecked at the ground and hopped its way closer. "I did what I had to do," I said to it. "I had no choice. He'd hover around me all day with worry."

When a car blaring loud music zoomed by, the wren flittered away into the colorless sky. That became my cue. I slunk to the backyard, hopped the fence into the Barringers', and took off down the rickety stairs to the rocky path.

I'd always had Shawn by my side coming down to the ocean. It wasn't right without his presence.

My heart beat rattled in my ears, deafening the spiteful winds as I hopped over the rocks. I fell to my knees on the pebbled shore, to gather my breath. How badly I wished to curl up there and go no further. Fear made me doubt. But I didn't want to let Shawn down, or Jack O'Sullivan, who needed him to be found just as much as me. Going from a crawl, to a kneel, to standing, I trekked ahead.

The moment I came face to face with the ocean, the waves coming toward me, white fingernails reaching, my head began to hurt. I closed my eyes and my body teetered, unbalanced. *I'm back in the boat. God help me, I'm back in the boat.* When I collapsed to the ground, the dory had been obliterated to pieces again. Pummeled by tons of seawater. I held my breath, preparing to plunge into dark, awful places. A high-pitched noise in my ears turned into the frightful sound of Shawn screaming. Drowning. I cupped my ears, but the noise went on and on. When I panted for breath and opened my eyes again, hoping to force myself out of the horror, the Grim Reaper stood before me. Tall, heavily cloaked, black smoke enveloping him.

My stomach leapt in alarm. *I thought I left these drug-induced illusions behind at the hospital.*

The Reaper's decayed, spidery hands held a six inch, Victorian pentacle hourglass. There was no sand within, but water dripping one drop at a time. "Look closely," his sinister, baritone voice said.

When I did, I noticed a tiny version of Shawn splashing in the water, trying his best to avoid getting sucked down. But with one swish of the Reaper's hand, a storm brewed and waves slapped around the hourglass. The water no longer dripped down, but created a sucking vortex.

"This isn't real," I shouted, curling up into myself. "You aren't real." I cried hard, not wanting to see Shawn struggle and get pulled down. "It's all in my head. It's all in my head. Shawn is still alive."

"He is dead. And he's mine."

With daggers, I glared in the Reaper's direction and repeated, "You. Aren't. Real." Without hesitation, I leapt for the hourglass, but the Grim Reaper swiftly floated over the ocean. Out of reach.

"Come, child…come into the water. Save him."

I stepped toward the shore, but my legs jittered and I fell hard on my knees. "I…I can't."

His stentorian laughter shook the skies. Turning away, quivering, I doubled back until I collapsed at the back gate of the Barringers'.

"I'm afraid…I'm so afraid, Shawn," I whimpered. "Have I've failed you? Failed Jack? Failed us? You have to be alive." My words disintegrated in my throat.

"Becky?"

Through bleary eyes, I looked up. A boy wearing a ball-cap stared down at me.

"I heard the gate rattle, and thought you were someone else for a moment."

"What do you mean?" That last statement made me pause and wipe the tears from my eyes. "Oh."

Upon seeing clearer, I understood. Aaron Barringer reached in front of me and helped me off the ground. With the ball-cap covering his dark hair, he looked just like his brother.

"For a minute there, I thought you were someone else, too," I said, deflated and queasy at the sensation of hope stripped out of my body. My heart ripped from my chest.

"Shawn, right?"

I nodded, bit my lip, fighting more tears.

"What were you doing out there?" Aaron asked, picking at his heavy sweater.

I couldn't tell him what just happened. "Nothing."

"Nothing," he repeated. "Everything pretty much feels like nothing now, doesn't it?"

Staring into his eyes felt too much like staring into Shawn's. I turned my gaze for a second, but not for long. I couldn't help but watch Aaron's every move. The way the voice of Shawn left his throat. How those guitar fingers kept flicking away imaginary lint.

I knew if I closed my eyes, it would be like the love of my life had returned. That comforted me a great deal and then made me think myself pathetic.

"Yah, you know…I should get going," I said. *Before I reach out to touch your face.*

"Sure, yah. See you tomorrow, I suppose." Aaron tucked his hands into his pockets and traipsed to the patio steps. He picked up his guitar, while I hurried over the fence back into my yard.

I stayed there, on the ground in a crouched position, and listened to the song he played, trying to forget about my encounter with the Grim Reaper. When my body began to protest the cold by numbing my hands and feet, I left and went inside the house. Aaron and I would *not* be seeing each other tomorrow. I had no intention of going to that memorial service.

***

"You don't even want to go for Phillip and Margaret?" Andy asked, cracking an egg into the frying pan.

"No."

"Alright then. I respect your decision." He cracked another egg. "How do you want these?"

"I'm not hungry." I said, realizing my hands were clenched in fists. Opening them, I looked down at the nail marks on my palms. I wandered from the kitchen to the living room at a snail's pace. Still in pajamas, with no intention of changing out of them. Meaninglessness occupied the space where my heart once sat, and the Reaper's laughter echoed in my head. I wanted his taunting to go away. But I couldn't distract myself enough. "*I knew you didn't have it in you. You are a disappointment*," his voice whispered from all corners of the house.

After several minutes of repeating, "Go away," I decided to have a drink of juice to flush what felt like a pasty film off my tongue. When I entered the kitchen again, I found Andy at the table, his head in his hands and a glass of ice melting in front of him.

"What are you doing?" I asked.

"I'm just chewing on some ice. I wasn't really hungry either."

I nodded and got myself a glass. "Is ice all that was in that glass?"

"Yes. I've sworn off the drink again. And this time, I mean to as long as I live."

I looked through the fridge and pulled out the apple juice.

After it was poured to the center of my glass, I drank it quickly, my expression blank when turning back toward Andy.

"I'm sorry," he said, swishing the ice around in his glass. "It's all my fault, you know." Tears streamed down his face. "Every time I saw you two together it bothered me. I worried he'd hurt you, disappoint you. Like I did. But, he was nothing like me. He was better."

"He is better. *Is*. Use present-tense," I said.

"I never wanted any of this for you. I need you to know that."

"Just stop...please." I slammed my glass on the counter. "I don't want to hear it. I *can't* hear it." I ran out of the kitchen with my hands over my ears and upstairs. I locked myself in my room.

I sat on the edge of my bed staring at the clock. I stared at it until it read 12:30.

The memorial service began in a half-hour.

Acidic fluid pushed up into my throat and vertigo hit me. Covering my mouth, I ran to the bathroom, locked the door, and started to gasp heavily. I expected to see Jack, but he wasn't there. I looked at myself in the bathroom mirror. Eyes swollen and blood-shot.

I grabbed a face-towel, ran it under cool water, and dabbed at my skin.

Andy lightly knocked twice on the door. "You sure you're not coming?"

"Stop pestering me," I said through grit teeth.

His voice softly replied, "I'll see you afterward, then."

Every sound in the house amplified—Andy's shoes on the stairs, the furnace kicking in, the throbbing pulse in my temples. I had to sit. I leaned against the tub and flung the towel by the sink. I recalled deep-breathing techniques I used at the hospital and started to do them. "One...two...three."

Regardless, when the surge of acid returned, I opened the toilet lid, threw myself over it, and vomited.

Standing again, and using the same towel, I wiped my mouth

clean. I looked in the mirror at eyes void of any light. I barely looked alive.

Reaching for the doorknob, I turned it, and stepped out into the hall. "Where are you, Shawn? Why haven't you come home, yet?" I hollered. "Prove everyone wrong and come back."

The image of a crowd huddled together on the sliver of beach—just after the jagged rocks behind the Barringers' house— sobbing and letting go, brought the taste of vomit back in my mouth. It had to be put to a stop.

I dashed into my room and raided my dresser drawers for anything to wear, pulling out clothes fiercely and whipping them across the room. I emptied all drawers and fell to my knees, crying. Eventually, I got up, changed out of pajamas, and, from out of the jumble of clothing, threw on a cotton pullover sweater and skinny-jeans. I left my hair down, messy.

While passing through the Barringers' backyard, I felt sick again. I looked up at the widow's walk on the top of their house; the hollow in my chest seeming more cavernous by the second. I pictured myself up there, looking out at the ocean, believing the love of my life might come home.

My feet took me down the same rickety steps. My knees went weak and I almost hoped to fall down the stairs and never wake up. I heard the somber hum of people chattering, weeping, and the grating interruption of seagulls. It sounded like the service hadn't started yet.

After the rocky path, I faced the backs of people sitting on foldout chairs. I chose a far side, so that I might look on at those toward the front. The whole school and half of the town had come, it seemed. People who, in my opinion, never knew Shawn nor cared for him. Even with the nasty ocean out of sight, I wished that I hadn't come at all.

Margaret's face stayed buried deep into a floral-print handkerchief. Phillip gently stroked her back, fighting tears of his own. After some time, I realized I'd been staring at Aaron's side profile. He wore a black suit, and his eyes were tear-filled, jaw set.

The Pastor stood at the center of the rows of chairs and slid his square glasses up on his nose before adjusting the cordless microphone on the stand in front of him. I held my breath as he began. "Though we gather here this September 24th, to mourn the tragic loss of Shawn Tyler Barringer with heavy hearts, let us remember what the Bible says—that though our earthly tent has been taken down, our Lord Jesus has given us an eternal body and a home in Heaven. Let's bow our heads in silence and then in a word of prayer before we continue."

I breathed in and wrung my hands, keeping my eyes open while everyone had theirs closed with heads down. I watched them beginning to forget—so convinced Shawn was gone. My breathing quickened, my hands fidgeted more. Quickly jumping from my chair, I moved fast and had the microphone off its stand, right from under the Pastor's nose.

"Stop!" I hollered.

Heads shot up, eyes opened. A wave of loud, confused whispers filled the air.

The Pastor tried to take the microphone from me. "My dear," he said, "please, kindly return to your seat."

I dodged his reach and began to pace up and down in front of the crowd. "I'm sorry, but I can't stand here and let this happen. I can't stand here while you all lose hope. Shawn is still out there," I pointed toward the ocean, without looking back at its evil grimace.

"Rebecca Leah Stafford." Andy stared at me from his seat, mouth agape.

"No. I don't care what anyone thinks. Shawn's body hasn't been found. I tell you, he's out there and we're all giving up on him!"

"Young lady." The Pastor couldn't keep up with me. I ducked underneath his arms several times to avoid him.

"I believe in him. Why don't you?" I began to cry, my voice hysterical. "We'll start a search of our own. Phillip, you have boats. I'm sure everyone here owns a boat. Come on!"

Looks of sympathy and pity were traded among the audience.

"Stop looking at me like I'm crazy!" When my eyes darted around, I swore I glimpsed a smoky black presence standing amongst the crowd. The Grim Reaper mocking me, yet again.

Andy shot up from his seat that moment and wrapped both arms around me in a tackle.

"Get off me." I screamed and kicked.

Andy wrestled the microphone from my grasp with one hand, the other hand tight around my waist. The Pastor ran up quickly to take it and put it back on the stand. Andy threw me over his shoulder and said loudly, "I'm so sorry, everybody."

"Let go of me." I slapped his back and fought all the way to our doorstep. When Andy put me down slowly, I pounded on his chest.

"Hit me. Hit me if you have to."

I slapped him across the cheek and then fell to the concrete and drained myself of my tears. He sat there with me until I had nothing left.

"I didn't mean to make a scene…" I sighed. "And, sorry I hit you."

"Hey, I deserved every bit of it."

"Huh…" I sighed, and said the morbid thought in my head out loud, "Now we're even."

TWENTY TWO

The day felt weird. Not only due to my demented moment at the memorial yesterday, but also because I'd had a dream that night of Aaron. While the man in the dream had more of Aaron's features, I referred to him as Shawn. Either way, it brought awkwardness, confusion, and guilt. We were in the lighthouse in the dream, on the chaise together. Under a blanket naked. Kissing.

I missed Shawn's lips on mine. The warmth two bodies brought one another snuggled together. The safety. The completion. So much that I mentioned to Andy in passing that we should invite the Barringers to our place for supper. This way, they didn't have to make anything themselves and perhaps they needed a change of scenery. Equally, though this next part I kept to myself, it would get Aaron here—or, how I needed to view it, the Shawn from my last dream. *This is the distraction you need to be rid of the Reaper's taunts*, I told myself.

Andy prepared a roast with potatoes and a spinach salad. The house smelled like salty pork and gravy. As much as I hardly ate these days, the savory aroma made my stomach grumble.

The Barringers came a few minutes late. Margaret whispered to Phillip in the doorway that she really ought to have brought something to add to the meal. When I took Aaron's jacket and hung it on one of the sailboat hooks, he barely mouthed thanks and drifted by without returning the smile I offered. Without a ball-cap on, my fantasy of imagining him as Shawn didn't quite take effect.

We sat at the table, handing dishes back and forth to one another. Andy made small-talk with Phillip about the milder weather we were now getting. Margaret stared down at her plate, silent, until Aaron handed her the bowl of mashed potatoes. "Oh, thanks my dear," she said softly.

She put a spoonful on her plate and directed the bowl at me.

All of us ended up with snack-sized portions in front of us. It appeared none of us here had an appetite. Aaron forked a piece of lettuce and ate it, chewing on that single leaf for far too long. Grinding it into inedible pulp in his mouth. The swallow appeared dissatisfying. He hadn't even added dressing to his salad.

No, I shouldn't have been watching him at all. Or, at least tried being subtler. But even without a hat, he gestured a lot like his brother and moved his lips the same. It distracted me. When he glanced up at my ogling, he went right back to staring down at his food. My stomach sank and it hit me how terrible of an idea this was.

I ate my tiny portion quickly, washed it down with some water and removed myself from the kitchen to go sit in the living room. For noise, I flicked the television set on.

It surprised me when Aaron joined me minutes later asking, "Anything decent on?"

"Nah, just news."

He sat on the far end of the couch from me. "Nice of your pop to invite us over. I hope he doesn't mind I didn't eat much. It's not his cooking, I just…"

"Can't."

"Yah," he replied.

I kept my eyes on the screen. "He won't mind, I assure you."

"Good," Aaron said. "I might head home then."

I turned to him, this time unable to resist looking his way. "So soon?"

"Just don't feel much like talking. I want to play guitar and get lost in the music for a while."

"I don't blame you," I sighed. "Do you mind if I come and listen in? I've got nothing better to do."

Aaron shrugged. "Sure, if you want."

"We're going for a walk," I hollered in the direction of the kitchen before we got jackets and shoes on and stepped outside into the pale-yellow evening.

The neighbor across the street raked his lawn and gave a nod as we disappeared behind Phillip's truck and Aaron's smaller, teal colored Ford Ranger. When Aaron stepped inside his house, I didn't.

"You coming?" he asked, holding open the door.

The burst of warm air, scents of varnish and Earl Grey, hit my face from inside the Barringers' house and made me want to faint. Taking in a breath, I answered, "I...I don't know."

Aaron read my reluctance and knew. "Let me grab my guitar. It's not too bad for temperatures, we can sit out here."

I nodded, and when the door closed I clutched my chest and leaned my head against it. "Don't start crying. Not right now..."

When the doorknob turned on the other side, I removed my head and stepped back to let Aaron through. He clutched the neck of his black acoustic and walked to the back of his truck, dropped the tailgate, and sat on it. I took a deep breath and went over to join him. This felt far too much like the time at school when Shawn played.

Aaron did some tuning and then plucked at the strings playing something slow and then breaking into a faster tune. Was this a cruel joke? The song. Everything about this moment. "Hey, what are you playing? I know this..."

"It's something Shawn and I came up with before I moved to Halifax."

"He played it for me once," I said. "At school."

"I can stop if—"

"No, don't." I closed my eyes. "Keep playing." Unable to fight it, I went back. Welcomed the memory of Shawn leaned against the back window of his father's truck. How after he'd shared that song with me, and we were rudely separated by the principal, that it compelled me to say I loved him for the first time.

As Aaron concluded the song, I mumbled, "I love you."

"Huh?" His thumb twanged off the strings.

"I love the song. The song." I slid off the tailgate. "Thank you for, uh, letting me hang with you." I blew into my hands, taking steps back toward my house. "I'm feeling chilled now, though. Going to warm up inside. The doctor said I shouldn't be out long."

"Okay..."

I gave a quick wave. "Bye."

Aaron already began to play something else, looking down at his guitar. "Bye."

I slid off my shoes in the entrance and hit myself in the forehead and muttered, "You idiot."

Meandering around the corner, I witnessed Margaret asleep on the couch, using Phillip's lap as her pillow. Andy sat on the coffee table in front of them. I turned on my heel, hid myself, and listened to the conversation.

"Would you believe, Andy," Phillip said, "that the other day I went right up to the boy's bedroom to ask him something? Completely forgot." He laughed weakly and then began to sob loudly. "Where's my boy?"

At that point, I turned around and escaped up to my room, bursting into tears of my own.

***

Aaron's presence in Lunenburg seemed to keep me together like a paperclip holding paper shreds. Death ceased stalking me with him around.

We'd spent practically every day together, hanging out with his guitar. I even gave him the pick I'd once stolen from his brother's bedroom. It felt like giving it back to Shawn.

Naturally, on the last few days of September when Aaron decided to return to university, I panicked. If he left, so did the paperclip, leaving all the shreds of me to fall in disarray.

Spying from around the corner of our house where the stair to our deck was, I fastened the uppermost button of my jacket, as he threw a few bags and his guitar inside the Ranger. Margaret hovered, repeating, "I wish you didn't have to go."

"I know, Mom. I'd stay longer if I could."

"Be safe." She hugged him and then wiped tears from her eyes.

He kissed her on the forehead. "I will."

Phillip showed up outside with a framed picture. "Thought you'd want to have this. It's a picture we took of you two at your birthday."

Aaron swept the frame up. "Thanks, Pop." When he glanced at it, he smiled and heaved a heavy sigh. "I regret not coming around a lot. The band, friends, school…it all could've waited. None of them matter as much as family."

"You can't beat yourself up about these things, Son."

He gave a weak nod. "I'll be back home as soon as I can."

"Call when you get in," Phillip said squeezing Aaron's shoulder and then swept him up into a hug.

"Sure thing."

Phillip and Margaret took one another by the hand and made their way back inside. The panic grew within me, until Aaron opened the driver-side door and stood there, hesitating. He furrowed his brows in thought and then took off inside the house. He probably forgot something.

To me, it couldn't have worked out more perfect. In the spur of the moment, I positioned my headband over my ears better, and slithered from behind the bush, climbed the bumper, and fell into the box of the truck. I moved right up to the back window and hid low so he wouldn't see me.

When the door to the house slammed and then the truck's door next, I took a deep breath in and whispered, "Goodbye, Lunenburg."

Aaron's truck roared to life and pulled onto the street. I turned on my back and looked up at the blue sky littered with cotton-fluff clouds. As birds soared overhead, freedom under their wings, I imagined myself as one of them.

The further out of town we rode, the wind picked up, the sky turned deeper shades of blue until heavy drops pelted my face. "Ah, stupid rain." I turned onto my stomach and covered my head with my hands, but the rain wasn't about to stop anytime soon and the cold bit deep inside my coat to get to my bones.

I reached up and rapped on the back of the window, then waited. When the truck didn't slow, I did it again. In one crank of the wheel, causing me to tumble the other way, Aaron had the truck pulled off onto the side.

He slammed the door and peered into the truck bed, the rain pressing his dark hair flat. "Becky? What the hell are you doing here?"

"I'm sorry," I said.

"You scared me shitless knocking like that." He shook his head, and wiped the water from his eyes. "Get inside the truck."

When I got up and wiped muddy hands on my pants, I guessed we were past Mahone Bay going toward Chester on the 103. The ocean scowled through the sheets of rain and made me trip over my own feet. I shook away my fear and scurried out from behind the truck and opened the passenger door. Before stepping in, I squeezed my hair out. The windshield wipers were on full-speed, creaking back and forth, throwing thick streams of water to the side. A small hula-dancer with a ukulele in hand, swayed her hips on the dash. All the motion made me dizzy. The rough ride in the back hadn't helped matters either.

"Aaron, I'm—"

"Sorry," he answered for me. "I know. You said that already."

He turned up the heater and rested his hands on the steering wheel. "Listen, I hope I don't come off as a jerk saying this to you, but...I know why you were back there. I know why you've invited us over a few times, followed me around since I've been here."

Followed me around. How pitiful he made it sound.

"I don't doubt what you and Shawn shared was special. That you loved him. But...I'm not him." Traffic blurred by, rocking the truck gently as they did so.

"Things got weird. I admit that. You share so many similarities, and I don't mean to discount the differences...it's that, you're a part of him. You sound like him. You gesture your body like him. I just needed...something."

"I know," Aaron said. "The difference between you and I is, you want to see me and I can't stand to look at myself in the mirror. I see him there, too. Heck, I see him everywhere in Lunenburg. It's why I couldn't stay at home. The place doesn't have that same atmosphere it once did. It's like the roof got demolished and we're pretending it's still there. Maybe I'm running away, and maybe I hate the ocean and am considering transferring to a university inland, but that's my way of coping with this brutal unfairness." He sniffed and wiped a hand under his nose.

Tears pooled and when I blinked, they cascaded down. "Aaron, do you really think he's dead?"

"Dead. It sounds so final...and conventional," Aaron said. "Very unlike Shawn. See, he never ceased to amaze me by doing unusual things, like with all the legend business. I will always hope he found a way to a better place than this world. Someway, somehow."

The talk of a better place, though reassuring, still meant Shawn wouldn't be coming back. That I'd have to go through life as a widow. I fluttered my hands, grief-stricken. "But I can't live without him."

Aaron leant in and engulfed me in a hug. I cried into his

shoulder, uncontrollably. The ugly kind of cry that brought forth all matter of mucous. He didn't mind. I didn't care.

"I hate the idea of living without him, too," Aaron's breath was hot on my hair. When my cries grew silent, he rubbed my shoulder. "Hey, I should get you home. Your pop will be worried sick. He needs to know you're alright."

I sniffed, and wiped my face on my jacket sleeve. The whole truth about why I jumped in the back of Aaron's truck settled like an anvil at the bottom of my stomach. Like him, running away had given me hope, and appeared to be a solution. But the fact of the matter remained. Hurt thrived. Thoughts reeled. Maybe there was no getting away from the Reaper's hold.

TWENTY THREE

October began. Trees rustled in joyous conversation, adorned in their brightest, leafy attire. Some even covered in red or blackberry jewels. In vain celebration of their most beauteous form. Even the birds sung their praises. How foolish and unaware they all were. There was nothing to celebrate. Shawn's memorial service had long since passed, or at least it felt like an eternity. Magic died then. And more and more, I followed suit.

The days tolerated my existence. Blew against my now thinner, onion-skin form. My clothing hung over me, three sizes too big. I hardly bathed. I ate and spoke only when necessary. Sleeping and crying seemed all I knew how to do.

Andy enrolled me in a distance education course, hoping I might start my school year decently. But I didn't crack open a book or complete one pointless module. School required focus. I had none.

He returned to work the first Monday of the month and worried about me constantly. Calling the house every half-hour to an hour. Margaret stopped in from time to time, bless her heart; her hair never as tidied and silken as before, eyes dimmer and accompanied by dark circles. Even in her pain, she took the time to consider me by dropping off a homemade lunch or a dessert, going beyond the normal realm of kindness. She'd ask if I wanted company, and I'd lie that school work had me occupied to avoid having to discuss feelings or be seen feeble with emotion. Selfishly, I just wanted to stay in bed. Away from people.

My mind turned off during naps in the day. However, the night was the Grim Reaper's favorite time to toy with me.

"Be kind..." I begged, before closing my eyes and sinking into my pillow just after nine o'clock.

***

"Becky," a distant, ghostly version of Jack O'Sullivan's voice called. "Yer starting to give up."

"I'm here, just like you asked. Aren't I?" I answered, standing on a long dock, somehow reaching the middle of the ocean. My nightgown's hemline danced in the light breeze. My knees weren't knocking, my hands were still. Oddly, being near the water didn't frighten me. Even when the spray from waves hit my skin.

Jack emerged from behind a tall post on the dock. "Tis true. "

"And where were you while the Grim Reaper terrorized me? I've been very alone."

"Ah go way outta that, yer never alone." He took out a pocket watch I could've sworn was the *Tree of Life* one Shawn had before, and put it to his ear. "There is much goin' on behind the scenes o' time."

"The Grim Reaper owns time. I saw it in his hands."

After I'd said that, the sea became unsettled and churned under the dock.

"What's happening?"

Jack held on to the post he'd hid behind. "Yer lettin' the darkness in...it's gettin' to ye."

Fragments and chunks of white splintered wood invaded the surface of the water. The end of a broken paddle floated nearer. I crouched, dipping my fingers into the water to grab it. When I lifted my hand out, it was covered in blood. Losing consciousness, I fell off the dock.

My eyes opened before hitting the ocean in my nightmare that had been in stark black and white, apart from the horrifying red blood. I gasped and threw the blankets off me. I'd fallen from bed.

The light flicked on and Andy rushed over to me. "Good Lord, Rebecca, you fell. Did you hurt yourself?"

I checked my hands, my heart beating out of control. "It was just a dream."

"Let me help you." Andy reached out.

Staring up at him, I asked, "Can you pick me up in your arms?"

His eyes softened. "Sure, sweetheart."

When he did, I nuzzled into his chest reverting to a child needing comfort by their parent. How I wished to be a baby again. Unaware of life's hardship. Unaware of the suffocating depths of sadness. The morbidity of nightmares.

Andy tucked the blankets up to my neck, snug around my body, and then kissed the top of my head. "Do you need me to stay with you until you fall asleep?"

I nodded.

"Okay." He shuffled to the other side of the bed and propped himself up on an elbow. Eventually, his eyelids weighed too much, his elbow slid out from underneath him, and his head lazed onto the mattress. Worried to have another nightmare, I stayed awake listening to the high whistles of his snores.

I turned my head left and before I shouted aloud, Jack cupped a hand over my mouth. I couldn't feel his touch, but the action made me keep in my breath.

"Follow me," he whispered.

A lone tear of dread fell from my eye after being taken off guard. Shallow wheezes escaped my nose. I crept out of bed, into the hall, and down the stairs. "To be clear…I am awake and you're a vision?"

"That's roy." He leaned against the front door and removed a small knife from somewhere within his coat to pick something out of his teeth.

"Why are you here?"

"Waitin' for it to shine."

"For what to shine?"

"Silly girl, why the lighthouse o'course," he pushed open the door and pointed out at the black wall of night.

"But, the Grim Reaper took the lens."

Jack's smile stretched to the side. "Did he, now?" He took one step and disappeared in the dark. "We'll just see about that."

***

"Rebecca," Andy's voice echoed as he ran toward me. "Rebecca!"

My eyes were wide open and watering from the sharp wind. He laid a hand on my shoulder. "You aren't supposed to be in the cold. What are you doing out here?"

I stared straight in front of me, dreamily, with the texture of gritty sand on my teeth and the taste of grass. "I can't remember. Where am I?"

When I looked up, I saw Shawn's monument for the first time. It gazed down on me—a marble stone, with his picture upon it and words underneath. I backed away in a crab-like motion, kicking up pebbles. "No. How did I...?"

"Your skin is beet-red and you're shivering. Let's get you back into bed." Andy helped me up, threw my arm over his shoulder, and steered me back home. "You worried me senseless. I had no idea where you were for a while."

Margaret and Phillip were at our house, wearing looks of relief on their faces when Andy walked me across our backyard to the patio door. He must've let them know I hadn't been in bed that morning.

The next night, Andy found me out in one of Phillip's fishing boats. Just sitting, staring out at the ocean, hypnotized in immense horror. When he approached, he crouched down on the dock. "Did you come out here awake?"

I shook my head.

"Then, this is like last time?"

I nodded, and after a moment of silence, said, "I wanted to…but I couldn't."

"What do you mean?"

"I'm never afraid of it while dreaming, but when I wake up, I can't face the waves and the noise." I cupped my ears.

"Okay. It's fine now. I'm here to bring you home. Take my hand."

"But I have to help find it. Jack is counting on me," my voice teetered along with the boat.

"Who's Jack?"

"Jack O'Sullivan," I said.

"Rebecca, take my hand," Andy pleaded.

I weakly turned to him and stared at his steadfast reach. He wanted to be the one to anchor me now from uncertain winds. But I couldn't let go of Shawn.

"I can get up myself."

Andy dressed me in thick pajamas, wooly socks, and light shoes before tucking me back in. "Just in case you go off again without me knowing," he said. I reluctantly went along with this absurd charade.

"So…who is Jack O'Sullivan?"

"Don't eye me up like I've lost the last bit of my sanity," I said, rubbing my eyes. "He used to be the keeper of the lighthouse. Shawn told me stories about him."

"Hmm." Andy tilted up his chin. "So, what's he got to do with anything?"

"It's a long story." I yawned. "I don't want to talk about it."

"I'll let you get some shut-eye, then." He fell asleep in the living room on our sofa, waiting to catch me if I sleepwalked out of the house again.

I closed my eyes, and they fluttered open when I received a gentle kiss and heard birds chattering and singing overhead. My room had fallen away and turned into wilderness. I slept upon a bed of silky, hare-bell flowers, and couldn't recall what Shawn once told me about them.

"Hello, Wendy Darling." Shawn's bright smile beamed at me. A shimmery, golden glow bathed him and he appeared to float around.

"Good morning, my dear Peter," I replied, sweetly laughing. When had I last laughed? I couldn't recall that either.

I rose off the bed of flowers and frightened off a cluster of red birds from a nearby bush. The more I focused, the more I came to see the birds were tanagers with hints of white trim on their wings. "Are we in—"

"Yup, kind of," he said.

"Looks like O'Sullivan Island here."

As he moved across sunbeams, they made him glimmer even more. "Isn't it great?"

"Yes."

He stretched out his arm and five birds soared toward him to perch on it, whistling. I pet one's stiff, crinkled belly. They were made of origami paper. "Aren't you beautiful?"

It chirped in response.

"Walk with me?" Shawn offered his hand, and I didn't hesitate once to take it.

We hovered just a few feet off the ground with all the birds following behind. Further out of the forest, where the trees shortened in size, the lighthouse's grandeur showed itself.

I squeezed his hand. "Does this one light up here, during the night?"

Before I took a step forward, someone else took my other hand. Looking at who it was, a flash of the Grim Reaper's macabre, scaly toothed smile met my eyes.

I shrieked, and the forest disintegrated, along with the glory of the place.

"Come back to me…" Shawn whispered.

I blinked hard. The scenery of the Barringers' backyard surrounded me now. "What? How did I get here?" I asked, retracting my hand.

Andy took off his jacket and put it over my shoulders. "You've been sleepwalking."

I glared at him, puzzled. "You were the one who took my hand? What have you done?"

"I'm bringing you back to the house before you get hurt," Andy said.

"No." I shook my head. "I walked with Shawn. We were somewhere beautiful…somewhere better."

"You dreamt it, sweetheart. I'm really sorry."

"No." I moved away from him and cast the jacket to the ground. "You ruined everything."

"I wish I didn't have to. Honestly," he said, sincerity all over his face. "I'd like nothing more than to keep you happy, even if it means in dreaming. But, I couldn't let you go off again."

My bottom lip trembled and I crossed my arms over my chest.

"Will you come back with me?" Andy asked.

I followed, regardless of his cruel robbery of the rare, feel-good dream with Shawn. Maybe if I fell asleep again, we'd be back to where we left off before the Reaper.

Once blankets cocooned me, Andy said, "I'll call the doctor in the morning. We'll think of something to do about this sleepwalking stuff. Good night." He flicked off the light, shut me in, and I heard the screeching of a stool or chair outside the door and knew that's where he planned to sleep the rest of the night.

As much as I tried to resurface the images and beauty of the last dream I had, it never returned. Depression crushed me like a paper weight, growing heavier and heavier. It never left, even when I wanted it to. It never stopped crushing.

***

Completely exhausted, even after sleeping in until noon, I dragged myself out of bed and went downstairs. Per the calendar, it read early November. Days continued to breeze by without me. The whites of my eyes took on a permanent shade of milky-red.

"You didn't have any episodes last night, did you?" Andy asked, dusting the railing of the lowest stairs with a rag after giving it a spray with spruce-scented cleaner.

"It's kind of hard when you're a prisoner in your own room," I said.

He'd taken the doctor's advice weeks ago, to put a lock outside my door and one on the window in my room, only opening them when he woke. If it hadn't been Saturday, Andy would've made me get up sooner before he headed to work.

Putting the cleaner and rag aside, he picked his cup of coffee off the floor and took a sip from it. "If it keeps you from wandering, it's not all that bad." He put his cup back down. "You still having nightmares, though?"

I tired of Andy having conversations with the doctor about me over the phone. Making me sound like a lost cause, fit for the nut-house. Fine. Maybe he didn't go that far, but I didn't want them discussing the wellbeing of my mind. Or how a mental-health therapist might be the only thing to help me now that I've probably come to grasp Shawn being de…well, in Neverland. Which, truthfully, I hadn't. Even after Aaron's take on things. Even with my hope threadbare.

"No. Nothing since the locks," I lied.

"Good."

Jack visited me often whenever the sun went down, telling me stories to keep the nightmares at bay. Sitting on the edge of the windowsill or against my dresser. Last night, I picked his brain and asked why my visions consisted of him, and occasionally the Reaper, over Shawn. "Ye can always beckon a dead man, love. Still, to ye, Shawn isn't a dead man."

"Andy, everyone…they think if I say he is, that I'll be reformed of my pain. You told me to never give up on him. Keep having hope."

"I did so. But we can keep hope for many other reasons." Jack nodded, pulled a flask from his coat and drank from it. He wiped the drippings of liquor on his beard across his sleeve. "Besides, how long will ye listen to an old ghost with reserves toward death. Who clung to life, and yet lost it all the same?"

"Rebecca?"

"Huh?" I snapped out of my reflection.

"Can we talk for just a moment about seeing a therapist?" Andy asked, already wearing an expression as if to say, "*Please don't get mad at my suggestion.*"

I slumped my shoulders. "I told you, I don't need to talk to anyone."

"It's not alright to bottle it in," he countered.

"A stranger doesn't need to hear my problems."

"Fine. Talk to me then," he said. "Let's go into the living room. I want to hear about everything. Jack O'Sullivan, the whole bit."

I lowered my head and my hair slid over my face. "What's the point? Jack's dead and gone. And so is Shawn, I guess. That's what everyone keeps saying."

"Don't do that," Andy pleaded.

"I love him…I always will. That's all anyone needs to know." I slumped back upstairs. My feet dragged down the hall as if an invisible ball and chain was attached to my ankle.

Andy knocked at my door a minute later. "Listen, I know it's still fairly new yet, and I'm sorry. But if you change your mind, I'll be here to listen."

I ignored him and pulled a shoebox from under my bed where I'd stored the red tanagers I'd made the time I tried to recapture visions of Mom. The ethereal dream of Shawn on the heavenly version of O'Sullivan Island made me want to make more. I pulled out my supplies, all the red washi I had left, and began folding and cutting. Every evening, I worked on at least three to busy my mind and recreate the happiness I felt in that blissful place.

The shoebox overflowed with birds now. I took clear fishing line out of Andy's old tackle box he stowed on a shelf in his closet and then sat back down next to the box. I grabbed scissors. With fluid sweeps through the air, I cut several pieces of line. Some long, others shorter, cascaded to the floor. Picking up one bird, I drilled an imperfect hole out from its flat back with the sharper end of the scissor, slid fishing line through, and tied it tight. As it dangled before me, I smiled and began to do this to the rest of the flock in the shoebox.

Once all my birds were strung to lines of varying lengths, I rushed out of my room to grab a Ziploc of thumb-tacks from the junk drawer I'd come across last I perused through it for a magnifying glass (which, like every other event in my life, seemed like ages ago), and then grabbed a stepping-stool from within the broom closet behind the stairs.

"Getting back to your crafts?" Andy inquired a few strides away in the laundry room. "What are you up to?"

I avoided giving an answer and disappeared back upstairs.

Manically moving about my room on the stool, I pinned all the birds I could to the ceiling until I ran out of tacks and breath. I inhaled deeply, lying in bed and looking up at my handiwork. I swore I heard the whistles and calls of every tanager. This space became a bird sanctuary.

Mesmerized by the twirling of red, the usual, thick miasma of despair in my head commenced thinning. I considered Jack's comment again. *Ye can always beckon a dead man, love.*

The time-span between the horrifying event at sea to now, the weather growing colder; it all led to the conclusion I never wished to face. But if I faced it, I could use my gift of visions to bring Shawn back. And if I had success, could keep his vision with me. Forever.

TWENTY FOUR

To bring Shawn about as clearly as I remembered him, I needed a picture. I thought about confronting Margaret for one, as I had none for myself. But, I hated to be a bother. Instead, I figured it time to face my fear of the ocean. I lifted a finger and spun one of my tanagers. "Wish me luck," I said before leaving.

With Andy at work, I had no one looking over my shoulder and plenty of time. The sun shone, dulling the crisp wind sweeping between houses and trees. Brittle leaves were pulled from their branch and scraped upon unforgiving pavement. A gentle smell of firewood smoke puffed out of chimneys, families already prepared for the upcoming winter months.

Ambling through the backyard, I hopped the fence and through the Barringers' gate to get down the stairs. With eyes fixed downward, a small, determined pale-blue flower peeked its head up at me through tangles of shriveling grass and rocks in between the third and second last step. "Is that a...? It *is* a harebell." I plucked it and carried it with me onto the beach. Paused, I took a deep breath, and then moved on toward the monument. A subtle trail in the stones told me Margaret and Phillip must've visited the site often. Such strong people. I had only been out here once, and not fully conscious when I'd done so. I felt the guilt of my judgement toward them in regard to the funeral.

While facing the monument, I placed the delicate flower shakily at the base and suddenly Shawn's voice echoed in my head. *It's a harebell, the flower of memory.*

"I never want to forget us. And so...that's why I'm here. To ask you to come back to me, if in fact, you are...gone." That particular word wounded the last part of me left untouched by grief. Streams of tears fell from my tired eyes that looked achingly at his photograph on the stone.

The ocean behind me boisterously taunted. Slapping greedy hands against the shore in a tantrum. It grew louder and louder, seeking my attention.

"Fine! Here I am," I turned around to face it. "You took Shawn away, you selfish squall...you...you bitch." I hardly swore. The words always felt filthy on my tongue. Not this time. I picked up several pebbles from the ground and threw them hard at the ocean's face, one by one. "I'm done being afraid. I want you to see me right here, right now, and watch as I take him back." The wall of denial toward his death crumbled and forced my heart up into my throat.

When I turned away, chest and nostrils flared, I froze. Jack had one arm leaned against Shawn's monument.

I fell back onto my hands, hyper-ventilating. "No," I cried, tears coming harder and faster. "What is all this? You said I wasn't seeing Shawn because I didn't believe him to be gone. You made me admit to...to his...you lied to me!" I clutched my chest.

His hands were up in surrender. "Hold on, now."

"No. I won't do anything else you say."

"Shawn sent me in his place. He can't be here, but for good reason. I—"

"Shut up, you liar!" I threw my hands over my ears. "I won't listen to you anymore."

Jack went to grab at my shoulders to stop me from running away, but went right through me.

"Listen to me, damn it. He's fighting for the light," he shouted at my back. "He needs yer help!" Air breezed by and nipped at my eyes and cheeks. Tears spread all over my face. My mind got thick with sludge. Black sludge consuming any logic, emotion, sliver of strength left within me.

I hurried across the Barringers' backyard, in my house, up the stairs, and into the bathroom. "There is no magic without you, Shawn," I said to my frail reflection in the mirror. My hands shook, grasping the rim of the sink. "And if I can't have you with me as a vision, then I want to die with you."

I cranked the faucet of the tub, put the plug in, and let it fill for a few minutes. Knowing full well panic would set in, I made the decision something had to be done to dull that. My lip trembled as I opened the medicine cabinet and swept Andy's Ativan off the shelf where I put it last.

Through the thick brain sludge, the familiar, baritone voice whispered, *"Take all of them quickly and leave no room for second guesses. You want to be with him. This is the only way."*

I hiccoughed a cry, put the medicine on the edge of the sink, and covered my mouth to stifle the painful sobbing pushing against my throat. "I can't."

"Do it for him."

I picked up the bottle again and dumped the cap and pills into my tremoring hand. What did Jack tell me before I ran? It sounded important. Trying to pull anything out of the sludge proved impossible. I stumbled back a few steps, my body shaking along with my hands now, and watched (as if in slow motion) the pills and cap cascading out of my palm into the bathwater. As I wiped my eyes, and kneeled to retrieve some, I noticed the cap floating on the surface and one pill inside it, moving over waves from the rushing faucet. An epiphany hit me.

If I sink too, then there's no one to finish what Shawn started. If I die, who will tell his story?

The cap symbolized a boat, and the pill in it *could* be me.

See, all this time I figured it selfish to consider myself. To go on each day, when Shawn didn't get that chance. I figured I'd failed him. But the only failure would be giving in. Letting the Grim Reaper talk me into going to a place entirely different from Neverland. Likely a place separating Shawn and me. I needed to hold onto hope to stay strong. Is that what Jack meant when he'd said something to the effect of hope being kept for many other reasons? I pulled the plug out of the tub and as the water drained, the black sludge in my head went with it.

I retrieved the cap and lone pill from getting sucked down the drain, and said, "You can't kill magic."

"Now you finally understand, in a way I never did," Jack said appearing atop the sink. "Legends never die, love."

"Just so long as there is someone willing to tell the tale."

"Aye." He slid off and blew me a kiss. "Farewell, girly. We'll see ye on the other side."

Andy's loud knocking startled me and the pill and cap slid between my fingers. He swung the door wide open, taking in the scene. The last bit of water in the tub got sucked down the drain in a loud *shhhllp*. "You were…"

"I didn't," I said.

Andy let out a loud exhale and ran his hands through his hair. "At first, I heard the water come on, I thought nothing of it. But then, this sick feeling overcame me." The hard swallow moved down his throat so ruggedly, I could see it. He then knelt to pick something up. The pill and the cap. "I love you, Rebecca. I need to say it a lot more. I love you, and I don't want you to ever feel so lost that you—"

When his hands fell at his sides, I took one of them and pressed it firmly in mine. I could hold onto Shawn no longer. Andy and I were now responsible for keeping one another from blowing away, and I wanted that. "I'm ready to tell you everything," I said.

His arms wrapped around me. "And I'm ready to hear it."

We left the bathroom and down the stairs to speak in the living room. I told Andy how my visions sparked a lot of fever in Shawn over the legends of Jack O'Sullivan. I talked about the stories, the lens, the sacred water, the Grim Reaper, and our short time surviving on the island. How close we'd gotten to piecing the map together and finding the vial.

"This saddens me, Rebecca," Andy said, eyes downcast, sitting on the opposite end of the couch. "How near you were to finding it. I told you before, I feared Shawn being a guy like me. Head in the clouds, not ready to come down. Likely to break your heart somewhere down the line. But he's nothing like that. And, if it hadn't been for my insecurities, maybe you two would've finished this adventure. Shawn might even be..." He stopped, sighed, and continued with, "I am so sorry for showing up in your life expecting to father you after all this time. For having no patience. For biting at you and calling you down. You deserved none of that."

"Thank you for apologizing. I wouldn't admit it to myself, but I was glad you came around after mom passed away. Glad to have a parent at least."

"Yah..." Andy scratched the scruff on his chin. "I have a long way to get to parent-status, I think."

I smiled. "Not that long."

He returned my smile. "I can never make up for what I've done. But can I ask for your forgiveness?"

"I forgive you," I said. "And I mean that."

We discussed in further depth my visions, grief, dreams, nightmares, my linking Aaron to Shawn. "I was grasping at straws. He felt like the closest thing I could get."

Andy nodded slowly. "I understand all that. You look for what you've lost in everything. People, places, music, you name it."

"How can one family be so acquainted with death?" I asked.

"I don't know," Andy said. "I question that myself. But then, if what you say about the Grim Reaper is true...you broke the cycle. You won over. I mean, he...it...whatever, wanted you, too.

Tried to lie to get you to end it all. But you persevered."

The paper-weights on my shoulders were lessening with each part of this conversation. I felt lighter. Less pressed. "I did, didn't I?"

"You better believe it."

"So, what now? How do I move on?"

"You don't," Andy said matter-of-fact.

"What?"

"You take each day at a time. You move forward, but you never forget. It always stays with you. That's why it's good to talk to someone when those hard days come. And they will."

"I see."

"So, these visions of yours," Andy began, "do you ever see Shawn?"

"No. I tried," I said. "But I think there's a reason why. I've got to finish what he started. Somehow, I have to decipher the map and get that vial."

"There's no other way to complete the task?"

"I told you, there was…but the lens in the lighthouse is gone."

A determined expression fell on Andy's face. "We're going to do this together. You and me. If I've got to read every journal entry, examine every artifact…you and I are getting that vial."

"You'd do that?"

"Rebecca, I'm a lonely old guy who needs something to do with his life."

"This means a lot. I want you to know that. Shawn would be happy."

"I admired the boy a lot. Though impulsive, he sure knew how to make life interesting. He was always looking to the future for the next adventure. It's not a bad thing to have dreams. See, for me, I based my life around my work. It kept me from thinking about the past, present, or future. Like some programmed machine. But my body is tiring out. I need to do a little dreaming mixed in with the reality."

"I'm stuck in the past," I said. "Ever since I lost Shawn, I just can't help but look back and want every single day I shared with him to come back. I don't see a future ahead. I did before…but not anymore."

"I hope for you that someday, that'll change. I think doing this will be a good start." Andy pressed a hand on the armrest and got up off the couch. "So, let's go do Shawn proud. Before the weather turns on us, we can pack up camping supplies and stay out there. I'll call Manny, a guy I work with who has a few boats. I'd ask Phillip for one of his, but I'm not sure that's a good idea." He paused. "You okay to go out on the ocean?"

"This is for Shawn. If I have to go out in a boat blind-folded with cotton in my ears, so be it."

***

Overnight, a cover of snow fell on the ground, and crystallized the trees in sheaths of hoarfrost. I heard the loud whistles of wind, like trains breezing by my room's window and woke. I turned the lamp's switch on my nightstand. The clock read 3:38 am.

At the window, I rapped my fist against the glass. "Why is everything against me?" The imprint I'd made fogged up and frost grew in the blank space. I decided to make my way downstairs. All the supplies we'd packed were piled next to the bottom step. Our journey halted until further notice. Maybe even until spring. I kicked a sleeping-bag roll and then sat next to it. I wrapped my arms around the roll and silently cried myself into a dream.

A cold, shadowy cave surrounded. Drops of water trickled and dripped from above onto my head.

I treaded guardedly, my bare-feet plunged into puddles of ice-water I tried to avoid, but couldn't in the dark. Voices echoed ahead, around a sharp bend where hints of light filtered from somewhere. I saw Shawn trapped, arms tied behind his back, inside a glass case, reminiscent of the vision I'd had with him in the hourglass. The case was placed underneath a stream of water flowing heavily from a crack in the rock. The water level reached

217

his knees. Soon it would reach his chest and then he'd be submerged under. I shouted for him, but had no voice to accompany my effort. Nothing more than a bystander as the scene unfolded.

"You are all alone," an evil voice hissed.

"You're wrong. She's fighting for me," Shawn contested.

I tip-toed in the shadows, and made my way behind the case. Ducking low, even though I felt certain I couldn't be seen, I tilted my head to observe where Shawn directed his scowl.

Upon a strange throne of rippled glass, the smoky presence of the Grim Reaper sat with rotting nails drumming against stone. "She is not, dear boy. Little by little I've whittled her down. I may not have been able to find that infernal vial, but neither did you. I did, however, take the lens and your life. And I'll take hers next."

"I won't let you," Shawn shouted and thrashed in the prison, the water now level with the bottom of his ribcage.

The Grim Reaper rumbled with laughter and neared Shawn in one swirling sweep. He pressed his dead hand upon the glass in front of Shawn's face. "Let me show you."

The jaundice skin folded away inside the middle of the Reaper's palm, in the shape of an oval. Within it, flashing scenes from my life showed until I saw myself in the bathroom of my house starting the faucet of the tub.

I cringed, knowing this moment too well. The one where I wanted to end my life.

With the Ativan in my hands, the Grim Reaper smirked an unsettling grin and then said the same taunts he'd given me then. "Take all of them quickly and leave no room for second guesses. You want to be with him. This is the only way."

"Don't do it," Shawn cried. "He's lying to you."

"She is unable to hear you, cretin. I've made it so she cannot hear anything else but me."

When I'd choked out that I couldn't go through with it, the Reaper slithered, "Do it for him."

Shawn body-checked the glass. "You bastard."

Seeing all of this, I beamed. I wanted to tell Shawn not to worry. To watch what comes next. I yanked the plug from the tub, and triumph rose in my chest watching myself do it.

"Yes!" Shawn whooped, as the water in his prison lapped against his collar-bone now.

My statement, "You can't kill magic," brought an angry roar of defeat out of the Reaper.

Shawn's bindings disintegrated. He body-checked the glass again. As it shattered, and the water dispersed, he lunged at the Reaper and forced him to the hard ground. "You can't kill magic," he repeated.

Shawn squeezed hard around his deathly neck, and the Reaper turned to smoke completely and faded down into the earth's fiery depths.

Shawn turned to the throne and I understood now that it was the Fresnel lens. "Thank you for believing, Becky," he said.

A blinding light shattered the scene to an all-white blur. I covered my arms over my eyes and woke immediately after my head rolled off the sleeping bag and hit the floor. I rubbed at the pain. I groaned myself to a standing position and then brought my hands over my eyes again when, from the kitchen windows, a rotating white beam cut through and briefly lit up the entire main level. *Am I still dreaming?*

I stayed watching it for several revolutions, until bolting upstairs into Andy's room.

"When did the town get the lighthouse on O'Sullivan Island up and running?" I asked casually, no regard for the time.

"Hmm?" Andy rolled onto his side. "Up and running? What time is it?"

"Technically, it's morning," I said. "There's a super bright light coming through into the kitchen."

Andy rubbed his eyes. "Maybe you're dreaming it?"

"Just come and look with me," I implored.

He tossed the blankets off and got up out of bed, wearing a white undershirt and plaid pajama pants. Following me downstairs into the kitchen, he stared out the patio window into the night and then winced. "Well, I'll be…"

"So, you see it?"

"I do."

I couldn't tell whether he said what he did just to humor me. "Really?"

He nodded and turned around. "It snowed, too. Pretty early for around these parts. Our expedition will have to be on hold until it melts. If it melts. Maybe it'll push us back until Spring."

"I know. But everything happens for a reason, like they say. The lighthouse shining is a message. There's no need to find the vial any longer."

"Right," Andy's eyes widened. "Because if it's as bright as this, the lens must be back up and you can…"

"Finish what Shawn started. I can touch it with my hand."

TWENTY FIVE

The snowy storm last night eventually ceased, but covered the town in a foggy grey blankness that morning. The bright homes tried to peer through, their colors dulled. No one had any inclination whatsoever to leave the comfort of their homes. Only Andy and me.

After breakfast, he'd made some calls and we bundled up in winter gear and headed out to Puffycup Peninsula. Manny pulled through and allowed us to take out his sea-foam green and white lobster boat he called *Snotty*. He seemed to be a comedic old man living the bare-minimum life surrounded by trees. His cottage had three simplistic rooms. A bathroom, a kitchen, and a bedroom without a door, where he kept a tiny television set propped on a chair beside his twin-sized bed layered in quilts. A few faded, frameless pictures full of people (who I took to be his family) were pinned to the baby-blue walls with nails.

He took us through his humble home to get to a long white door that led out into the backyard, which banked toward the ocean. Shimmering tall grass and shrubs popped up along the pebbly shore that looked like sparkles as the sweep of ocean waves spilled over it. The snow melted the moment it got touched, like sugar in hot water. Small chunks of ice fell off the dock and into the water while we strode down toward *Snotty*.

Manny climbed aboard first, Andy then stepped in and helped me. Flashbacks of dark waves, thunder, and screaming echoed in my head. I stumbled over Andy's feet.

"You sure this is okay for you?" he asked.

I nodded, trying to fight all the forces that acted against my body, making me want to jump out and head back to the cottage.

After a tour of the boat, Manny said, "Hope all of that made sense. Now, I'm getting back inside, before I freeze my assets," he chuckled, patting Andy's back. "Oh, and lifejackets are in the aft stowage locker. You clear where you're heading from here?"

"Got some charts to use with the marine compass, but even so, pretty certain."

"You're on your own, then."

"We appreciate your help, Manny," Andy said.

He waved us off and retired back inside.

Andy pulled out two lifejackets from the locker and we put them on. A recollection of Shawn placing his under my head after I'd fallen out of *Old Broken Down* made my stomach lurch. And then an image of his face hovered over me and waves crashed around us. The boat began to break down. *I'm so sorry, Becky. I failed us, and not just in the attempt to be a hero out on the ocean, but...* The rest faded away. The thought incomplete and as broken as me.

As we went up to the bow and raised the anchor, I said to Andy, "I'm scared. I thought I might be able to do this, but now I'm not sure."

"Follow me to the helm," Andy said. Once inside the enclosed space, he untied the flaps of his hat so that they fell over his ears and then removed his scarf. "Turn around."

"Why?"

"I know you want to do this. That you *have* to do this. And you said you'd do it even if you had to be blindfolded. Here," he said, digging into his coverall pocket. "I brought along these earplugs, too. But the idea is not to let your mind play games with you while you're stuck in the dark and can't hear anything. Think happy thoughts." He winked.

The reference to Peter Pan brought a flutter in my heart. "Right."

He smiled and placed the earplugs in my hand. "Go ahead and turn."

I stuck one in each ear and let Andy wrap his wool scarf over my eyes gently. Once he led me to a seat, I tightened it.

The boat came to life and vibrated under my boots. *Happy thoughts. Happy thoughts.* As Andy steered us out to sea, I shook hands with Shawn again for the first time at the front door of our new home. I swam with him in the ocean and attempted to go to the island. We snuck out at midnight and I learned about Jack's legend. Had our first kiss on the firework finale during Canada Day. Every moment shared, from the start to the last, surfaced. How brief it all was in retrospect, but how long it felt I'd known Shawn. Certain people come into your life for a season, and they leave no less a mark on you than someone you've known for ages. Shawn left a large mark on my heart—call it a scar if you want—and I wasn't sure I could love anyone else the same way I loved him.

We arrived on the part of O'Sullivan Island where we had to climb, and I pulled off my scarf, amazed at how different it looked covered in snow. It made me feel less like I'd been here before, which eased some of the pain. Andy brought me to the metal ladder on the aft end of the boat. "I think it's best you do the rest on your own."

"You sure? We both can touch the lens and get many more years."

"One life of average length, if I'm lucky to receive that, is more than enough for me. That light came on for you. This is between you and Shawn now."

I took off my lifejacket and climbed down. Andy peered over

the edge and held a small lantern above me. "Take this, and take as long as you need. Be safe, and I'll be waiting here for you when you get back."

I accepted the lantern and began my walk along the bed of rocks, managing my way slowly up the cliff to the ledge. I sat for a moment, nervous and excited, then I dusted the snow off myself, looped the lantern through the belt of my jeans, and began to climb the ladder. *Clink, swish, clink, swish,* the lantern rattled against my thigh.

The lighthouse looked like an icicle covered in frost. I stared at it for a while, extremities getting colder as I stood there, before I brought myself to rush up and step inside. When I did, my boots clicked on the cement floor and the cool air shrieked in. I closed the door and my chest suddenly felt heavy, building with rage.

I looked up. "Why are you working now? Why didn't you shine for us when we needed you? You stupid lighthouse, you could have saved him!" Then I screamed…and I kept screaming in despair until the back of my throat went hot and my lungs ached. I fell back on the red stairway, and as I did so, thought I heard something—footsteps.

"Hello?" I turned around. "Anyone there?"

I began to go up each stair until I reached the quarters where Shawn kept all his artifacts. "Hello?"

My fingers caressed the edge of the chaise longue. Under a crisp, dusty blanket—the white and blue one Shawn and I had taken out there—the book of Peter Pan sat. Right where I'd left it last. Dust covered, too. Cold. I flipped through the pages and a shriveled harebell twirled out. *The flower of memory.* It seemed to crop up everywhere now, not wishing to be so rare. *Never forget,* it seemed to say. I picked it up by the shrunken stem and slipped it back inside the book, that I then placed on the bookshelves along with all the other stories. The tale of Peter Pan was over.

Leaning hard against the window in the room to break it open from the frost, I let the stale air leave the space before taking in a deep breath. *Too many things to haunt me here. Why did I come?*

Jack O'Sullivan's jewelry box sat ajar. Where Shawn pulled out my ring to propose. Clingstone peaches, withered and frozen, along with the food we'd brought and so badly wanted before Shawn got apprehended by Phillip and Andy, remained where it'd been dumped. This room waited for our return, but we didn't come back.

I wiped tears away, looked up to the ceiling, and said, "I got called here, didn't I? Was it to torment me more?"

"I'm so sorry, Becky. I failed us, and not just in the attempt to be a hero out on the ocean, but I failed our love."

Shivers pulsed through my body. I turned my head very slowly to the door and then fell to my knees. Shawn was there, looking very real. Very much alive. A deranged laughter burst out of me. I fell to my knees in disbelief, my laughs eventually turning into hard sobs.

Shawn moved from under the doorway and walked toward me.

"You said that to me before our boat shattered."

"You were under such trauma, you didn't hear it then," he said. "But I'm here to tell you everything I said that night before I died. Because you need to know all of it."

"So, you aren't really here?" A small hope inside me shattered. "This isn't you having waited for me all this time. I'm envisioning you?"

"Yes."

"Can I touch you at least?"

"Like all your visions prior, you can…but you won't be able to feel me. That's the rules. And as much as I'm not keen on keeping things by the book, there's not much I can do about it."

"I miss you so much."

"I miss you, too," he said.

"The Fresnel lens…you got the lighthouse's light to work again."

He knelt. "You did. I never would've been able to had you not believed."

We both rose. Streams of burning tears fell from my face as I looked into his eyes. "I don't want to live my life without you. I can stay right here with you, forever."

"You know that can't be done."

"What about the life we were supposed to share together?"

"I know," he whispered. "And maybe we can't share it together anymore, but you will have another someday. Someone who loves you a lot, who you'll get to live a proper life with."

"I don't see anyone else but you."

"In time...you will. And at that moment, promise me you won't feel guilty. It's what I want. I wish for you to get the fairy-tale wedding, the big dress, the works. You deserve a great life." Shawn pointed up. "Follow me. We need to go upstairs—right to the top."

He led me all the way to an enclosed platform outside. Directly in front of us were long, egg-shaped frosted sheets of glass covering a large bulb. "This is the lens," I said in a matter of fact tone. "I've seen it in my dreams."

Shawn leaned against the ledge, staring out at the ocean. I went to join him. From up here, the town looked quaint, as if tucked inside a snow globe. "Wow—it looks so pretty out there," I said, saddened. Experiencing moments like this with Shawn had always made me happy, yet though he stood there, he really wasn't with me. "You said you had to tell me something?"

"Regrets." He eyed me from the side. "I wanted so bad to bypass the present. Ignore all the steps for one selfish goal. In doing that, I missed out on what was right in front of me. Family, special occasions...you. Especially you. I endangered the girl I love because of recklessness and cockiness."

"Shawn, I don't blame you for anything. You need to know that," I said, my breath a visible vapor. "I've made mistakes, too."

"Yah, but I wish mine didn't cost me my life, and nearly

yours. I strived to get more time and be just like O'Sullivan, and in the end got cut short. The truth is…Old man Hook got it right. The Grim Reaper is time. And time is chasing after us all. We are our own worst enemies when we squander it.

"I shouldn't have concerned myself over how much I may or may not get, but just live. That's why I need you to do that, Becky. Don't repeat my mistake. Take in all that's around you. See the beauty in everything. See the small things. Dream, not to escape reality, but to enhance it. The *here and now* is your greatest adventure."

I started to pace the walkway anxiously, thinking about every vision and dream I'd had involving the Reaper. "I don't like that death took you from me."

"You give old death far too much credit. You think just because my body is gone that that's it?"

"Then where are you, Shawn? I just need to know you're okay."

"I'm in a place even Peter Pan could never imagine up."

"So…not Neverland?"

"Better. See, before the boat broke into pieces, I had time to make peace with my maker. I'm being well taken care of, and exploring many great lands with Grandpa Barringer." Shawn's eyes gazed at the sky, reflecting the snowflakes that began cascading down like crystals.

"That sounds nice."

"Oh, it is." He nodded, drawing nearer. "There's another special person I met there…a woman. You look just like her."

A wave of warmth entered my heart. "My mom?"

"She said to tell you she misses you very much. But it's okay now. The cage of your pain is wide open. It's time to fly free. Be rid of it."

As he said that, a red bird darted just above our heads and took to the sky with wings stretched wide, concealing itself between the grey clouds and beyond.

"Shawn, I want you to know that you will always be the light of my life. That won't change."

He ran his thumb down my cheek.

"Your death left me devastated, and yet you've helped me see more clearly than I ever have before. I shouldn't have gripped on to you as my savior. You didn't ask for that responsibility. It's time I find my own way. Find out who I truly am. But this isn't goodbye."

"Never," he said.

I reached out. "Put your hand over mine and link fingers."

When he did, I stretched out our arms and pressed the palm of my hand firmly against the Fresnel glass, melting the frost underneath.

Shawn's smile grew on his face. We both glowed with a love that could disarm all the dark corners of the world. I closed my eyes to remember this instant we shared, not feeling lost anymore, but peaceful.

Our hands slipped from each other's. Shawn whispered in my ear, "Thank you...for finishing my journey."

He would no longer be standing there when I opened my eyes. I knew after this, I'd never again have another vision of him, of anyone. And whether I got granted long life or not, one thing was certain, his memory would live on through my stories of the lighthouse. He would become the legend he always wanted to be.

So, maybe we're not paper dolls after all, but something far more resilient. Stones being skipped across an ocean. Getting chipped away at, tested, until polished. While skipping, we are only able to see very little on the surface. At one point, we will stop and find ourselves sinking into something deeper. Something wonderful.

As I made my way back to the boat, I was a stone moving in Andy's direction. All the resentment and rejection fell away, and made smooth the path we were on together. When our eyes met, I knew everything would be okay because I wasn't alone. I had my father. Who from here forward, would never be called by his first name again.

Though I couldn't keep Shawn on the surface of my life, and I had to continue skipping on without him, one day when I stopped…he would be there.

IF YOU SUFFER FROM DEPRESSION OR OTHER MENTAL ILLNESS AND ARE HAVING THOUGHTS OF SUICIDE, PLEASE CONTACT THE NUMBERS BELOW:

1-800-SUICIDE
(1-800-784-2433)
OR
1-800-273-TALK
(1-800-273-8255)

YOU MAY ALSO WISH TO VISIT THE WEBSITE:

HTTP://WWW.SUICIDE.ORG/INTERNATIONAL-SUICIDE-HOTLINES.HTML

THE LIGHT OVER BROKEN TIDE PLAYLIST

Music that inspired the story

1) Times they are a changing-Bob Dylan

2) The Lighthouse-The Hush Sound

3) Stay Gold-First Aid Kit

4) Paper Doll-Rachael Yamagata

5) Ring Around The Moon-Elephant Revival

6) Watch You Sleeping-Blue Foundation

7) Salt Skin-Ellie Goulding

8) Luna-Smashing Pumpkins

9) Adore-Amy Shark

10) Flume-Bon Iver

11) Deep End-Ruelle

12) Sail Away-David Gray

13) Heart Of The Sea-Flogging Molly

14) Come Back-Pearl Jam

15) Asleep Underwater-Caracol and David Usher

16) Watermark-Enya

WHAT DID YOU THINK OF THIS BOOK?

Why not review it on your blog, Amazon, Barnes & Noble, Goodreads, and/or your other preferred online book retailer sites?

Reviews support authors. Leave one for The Light Over Broken Tide today.

Thank You

ABOUT THE AUTHOR

Holly is a creative writer and award-winning poet from Canada with two published poetry chapbooks, Hiding Bones and Confetti Confessions. The Light Over Broken Tide is her first novel.

Her writing has been showcased in magazines, various online sites, Wattpad's featured list, and inside book subscription boxes. She is a member of an exclusive writer's group called The Underground Writing Cohorts. Aside from honing the skill of writing, Holly spends time with her family, goes outside a lot, gets lost in the magic of music, and collects books, antiques, and Funko Pops.

Currently resides in a modest lake town in Alberta with her husband, daughter, and two cats.

WWW.HOLLYDUCARTE.COM

Made in the USA
San Bernardino, CA
22 March 2018